THE INSTITUTE

Jakub Żulczyk

Translated by Danusia Stok

Legend Press Ltd, 51 Gower Street, London, WC1E 6HJ
info@legendpress.co.uk | www.legendpress.co.uk

Contents © Jakub Żulczyk 2016
In agreement with Author's Syndicate Script & Lit Agency
The right of the above author to be identified as the author of this work has been
asserted in accordance with the Copyright, Designs and Patents Act 1988. British
Library Cataloguing in Publication Data available.

The Institute was first published in the Polish language under the title *Instytut* by
ŚWIAT KSIĄŻKI Publishing House in 2016.
This English edition of *The Institute* was arranged via Red Rock Literary Agency Ltd.

Print ISBN 978-1-78955-8-999
Ebook ISBN 978-1-78955-9-002
Set in Times. Printing managed by Jellyfish Solutions Ltd
Cover design by Simon Levy | www.simonlevy.co.uk

This publication has been supported by the ©POLAND Translation Program

BOOK INSTITUTE

©POLAND

Jakub Żulczyk is a rising star of the Eastern European literature scene.

His 2014 novel *Blinded by the Lights* was adapted into a TV series by HBO Europe and listed as one of the best TV shows made in Europe in 2018.

He is a successful screenwriter as well as the author of the bestselling Polish novels *Do Me Some Harm, Radio Armageddon, Hound Hill* and *Black Sun*.

Follow Jakub on IG
@jakubzulczyk

Danusia Stok is a freelance translator of interviews, novels, short stories and film scripts. She has translated, among others, works by Krzysztof Kieślowski & Krzysztof Piesiewicz, Andrzej Sapkowski, Marek Krajewski, Mariusz Wilk, Grażyna Plebanek and Jacek Dukaj, and compiled, translated and edited *Kieślowski on Kieślowski*. She lives in London.

Whoever you are.

My name is Agnieszka, and the Institute is my apartment. Twelve hours ago, I became a prisoner here. Nobody can go out. Nobody can come in.

The Institute is on the fifth floor, at the top of a pre-war tenement on one of the main thoroughfares of Cracow. The address: 20 Mickiewicz Avenue. It measures one hundred and thirty square metres, has four bedrooms and, as do most of the apartments, a kitchen, a toilet and a bathroom.

There is a large living area, at least in theory. When couples boasted that they had two rooms, my "one hundred metres" gave rise to envious tutting, enquiries and taunts, such as: "Ride around on a bike in here, do you?" But it seems to me that space doesn't mean all that much when you're locked in. A cell is always a cell.

The name "The Institute" was on the entryphone when I first came to look at the apartment. I asked the solicitor who was viewing it with me, why Institute, and why was that up there instead of my grandmother's name – what kind of Institute? She had no idea. Later, once I'd moved in, the administrator asked whether I wanted them to change the tag beneath the entryphone to one with my name on it. I said no. I thought it'd be easier that way. I wouldn't have to drum my name and the number of the apartment into the heads of those intending to visit me. *It'll be enough to say "phone the Institute,"* I thought, presuming I'd meet people in Cracow who'd want to visit me.

Very soon, I wished there were far fewer visitors. When

mentioning my apartment, people said "to the Institute", "in the Institute", "from the Institute", "at the Institute", "not far from the Institute". That's what they said, people who popped in for a coffee, people who came a little more often and then moved in, people who visited those who'd already moved in. There are hundreds of apartments on Aleje Trzech Wieszczów. Tens, hundreds of thousands in the whole of Cracow. And so, "the Institute" simply became the Institute. When that happened – and I can't say exactly when – I realised that I really didn't want the Institute to be just an ordinary apartment that belonged to Agnieszka Celińska, like those belonging to or rented by the Nowaks, Paprockis, Daszyńskis, Malickis, Dawidowskis. Even when there were forty half-comatose people still doggedly together on Monday at eight in the morning and I had to be at work in two hours, I didn't want it to become any old apartment.

But now, the Institute is no longer an asylum; in fact, it's the opposite – it's a trap.

We can't leave the Institute. That is, we can, but only to go to the landing. On the landing, to the left, is an old wooden lift with a two-winged door. Next to the lift is a stairway leading downwards, which is sealed off by a massive pre-war grating with densely set struts twisted into Art Nouveau knots. The grating has always been open, but now it's fastened with two locks. I haven't got keys to the locks. Mrs Finkiel, my neighbour, might have some. Opposite our door, on the other side of the lift and stairs, is the door to her apartment. Mrs Finkiel can't or doesn't want to open it for us. Or else she's not in. The lift has always worked, but now it doesn't.

Our phones aren't working. We can't get the internet. We're in the very centre of Cracow yet cut off from the world.

We call the people who've locked us in 'They'. In a way, that's how they introduced themselves. A few hours ago, we'd found a sheet of squared paper on the doormat, torn out of an exercise book, with **THIS IS OUR APARTMENT** scribbled on it in gory red letters.

We don't know who 'They' are. 'They' could be our neighbours. Could be somebody one of us knew a long time ago and hurt: ex-girlfriends, boyfriends, husbands, family members. 'They' could be some psychopaths like those who pick a random mobile number and harass you for a month, calling at three in the morning and threatening to burn your house down. 'They' could be the tenement's administration. Could be the police. Owners of the vegetable stall opposite. The strange group of people in worn-out suits holding leather pouches and clearly well-used paper files, whom we passed in the street a couple of days ago. We haven't a clue.

Now all we can do is wait, sitting or pacing the apartment. There are seven of us: Veronica, Iga, me, Sebastian, Jacek and two of Veronica's friends, Robert and Anna.

We move from room to room to dilute the feeling of being imprisoned at least a little, but instead of fading, it grows by the second, enters every strand of every muscle like a turbo-charged tumour. We feel it most when we stand still, gripped by a rustling, a sound or banging outside. We wait a few seconds, peer out onto the stairwell, look out of the window at the street. But none of these sounds has, as yet, turned into anything concrete. They're just ordinary sounds, echoes from a world from which we've been cut off. All that's left is for us to go back inside, sit down, get up, light and extinguish cigarettes, boil water for yet more tea, turn the water on, turn it off, take our clothes off and put them on – over and over and over again.

We've calculated that we got locked in on Sunday at about ten in the evening. It's possible that we were locked in as early as the afternoon, but nobody can say for sure because of the day it was. Sunday at the Institute was a day of exhausted shuffling to the bathroom, throwing out the last of Saturday's wrecked bodies, eating pizza together in the evening, watching a stream of hopeless programmes about actors from Polish serials and Polish singers dancing, singing and doing handstands. Sunday was a day when it took half an hour to muster up the energy to run a bath, let alone leave the apartment. Sunday was a day usually forgotten.

The previous day, Iga and I had stood behind the bar of the Ugly Cat, a popular drinking hole not far from the Main Square. Papa, the owner, let us go home at half past nine, when the sad remnants of Saturday night were still knocking around. Comatose forty-year-old women who looked like prostitutes from an '80s Polish film stood on the counter, dancing to "Lambada" as it spun over and over again. Sebastian, Yogi and Papa cleared artists forgotten by the world – unemployed musicians, unpublished poets and art students, their heads on tables, faces in ashtrays. The floor was covered with a crunchy and slippery blanket of mud, slush and fag ends. We left as a threesome – me, Iga and Sebastian, holding on to the walls from exhaustion. Papa rewarded our trooper's stance with a bottle of wine each. If it weren't for it being December and several degrees below zero, we probably wouldn't have made it home and would have fallen asleep on a bench in Planty. Dragging ourselves along Karmelicka Street like a procession on diazepam, we finally reached the Institute, crashed onto our beds and lost consciousness.

As we were drifting off, I could hear some sort of gathering going on in Gypsy's room: Jacek was talking loudly to a group of gabbling young individuals whose voices I didn't recognise, and who were talking about some clever plans to throw yoghurt at minicabs and set fire to the bus stop.

Apart from Veronica, we were all still asleep at ten in the evening. Veronica had visitors, the same ones as the previous Sunday as it turned out: Robert and Anna. They're the ones who discovered it was impossible to leave.

I was just trying to get up when Veronica came in.

"Agnieszka, something strange has happened," she said.

I threw aside my duvet and our two cats, Black and White, got up and plodded to the door. I had to squint even though the apartment was in semi-darkness. My mouth was swollen and painful, as though I'd tried to swallow five glasses of sand. Some unidentified blunt instrument was thumping rhythmically within my skull. Veronica showed me the piece of paper she'd found. I took it and brought it up to my nose like an old woman trying to decipher a phone bill.

"It was on the doormat." She pointed to the expanse beyond the open front door. "Come on. Maybe you know what's going on."

"This is our apartment," I read once aloud and several times silently.

I do several things here, in Cracow: make-up for television productions, and interior decorating, but mainly I work behind the bar of the Ugly Cat every other evening. Like all bar staff, I drink staunchly on the job. A barperson works twelve-hour shifts on average and in that time drinks small beers and the occasional vodka with friends, then finally gets blind drunk when it's time to knock off. It takes a diabolically inhuman effort the following day to focus on even simple sentences.

Besides, I'm thirty-five, and deep down believe I'm getting to be an old woman. I find it harder and harder to live the life of a twenty-year-old with impunity and still function. I get out of breath. Find it harder to tolerate alcohol. Need more sleep. My back aches just standing too long or sitting.

In short, I had to concentrate very hard to understand what Veronica was saying and showing me.

"Veronica, somebody's made a mistake." It didn't surprise me that instead of my own voice, I heard something between an angle grinder and a dying blues singer.

"Come to the landing with me." Veronica beckoned with her arm.

Her friends were standing on the landing: a slim, tall, crooked lad in a long women's cardigan and horn-rimmed glasses, and a petite blonde wrapped in an over-stretched T-shirt and leggings with the logo of a washed-out rainbow on them, her face and hands the colour of old porcelain.

"Okay, so someone's taking the piss," I said, squinting as

though we were all on a beach on an August afternoon. *Back to bed*, I still thought at the time. *Under the duvet. Sleep.*

"We can't get out," replied Veronica. "The lift's not working and the grating's down. They've locked us in."

"Who's 'They'?" I asked.

Veronica showed me the piece of paper again, and again I read: "This is our apartment."

I came to my senses – enough to realise that my feet were getting cold. I was standing barefoot on the unheated landing.

I waved for them all to go back inside with me, returned to my room and slowly rummaged in a big pile of clothes for my phone. It wouldn't turn on. I began to search for my charger but realised it might take an hour to find. I made my way to Iga's room. She was sleeping on her stomach in her clothes, her head hanging dolefully over the edge of the bed; she looked as though she'd crashed onto her bed from several floors up.

"Iga, somebody's locked the grating to the stairs and left a crazy note on the doormat," I said.

Iga raised her head a couple of centimetres, opened one eye, choked out a hoarse "Oh my God" and got up. I handed her the letter from the doormat.

"It's Gypsy's friends." She shook her head. "They do things like that. They once nicked the keys to the bar on somebody's birthday and locked everyone in."

"They mustn't come here again," I said quietly. "We'll print their photos and stick them to the street door."

"Yes, you're absolutely right." Iga nodded. She stood up, passed me, shuffled along the corridor and started to thump her fists on the glass of Jacek's door. "Gypsy!" she yelled. "Phone your moron friends and tell them they're totally not funny."

After a good minute, Jacek, known in the Institute as Gypsy, opened the door. He resembled a piece of paper that had been crumpled and then flattened. We pointed to the front door. Slowly, shuffling past us, he went out to the landing. I stood in the doorway. Gypsy shook the grating once, twice, three times.

"It's anything but funny." Iga stood, hands on hips.

"It's not my friends." Gypsy shook his head.

"Of course it's not. It's my mum."

"I don't know where they'd have got the keys to the grating if we've never had them." Gypsy ran his hand along the bars, then walked up to the lift. Pressed the button once, twice, three times.

"It's not working," said Veronica.

"Strange if it did." He shrugged.

"A guy came to fix it yesterday." Iga approached the lift door and started to press the button in vain. "He caught me as I was coming back from the shop and spent half an hour showing me how it zips up and down like a Pendolino. Those were his words. 'Zips up and down like a Pendolino.'"

Nobody spoke for a moment. Then Veronica's friend asked:

"Does this often happen?"

"Every week. It's a tradition," replied Gypsy. The girl didn't even glance at him. She kept staring at the lift button. There was an uninhabited wilderness in her eyes.

"No, no, it doesn't," I replied after a while. I wanted to smile, but I couldn't. I just motioned at them to go back in. "Iga, give me the phone," I said. "I'll phone admin and ask them to open the grating."

Iga retreated to her room and returned with the phone and charger.

"Odd." She handed it to me. "It won't turn on."

The phone was out. The logo of a bitten apple and several dots ending in the symbol of a cable appeared on the screen. Gypsy took the phone from me.

"It's down."

"I'll get mine," I said.

My iPhone was missing its SIM card. I took Iga's charger, plugged the phone to power and tried to turn it on. An apple appeared on the screen, dots, charger symbol, dumb and stubborn. It was an instant sobering. Like bumping into a police patrol at four in the morning when you've got a bag of weed in your pocket, like driving into a car parked in front of you.

I showed Iga the screen, leaned against the wall and realised I felt scared. I wanted whoever was playing this joke on us to call it a day then and there, open the grating, come in and tell us we were on candid camera. And they'd better have some alcohol with them, good food and sweets.

"Calm down, calm down." Gypsy scratched his head and kneaded his face like it was made of plasticine; he gave the impression of being nailed to the ground in order to keep from falling. "You were at work, had a lot to drink… somebody's playing a trick on you. Or you fiddled with the grating yourselves."

"But why?" I said.

"I've no idea." Gypsy shrugged.

"Get your phone, Gypsy." Iga tried to speak as calmly as she could.

Sebastian emerged from his room and stood in the middle of the hallway. Wearing nothing but his tracksuit bottoms with the Banda company's name printed in Gothic letters on the left leg, he looked hard but fragile.

"What's up?" he asked.

"Somebody's playing a trick on us," I answered.

Sebastian scratched his head, ran his eyes over Robert, who, seeing him, had shrunk about ten centimetres, and said:

"I'll fucking kill him. As soon as I've had some coffee."

Robert startled, as though he'd been mildly electrocuted.

"Not you, pit bull." Sebastian patted him on the shoulder and went to the kitchen. Right then, Gypsy reappeared, holding his phone, an old Nokia. I never knew whether he used it through noble self-denial or because he'd coldly calculated that it would make him look hip; this collection of unknowns constituted his entire being.

In fact, he'd brought only half the phone: no battery, no SIM card, no back flap.

"Have you turned your laptops on?" he asked.

"Not yet," I replied.

"There's no network. It's not picking up any networks," Gypsy said and sat on the floor. "They wouldn't have thought of anything like this. Those friends of mine." He got up and sat on the couch and started kneading his face with his hands again. "Fuck me, I'd give a kidney for some coffee."

"None left!" Sebastian shouted from the kitchen. "Want some chai?"

Iga disappeared into her room. A moment later, she ran back down the hallway and swung by my room, but then returned and rested against the wall, trying to catch her breath.

"The cable's been cut," she said, "right by the window. The cable to—"

"The router," finished Gypsy.

"Has been cut," repeated Iga.

Sebastian returned from the kitchen, leaned against the wall and looked at us without the slightest sign of any emotion. Veronica closed her eyes and sat on the floor. Started moving her lips silently. After a while, she looked at me again, her eyes flashing with unease.

"I wasn't home today," she said. "I was at work. I met Robert and Anna by the Bagatela at six and we came here."

"And the note wasn't there then?"

"No, no note."

"The door was open?"

"Yes," she replied without hesitating. "The door was open."

"What's happening? You losing it, Hat?" Sebastian finally spoke. He called me Hat, as did Papa, our mutual boss. Both knew I hated it.

"I've told you so many fucking times to lock the door!" Iga raised her voice. I stopped her with a wave of my hand. I pointed first to myself, then to her.

13

"It doesn't make any difference, Iga, they've got the keys to the grating, so they could easily have the keys to the door, too," I said.

"You're taking the fucking piss out of me," said Sebastian, and he took a sip of tea.

I lit a cigarette. Cigarettes are meant to calm your nerves, but it didn't work this time. It was as if I'd swallowed a piece of metal along with the smoke, and it now travelled through my whole body, shredding it slowly from the inside. I looked at Veronica and remembered what she'd said when she entered my room, and then a heaving in my belly told me to lay off the cigarette and grab my stomach with both hands.

"You said it's strange. That something strange has happened." I turned to her.

"Yes." Veronica looked at me quizzically. "Yes, I did say something like that."

"I've known you for months. You've never called anything strange. Never used that word."

Veronica gazed at me as though trying to recognise me. But, as usual, it was really only her eyes that were doing the work – two hypnotising, green tunnels. Sometimes when I peered into them, it felt as though I was being X-rayed. She didn't answer.

Again, we all either stood or sat in silence for a long time.

Iga got up, walked over to the grating and began shaking it and yelling down the stairs. A while later, Gypsy and I joined her. We screamed "help!", "hello!", "open the door!", "emergency!", then we just screamed, our throats paring as though they'd been scrubbed with sandpaper. Gypsy threw a bottle through the grating. The sound of shattering glass echoed throughout the whole stairwell but to no avail. No doors opened, no lights came on, nobody came out or shouted that the police were coming. It was as if everybody had suddenly run away, driven out by an alarm through which we'd slept.

Sebastian tried to shake the grating with all his might, but it was useless. The only effect was a clattering that echoed to the lower floors.

The windows from my room and Iga's gave on to the street. We looked out, shouted, but there was hardly anyone around. A couple of cars went by. Besides, you wouldn't be able to see anything from the driver's seat.

Iga threw a wine bottle, which shattered against the pavement. Nobody reacted. Nobody ever reacts to such incidents.

The windows on the other side of the apartment, those in Seba and Gypsy's rooms, look out to the yard. It was even emptier and darker than usual. No lights were on in any of the windows opposite.

We began to stomp around the apartment, jump up and down, scream. Thump on our only neighbour's, Mrs Finkiel's, door – no response. We turned music on in all the rooms at once, full blast, waiting for the police to knock on our door and summon us to court, which had happened before, when we'd emitted far fewer decibels. Nothing. But we continued to leap around and make a noise in order to ward off the panic; fear was growing, filling our bellies, curdling our blood.

At about one in the morning, we stopped. We'd no strength left. We kept the music on in my room, closed the door and went through to the kitchen.

We discussed who could have done this and why.

The neighbours. Apart from Mrs Finkiel, we were on fairly good terms with all our neighbours.

Each of us examined our conscience. Betrayed girlfriends, ditched boyfriends, forgotten moneylenders, past friends, all the nutters we could possibly have come across.

We sat, taking turns to sip from the last two bottles of beer we'd found in the fridge, and waited for something, anything – a sign, a movement, a knock on the door, a rustle. We killed time and fear by exchanging ever less plausible theories.

At two in the morning, we tried screaming again, leaning out of the window, shouting into the empty, cold and sombre street and into the dark patch of Krakowski Park on the other side, but nothing came of it; our cries bounced across the city and disappeared without response. When a police car drew near, Sebastian threw another bottle in its direction and yelled something like:

"Fuck!" The bottle smashed right in front of the car. The car accelerated.

"When I get hold of this fucking moron, I'm going to drive over his legs then chuck him down Skałki," said Sebastian, taking it that one man was responsible for the whole thing.

At about four, we went to sleep. We spread some mattresses and blankets out on the floor for Robert and Anna and collapsed on our own beds fully dressed.

We didn't sleep long. At half past five, we heard a clanging. It was as though someone had struck the stairwell grating with a thick metal rod. Then we heard someone run up the stairs, followed by a forceful kick on the door, which resounded in all the windows and doorframes of the apartment.

The first to leap out of bed was Sebastian, emitting a guttural roar, which I understood to be something like "son of a bitch!" He held the kitchen knife he'd kept ready. We ran after him. But we didn't even manage to yank the front door open before there was another loud crash. The doors to the lift had closed.

There was nobody behind the door. The stairwell was just as empty, dark and cold as it had been a few hours ago. We just saw the cables slide as the lift went down. Heard someone get out a couple of floors down. We pressed the button as though trying to get a coin back from a broken coffee machine – the lift didn't return.

We heard the slow, measured sound of shoes hitting the stairs, two pairs, growing quieter by the second, by the tread. The regular stride of those living with impunity and the calm certainty that nobody's going to try to follow them. The stride of a prison warden.

I glanced under my feet. There was another piece of paper.

The same – squared, ripped from a school exercise book. I picked it up with two fingers, carefully, turned it over and read the message, scribbled again with a red felt-tip pen, the same unsteady writing.

SAY THAT YOU'LL NEVER COME BACK HERE AND WE'LL LET YOU OUT. SWEAR.

I was just about to say something, shout, but Sebastian was quicker. He leapt onto the grating, grabbed the bars and started bellowing down the stairwell.

"Come here! Come back, you bastard! I'll give you shit! Do you hear me? I'll get you back for this! Fuck you, come here now!"

But even if somebody had heard him, nobody answered. The footfalls had long grown silent at the tenement gate. The stairwell was silent and cold, dark and empty.

* * *

When my daughter wants to ask me something, she assumes the most streetwise expression possible. Legs astride, one to the side, the other forward, hands on hips. She carefully arranges the angle of her head, tilting it slightly in the direction of the leg to the side. She knows what she's doing. If I knew what I was doing as well as she does, maybe everything would have been different.

When my daughter finally asks me her question, it sounds rhetorical. Besides, my daughter never slouches. Always looks you straight in the eye. Doesn't cover her mouth when she speaks. And she speaks loud and clear. Maybe deep down inside she's unsure of herself, but, generally, she looks like an invincible warrior, even when all she's asking is whether there's any milk left. A twelve-year-old Valkyrie in leggings and with a collection of Japanese comics. I'd like to think that it's the result of something I'd been drumming into her since

I'd started to suspect that she understood Polish. But it's more likely that she was simply born this way. Must take after some great-great-grandmother.

"Ela, remember, you must never be vulnerable. Never show you're weaker than anyone. If somebody offends you, fight. If they hit you, hit them back twice as hard. Remember that you're the cleverest, prettiest *and* the best, and no piece of rubbish has the right to kick you around."

I repeat this to her non-stop, but really I'm repeating it for myself.

I kept drumming this message into her until, one day, I realised that she understood it better than I did. I was just preparing a silicone cast of a human jaw when I got a call from her form teacher. A quarter of an hour earlier, I'd received a call from the director with whom I was working at the time. He was a daydreamer and, that day, had fantasised about showing a fight scene with a four-second close-up of a guy whose jawbone had just been broken. He'd said:

"Aga, these idiots are making it look like something from a fucking cop soap, like Borewicz. Like when a guy works another over, it sounds like they're kicking sandbags and everyone knows their mugs are covered in ketchup. I want it to look real, you know. Like in *A History of Violence*."

"The guys making *A History of Violence* didn't work alone, from home, after hours and with a kid around," I said.

To which he replied:

"Look, we need to do it right so that they don't, like, fucking axe it in Paris and London, and you're going to be behind this, you know, it's your name that's going to be on it."

"It's definitely going to be shown in Paris and London."

"I won't ask again – get those casts and silicone scars to me by tomorrow night, or the production manager's going to kill me," he said and hung up before I could comment or say that if the production manager killed him, it would be a blessing.

Fifteen minutes later, the squealing cunt, meaning my

daughter's form teacher who spits dust and chalk even over the phone, called and squawked:

"Mrs Celińska, please come to the school. We've got a bit of a problem here."

I was just modelling some false teeth in mother of pearl, which I would then chip and paint yellow. Looking at a paused shot from *Dawn of the Dead* out of the corner of my eye. One zombie had a chipped jawbone exactly the way I wanted it.

I asked what the problem was.

"Ela pushed one of her classmates against the wall, scratched him and started kicking him. Marek has suspected concussion. He's a top student."

I released the pause button. The zombie's head turned into a green and red splodge. Unfortunately, the shooter had run out of ammo; a second later, another zombie ran up to him and bit off half his neck as easily as if he were chomping cheesecake. I pressed pause again. The scene had lasted two or three seconds. A whole team of special effects and make-up artists had worked on it for a week. And they probably weren't being shouted at down the phone by their daughters' teachers. Didn't have a twelve-year-old daughter. Weren't getting divorced.

"I'll be there shortly."

Ela was in the headmistress's office, which looked as though it hadn't changed since the days when I was my daughter's age: white eagle, ferns, subtle olfactory hints of rags and unwashed bodies. Except that instead of a typewriter, there was a computer and a photocopier. And there were colourful posters on the wall saying things like *Child's Day*, *All Children Belong to Us*, *Clean Up the Earth*.

When I entered, my daughter was standing in front of the headmistress's desk, arms folded and lips drawn into a headstrong line. She stared at me, sending a telepathic signal: "Get me out of here, surely you can see there's no point in talking to these people."

Behind the desk sat a nurse in a helmet formed by a

honey-coloured perm and a jacket that reminded me of the Balcerowicz Plan, the economic Shock Therapy of the nineties. The squealing cunt stood nearby in a long, black dress-like thing out of a bonprix fashion catalogue, her face plastered with powder. They were staring at me, sending me the telepathic signal: "You're another one of those self-made hussies who have their children up their arse and dump them here for us to look after like some friend's dog when they go on holiday. Oh, you'll get your just desserts in hell, you bitch, a kick in the arse for those *Wysokie Obcasy* magazines, all that sushi and yoga. Try teaching classics like *Knights of the Teutonic Order* to a bunch of hormone-charged half-wits, then you'll see what it's like."

I was wearing pink tracksuit bottoms and a fifteen-year-old World of Witches band T-shirt splashed with silicone and fake blood. My colourful turban was better than what was under it, meaning my hair, which I'd tried to dye the night before while holding five telephone conversations at once. I was the image of the end of counterculture.

I stood between them. Looked at the squealing cunt. She cleared her throat. The headmistress drummed an object that resembled a Chinese-like fountain pen against the table, hoping to add gravity to the situation. A bell rang in the background.

"We've got a problem here, Mrs Celińska," said the headmistress.

"Ela's been very aggressive of late," added the squealing cunt.

"Her classmates have said that Ela doesn't join in. She's been argumentative, unfriendly, has poor grades, and now—"

"He said I was a slut, Mum, that I do stuff with old guys for money." My daughter looked down and sniffed, but she didn't slouch; her arms were by her sides but not dangling uselessly. Tears glistened in her eyes, but I knew that she didn't have the slightest intention of bawling. "He said it during break in front of the whole class," she continued. "Then he followed me into the cloakroom and said he was going to post stuff on Facebook saying I give old men blowjobs…"

The headmistress cleared her throat. The squealing cunt wanted to raise her voice, but my glare stopped her. From that moment, I didn't have to act out the furious mother. I was so furious I had to hold back from throwing myself at her and biting into her aorta like the zombie in the film, the one with the jawbone.

"Watch what you say," I told my daughter.

"He went on and on about it, saying things like that," my daughter said loudly without a breath, like any child who has to speak out in their own defence and is simply trying to get as much in as they can before someone interrupts. "That I kiss boys on the willy, that I'm a slut and a chav. Maybe because I didn't want to kiss him at the school disco and told him that if he lost weight and washed more often, maybe I would. But he's really fat and ugly, Mum."

"What did he call you?" I wanted to make sure I'd heard correctly.

"Was I supposed to wait until he posted all that and smeared my reputation? I'd rather kill myself, Mum, he had to get what he deserved," concluded my daughter in defence, looking me in the eye. I subtly winked at her.

"You can see for yourself." The headmistress dotted her i's, so she thought.

"I certainly do." I dotted mine.

"We'll talk about it at home," I said, sweeping the air above Ela with my arm as though gathering her to leave. "I'm confiscating your tablet."

The headmistress glared at me, peeved and doubtful. The squealing cunt exhaled loudly and was at the door in a flash, cutting off my hasty retreat.

"Marek might be scarred for the rest of his life." She pronounced her medical opinion with deadly calm.

Personally, I regretted Marek had survived at all. Although we might have had a few problems if he hadn't.

"Olympian." The headmistress's voice reached me from behind her desk. "Winner of the Kangura Prize."

Actually, my daughter was the winner of the Regional Fine Arts Olympics for the best papier-mâché sculpture, which, according to her, represented the mysterious Japanese white magic symbol from her favourite Japanese cartoon. But I kept that information to myself.

"I'll talk to my daughter at home," I repeated, without turning around.

"Go to the car," I said, simulating an angry command aimed at my daughter. My daughter simulated outrage. Together we simulated slamming the door.

Once in the car, I hugged my daughter and kissed her about seventeen times until she started struggling.

"Mum, what's going on?" she asked while I, because of the silicone jawbone and missed lunch, pointed to the KFC looming on the horizon. She nodded and immersed herself in examining her nails, painted with some pink varnish she'd got as a freebie with a magazine.

"I'm proud of you," I told her, joining the traffic. My car wasn't exactly king of the road; it was a battered, bird-shit-spattered, sputtering, fifteen-year-old Volvo, which, in an act of great generosity, my husband had given to me when he'd bought himself a sparkling new Volvo to celebrate finishing some powdered soup adverts and a few episodes of *The Varsovians*.

My daughter scraped the varnish off her nails. I patted her on the hand and told her I'd give her some nail varnish remover at home.

"No moron's got the right to say things like that to you."

"Especially as it's not true, Mum," pointed out my daughter.

"That's neither here nor there," I said. "I hope he hurts."

"Alright, Mum, but it's not you who hit him. What if they chuck me out of school?" my daughter said and returned to scraping off the varnish. The sound reminded me of polystyrene being ripped and set my teeth on edge. But I was too proud of Ela to tell her off.

"You'll go to another," I said. "And finish one in the end. Ela, it's more important that you know how to punch somebody in the face when they've offended you."

I parked in front of the KFC and realised that my daughter knew this better than I did. She knew how to punch somebody in the face when they offended her. She could already teach me. She deserved some fried chicken and some hideous strawberry ice cream. We bought more than we could eat in three days and drove home.

Regardless of honour and self-defence, it's hard not to create what are generally believed to be problems of upbringing when you watch your mum at home trying to squeeze as many things as she can into small suitcases, compress her belongings, blouses, trousers, skirts, jewellery, tights, books, cosmetics, discs, laptop, documents, powders, fake blood, silicone, gum, foams, wigs, dyes and latex into a tiny space. When her eyes look like two huge swellings with a little, narrow slit in the middle; when she's pacing the apartment from corner to corner with fast but uncertain steps, when her movements are abrupt but not in the least effective.

"So, you're moving out, Mum?" asked Ela.

I nodded, blew my nose and once more started rearranging things. I couldn't allow myself to stop and sit on the bed in front of my daughter, wring my hands while tears ran silently from my eyes.

"You don't have to pretend to be a supermum, Mum," remarked my daughter.

I could see that she wanted to burst into tears too, and knew how bravely she was holding back. I started to look around the apartment in search of things that were indisputably mine, not bought together during mutual arguments conventionally known as shopping or given to me as a present to say "I beg you, please forgive me." I searched for things that were completely mine, those I'd brought to the relationship as a dowry – but there weren't many. More had been bought with the grand gesture of a momentarily independent woman, for what was undeniably her money, far from home and in loneliness. But these things – DVDs, French and English magazines, clothes, bags, other pieces of crap – I probably didn't need.

Thirty-five isn't a good age to suddenly have to choose your own colours from a smeared palette that won't separate regardless of how much solvent you use. Some things can't be easily divided between two people who have lived together and thank each other for cooperating. Even if that cooperation was a sham, purely professional, continued out of habit, even if its best moments meant mechanical sex and polite indifference.

My daughter doesn't cry, she shakes and whimpers like a broken toy. Now she shuffles up and puts her thin arms around me. They're smudged with paint and sticky with some gungy chewing gum. I sit down instantly and start to howl. We howl together, two broken dolls.

"I want to go with you, Mum," snivels my daughter, and I feel that I haven't got an ordinary heart but alien offal scratched with a rusty fork. I've never had a heart attack, but this is worse. "It'll be a fantastic adventure," she goes on. "The two of us will go on a long road trip. We'll even go to the States and see the Grand Canyon. We'll sleep in cheap hotels and buy hideous sunglasses. Eat hamburgers in cheap diners until we get terribly fat. It'll be fantastic, Mum, you'll see, like in a film. Like in your favourite film."

"Thelma and Louise die in the end, darling," I say to my daughter.

"No, they don't. They go to heaven," replies my daughter. She's the world's best.

I catch sight of my old CD holder, smeared with fluorescent paints and covered with stickers from long gone Warsaw techno clubs.

"Dad's not a bad person. He loves you, and you need to

stay with him for a bit." I try to speak like a reader on a tape teaching a foreign language; it's the only calm I'm capable of feigning now. My daughter snuggles even closer. My heart isn't pulsating of its own accord, more like leaping convulsively in some corrosive, boiling liquid. "But we'll keep seeing each other. More and more often," I add, my speech even slower, as though the tape has stretched. I don't feel I'm myself, more like I'm looking at a stranger who is saying things completely against their will, but the will gains the upper hand in articulation, stretches the vowels, stretches the tape.

"Dad's an idiot," declares my daughter.

"Don't say that," I reply.

"You're the only one who's allowed to say it," my daughter reproaches me.

"Yes, I am," I uphold.

Ela's father's nothing but my husband, someone whom I've already run away from once. I could have not returned. But it's pointless using the past conditional in the present. It can finish you off; besides, it doesn't suit rational people.

I met my daughter's father thirteen years ago. I was twenty-two and studying at the Academy of Fine Arts in Warsaw. You could say I was a party girl who painted terrible pictures. I copied images from leaflets handed out by Jehovah's Witnesses, for example, and gave the people on them heads of cows or pigs. My friends liked all that, because we took a lot of drugs at the time. I frequented the Blue Velvet, Paragraf 5ą and Przestrzeń Graffenberg clubs. Pre-Cambrian now, of course. Post-Second World War Polish history for today's youngsters, those from Barka and Plan. But for me they were a colourful and pulsating world made up of beautiful boys and extravagant girls, continuous glittering raves, non-stop balls and hundreds of far from clever ideas. In my mind, this entire period features as a swimming pool full of sweet wrappers. Everything rustled and glistened. True enough, I wasn't exceptionally degenerate, didn't do drugs every day, wasn't addicted to alcohol, didn't jump into bed with any man who came along; but I loved being surrounded by hundreds of people, laughing so loudly and for so long that my head spun. I remember, I adored ecstasy. I don't know whether it still exists.

Then I met Ela's father, who was twenty-five at the time and had just finished film school. I remember that he was the handsomest guy around, but I don't remember where we met; he'd have to remind me. Although, when we do speak now, we're not exactly inclined to reminisce. I just remember that I saw him and knew that it had to be him; these things used to happen to me very often at the time, but I walked up to him and said: "Come."

And he came.

Everything was great at first. It was like a hit song. Ela's father loved talking. He talked a lot and spun beautiful fairy tales. He really knew a lot of words, had written an erratum to everything. He read and watched as though his life depended on it and recounted everything with unparalleled vehemence. He loved the cinema. The heavier, the better. When he started talking about *Satantango* or *Cries and Whispers*, he really did tremble. On top of that, he had masses of great ideas. He'd get up in the middle of the night and wake me up to go to the Vistula. We'd walk until dawn and he'd say what a beautiful dawn it was, then talk for three hours about filming the dawn. He'd take photos of me naked, as many as five thousand a day. Once, we hitch-hiked to Sicily. Then we went a second time, in his car. He knew how to cook, and those were days when only our mothers cooked, so I was really impressed.

I was truly in love with him. Or perhaps he was so loud, there was so much of him, that he left me no room to realise that he'd simply beguiled me.

Then everything started to get screwed up, which is far more interesting because things get screwed up a little differently for everybody.

Ela's father was a young director. Like every young

director, he wanted to direct his own film, like every young director, he had a fascinating script and, like every young director, didn't have any money. He kept trying to improve his ingenious script and sent it to every Polish producer, all of whom turned out to be grey-haired guys in Italian jackets costing four times the average national wage, a golden chain with a medal of Our Lady dangling from it, and a signet ring. All of them made it clear: "Nobody's going to buy this, man, nobody's going to understand it. Wipe the snot from your nose and stop trying to be another Lynch." Ela's father really wanted to be a young Lynch and tried extremely hard to become one. At night, lying next to me in bed straight after sex, he'd say: "I see the first scene as being set in a corridor flooded with blue light. Hypnotic music – no rhythm, no tune, just a hum. And then somebody comes from the far end of the corridor and stands in the middle, in front of the camera, but far away. We don't see who it is, don't see where they've really come from, whether there's a door. We don't know who it is; they're a black smudge to the viewer. We just hear them start to scream."

Ela's father also had a lot of ideas regarding us. He wanted a house in the country. A large family. Wanted an apiary and to rear cows. Wanted a yurt in Tuscany and to tread fresh olives with his bare feet as he'd once done with a friend. Wanted us to go to Africa. He wanted a lot and talked a lot. But everything was a vague idea, a fantasy on the horizon. Nothing materialised because Ela's father was, and is, a man of ideas thrown at people who are supposed to catch them politely and make them real. He simply knew how to and liked to talk. Little else.

At first, I was drunk on his talk. Only later did I start to pay attention to the details. That Ela's father still lived with his parents. That he didn't really listen to me, that when I said something about myself, he turned the other way and jiggled his leg. That he was extremely nice to women, various women, including his past girlfriends whom he absolutely wanted me to meet. That he was sometimes nicer to them than to me. That he often didn't pick up his phone, especially when I wanted something from him. That he often spent the night at his friends' places, concocting scripts.

But by the time these details had become very clear, there was also a very clear Ela the size of a tennis ball in my belly.

Ela's father's parents gave us an apartment left by his grandmother. It didn't cost them a great deal because Ela's father's father ran one of the oldest law establishments in Warsaw. To make it clear, I didn't demand anything of them. I didn't demand anything of anyone, so I didn't demand anything of them either. But I started to realise, in that apartment, that I'd locked myself in a cage with a stranger on whom I couldn't particularly count and who didn't have much to say to me.

The apartment was lifeless and full of objects belonging to a dead woman I'd never known. We were forbidden to throw anything away, so we existed in a waiting room among unfamiliar books, flea-ridden clothes, plywood furniture. The grandmother's heavy, damp coats and furs hung in the wardrobe. I was scared of touching anything. Ela's father's mother hated me and thought I was a drifter, a drug addict, satanist and HIV carrier. Despite hating me, she managed to visit our apartment as though it were her own – it had, after all, been her mother's – and spend hours telling me that my child was going to be blighted because I was blighted. She was right, I was full of venom, I swelled a million times in her starched linen, couldn't hold my shit in, and blood kept pouring out of me. By night, Ela's father polished his script about screaming in a blue corridor. Or simply went off to Dębki with his friends. "On a recce," he claimed.

His mother came every day. Kept doing the laundry and disinfecting the house, although she'd have to throw out all the awful old flea-ridden things in order to disinfect it properly.

Ela's birth was inhuman. She came into the world without an epidural and without her father there. When I screamed that

I was having contractions, the midwife, without looking at me, came out with various encouraging phrases such as "go and pull yourself together". My daughter scored low on the Apgar scale, had the cord wrapped around her neck and was blue, and they only handed her to me the following day. After the birth, Ela's father's mother still kept coming to our apartment. She entered without knocking, then sauntered around, opened the windows, moved objects from place to place. Didn't speak to me. Sometimes, she'd take her granddaughter in her arms and perform typical, idiotic things grandmothers perform with grandchildren, all that "a coochie coochie coo" talk, or "Who's a beautiful little girly whirly?" It sounded like someone sanding the floor.

Ela's father was a broken man at the time because his father didn't want to give him any money for his film. He'd said that they'd already given him the apartment, that his career as the new Lynch could wait and that, all in all, he should stop making a fool of himself. But really, Ela's father's parents, both of them, just couldn't accept the fact that their son had had a child with a woman he hadn't married. They didn't know how to tell their families or friends. After some time, Ela's father's father told Ela's father that he was to marry me because, firstly, what did it look like? And secondly, if he didn't, then he wouldn't get any money.

I wasn't screaming yet. Ela's father told me that we were going to have a lot of money some day, that we were going to be happy, that his parents would be dead. He talked about this or about the first scene in his film, which changed every week; I couldn't get even an hour's sleep.

I was more and more out of it every day. I did everything on autopilot. Got up on autopilot, fed the baby on autopilot, carried her non-stop in my arms, gently rocking her on autopilot, because she cried when I put her down, listened to screaming blue corridors on autopilot, opened the envelope that contained the decision about my being crossed off the student list on autopilot – people still got crossed off student lists in those days. We got married on autopilot in the Ursus Registry Office at the beginning of 1998 or thereabouts. I don't remember much of the reception apart from the fact that I didn't even invite my best friend, and that Ela's father's drunk uncle pinched me on the backside as I danced with him to some jaunty song about summer, knickers and blueberries. And I also remember that my mum followed me to the Ladies', wiped the mascara that had run down my face and said: "You can still get out of this, darling." I wasn't screaming yet. A long time ago, before the wedding, my mum had wished me: "May you never scream. The only people who scream are those who are naturally bad or those driven to the extreme." As it turned out, it took much, much more for me to start screaming.

Ela's father said that it would be great if we had a boy to complete our family, one who'd be called Stanisław. "Stanisław, great," I agreed, staring at the many layered, pink christening cake. "Stanisław's my father's name," declared Ela's father. "And so it is," I replied.

A year after Ela was born, I ran away for the first time. Outwardly, everything seemed to be getting better and happier. Ela's father got a job as first assistant director on the soap opera *The Varsovians*. He adored it and soon forgot about his blue light, non-rhythmic hum and black, screaming figure. *The Varsovians* was about the adventures of three young couples who had just moved into their own colourful new apartments on the first best, newly constructed housing estate. These colourful people in the colourful serial had problems such as having nowhere to park, being stuck in traffic jams, smog in the city centre and unexpected invasions from their parents. All this set to a soundtrack of overly happy, farty music.

Ela's father earned a fair amount of money, bought a car with a child's seat in it and declared that we were going to rent a better apartment and let the one in which we lived. He didn't talk much to me at all any more. Sometimes picked up his daughter, tried to hide his unease.

Ela's father's mother bought some pink blinds and, without a word, hung them up in the window of the smallest room, which she decided was to be the nursery.

I slept two hours a day, spending the rest of the twenty-four hours in a state of stupefied wakefulness like a monitor with a flickering screensaver. I didn't have any friends; my friends had stayed behind at that unidentified party where I'd met the father of my child, and nobody had realised yet that I'd left the club. Maybe I didn't want those friends. I didn't really have anything to say to anybody. I fed the child, ignored my mother-in-law and surfed from TV channel to TV channel. Ela's father filmed the series, as well as some adverts for medicines. We painted the apartment. The dead grandmother's things were finally disposed of.

Finally, we moved out of there to a three-room apartment in Ochota. It was bright and white. I'd wake in the mornings convinced that I was still in the old one. Nothing had changed. In the newly bought wardrobes, I picked up the smell of damp furs.

I remember a time when Ela's father left in the early morning to shoot the Christmas episode of *The Varsovians*. Before leaving, he told me that Adrian, one of the characters, was wondering whether to buy Basia a Peugeot or a Renault for Christmas. He talked about nothing else. I didn't feel the need to talk. I couldn't, to be honest. Somewhere I'd lost the knowledge of who he really was. I forgot how to attach a first name and a surname to the face, stature, gait and voice. One day, when he got out of bed and traipsed in his underwear to brush his teeth, I saw an entirely different person. He, his mother, most people – all had lost their contours, had changed into smudges without outlines. That's exactly how my life as a mentally unbalanced person began.

I knew only that my daughter was my daughter and that she was called Ela, and that I was called Agnieszka and that I loved my daughter. I told myself over and over again: "I know that I love my daughter, I love my daughter, I love my daughter, I love my daughter…" When Ela's father talked about the happy Christmas adventures of *The Varsovians*, I stared at the pink blinds.

In the morning, I took one-year-old Ela and went to my mum's. That was when I ran away for the first time. I ran away peacefully. Stuck a note to the fridge. Lied that I'd be back soon. Everything was still alright. I wasn't screaming yet.

* * *

The hallway constitutes the main aorta of the Institute. It contains a white lamp from IKEA with a synthetic fabric shade on which a drunk and stoned Iga had once painted a cartoon of two philosophising bunnies; two run-down armchairs from the interwar years picked up from a rubbish dump; an old green fake-leather sofa from the Ugly Cat; and ashtrays, cardboard boxes full of unread newspapers, scratched discs, washed-out clothes, boxes creaking with unused objects that didn't fit in the improvised closet in the toilet.

Right now, we are all pacing the hallway, biting our nails, sharing cigarettes, gnawing holes into our sleeves, waiting. It's Monday, ten o'clock in the morning. We've spent the last few hours shouting and calling out through the window, but Aleje Trzech Wieszczów, completely deserted earlier, is now so choked with a stream of cars, hooting buses and lorries that nobody's going to hear a bunch of people screaming from the fifth floor. The windows on the other side of the apartment overlook the yard, where there's never anybody apart from residents taking their rubbish out; there aren't even any students getting drunk in the gateway, because the entrance to the tenement is always locked.

There are two bedrooms on each side of the hallway – all four of which have the same heavy brown door with glazed panes of thick cut glass. Beyond the two rooms on the left, the hallway turns towards a bright kitchen with a fridge, gas stove, table and an insurance company's calendar. The calendar shows the victims of accidents – a different pile-up for every month of the year. Above the stove hang cupboards pasted with cuttings from colourful culinary magazines. We stare at them while chewing on rice and hotdogs. Pictures of panna cotta with caramelised pears, eels baked in a sauce of caramelised lemons, black tiger prawn tart, Thai soup with marinated ginger. I'm sure that if I ever go to a Thai restaurant and order Thai soup, I'll stab the waitress in the artery with my fork if I find even a single grain of rice in it.

Straight up the hallway, your back to the front door, are doors to the toilet and the bathroom. The unused toilet is the size of a small wardrobe, ninety percent of its surface taken up by the toilet bowl; the rest of the space just about fits some toilet paper and a newspaper. We don't use it, because its stuffed with piles of old shoes, clothes and boxes. It acts as storage space because I didn't have enough money left to refurbish it. But I did have enough to do the bathroom, which is fitted with navy-blue tiles, a gleaming white bath, imitation marble taps and chrome towel rails. Now, however, a hardened, slippery layer of hair, dust and old skin grows on the navy-blue tiles, and even in the morning, only cold water runs from both taps. It takes forty minutes to fill the bath with water. We wouldn't have the slightest chance of winning a world championship in cleaning and home repairs.

Every hour we restart our ritual, stomping on the floor and turning the music up as loud as possible in every room. We've tried shouting to passers-by since seven in the morning, but they don't even look up. None of our actions get a response, so we carry on waiting until 'They' come, carry on sitting or walking around in circles, talking less and less, saving our voices for the next bout of shouting. Black and White make the most noise meowing, demanding food that has already run out. Yet in the intervals between their meows, they listen out like us, ready to attack, as though they know something is wrong. White lies on a radiator; Black sits on the gas meter. Two distinguished, fat and castrated tomcats with the monitoring abilities of military radar. We give them what we ourselves eat, but both are fussy. They sniff the overcooked rice and, wagging their tails, walk away from their bowls and, meowing, return to their posts.

Just in case, we've collected all the sharp instruments in one place. Screwdrivers, bread knives, scissors.

"These people haven't got the faintest idea what they're doing, sis. Because when they finally let us out, you're going straight to the police and reporting all this," says Iga for what must be the fifth time as she traces endless circles with her burning cigarette.

I nod. She's right, but my attention is preoccupied with the walls of my apartment, which we'd painted rainbow orange, blood red and fluorescent green, spattered with postcards from Berlin bars, posters we'd torn down in the streets advertising festivals, video installations, exhibition openings and gatherings of religious sects and raves at the Cat with names such as "Beach party", "American surf rock from the eighties", "Ladies in bikinis – first drink free" or "Alojzy Krzemień, Digging up the unknown". I remember the feeling surging in me as I painted the walls, previously mouldy, heavy and brown, covered with patches of old dirt. The sense of lifting a spell, drawing out the colours of the real home from under the enchantment cast over it. For two weeks I'd painted, sanded the floor, shopped and returned with carrier bags full of air fresheners and rowanberry scented candles from IKEA to kill the omnipresent bouquet of smells that pervaded the apartment – flowering mycelium, yellowing shirts, valerian and methylated spirits.

"I hope they get ten years," says Iga.

"For what crime?" asks Gypsy, barely raising his eyes.

"Attempted illegal possession of property, kidnapping, threat, blackmail, mental abuse?"

"What the fuck do we need the police for? We'll sort it out ourselves." Sebastian's standing in the hallway, still in the same Banda tracksuit, brushing his teeth, his mouth full of froth.

Iga asks me whether I want to eat something. I nod, although all we've got is rice, hotdogs and rusty, chlorinated running water, a bag of tea from the discount store containing four hundred teabags from which you can make a hundred and fifty relatively strong mugs of tea, and a carrier bag full of flowering potatoes. The packets of rice are what's left of supplies bought a few months ago – Iga had dragged them back after a campaign called "Food not bombs". The massive box of hotdogs was brought in one day by Sebastian who declared from the threshold that he'd received it as a gift. When we tried to press him to tell us which friend hands out such original gifts, he said something about an indebted cold meats wholesaler. Apart from being a security guard at the Ugly Cat, Sebastian occasionally makes ends meet as a debt collector.

So that's all we have. No cheese, cold meats, frozen fish, jarred sauces, milk, bread, no normal food, because none of us remembered to go shopping, nobody thought we were going to be incarcerated.

Iga shares a room with Veronica. The second on the right. It's the largest room in the Institute, divided into two different galaxies, something like a living room with a bed and a disorderly stack of books, CDs and photocopied posters on Iga's side, and a perfectly made mattress, table with television, Japanese pictures and amulets pinned to the wall on Veronica's.

Iga's the youngest of us. She's twenty-five and has black dreads with a forever backcombed fringe. My mum would have described her face as bright and chubby if it weren't for the many earrings and piercings. Iga's always swaddled in belts and pockets; her jackets, covered with sew-ons and pin-ons, have ninety pockets, just like her trousers and skirts, all in black. To go with these black multipurpose clothes of a leftist terrorist, she always wears glaring bright pink tights.

For Iga, 'They', for whom we are waiting, 'They', who are breaking into our apartment, are the sort of people who call and pant into the receiver or repeat one word – the German *raus*. 'They', like Sebastian, are bald and at their peak, dripping with testosterone, and use the words "faggot", "lesbo", "fucker". Just as Sebastian is big, Iga is short but thickset and strong, with a voice like a foghorn. She's got a PhD in Cultural Studies and has been a punk since she was twelve. She has a stiff, moral backbone and straightforward tenets. Loyalty and friendship, faithfulness and honesty, one for all and all for one. Iga can't lie, can't say "No, I'm not giving you anything to eat", "I'm not putting you up for the night", "I'm not going to lend you any money". She has the heart of Mother Teresa and, when necessary, the fists of a thug from Nowa Huta. And it is from her room – and not Sebastian's – that Polish hip-hop about fucking the police and a hard life behind bars sometimes thumps throughout the entire apartment and gives me a headache.

Gypsy has the first room on the left. Right now, he's sitting next to me on the sofa, trying not to touch me, gazing at my room with the look of someone who might be deep in thought but could just as easily be thinking of nothing. Gypsy is tall, sickeningly thin, unshaven, with wide-open eyes that give him the look of someone who's just experienced their first hallucinations. He's twenty-nine, but his unshaven and wasted face make it hard to guess his age, just as it's hard to guess the age of someone who's homeless or a drug addict. A strange, sinuous and clearly unfinished tattoo coils around his arm. He works for some obscure company that officially offers insurance and investment advice but, in reality, pours its clients' money into stocks, doubles it, buys crude oil, gold and shares. He's always got money. Once, having drunk a horrific amount of vodka, he confessed that he had a hell of a lot of it. But for some reason he prefers to rent a small room, unfurnished apart from the mattress, laptop, a few newspapers and a cardboard box for his clothes.

"It's easier that way, Agnieszka," he said, "because all those things are just a burden. And I want to be able to move from place to place and not be weighed down. Light. Besides, I'm not interested in money. I'm interested in the process of making it."

"Why's it so interesting?" I asked.

"Because a child could do it. I don't understand why everybody goes on about how impossible it is," he replied.

Gypsy got into the Sorbonne and got thrown out after a year for spending more time with the dossers in the Paris suburbs than studying. Back in Poland, he finished the Warsaw School of Economics with distinction. In three years.

Jacek became Gypsy because that's what Sebastian christened him due to his forever creased trousers and shirts, his habit of walking barefoot and his long beard, which is now sprouting shoots. I know Gypsy best. All in all, I'd like to know him a little less. Then at least he'd look me in the eye, not automatically try to leave the room when I ask him something, not move away from me when sitting on the same sofa. But that's not important at the moment.

What's important is what's going on now. The explanations we'd come up with throughout the morning had stopped making sense. All afternoon we'd tried to answer the question of who 'They' are and what 'They' want in vain. Our theories were illogical, a load of nonsense; after all, there's not the slightest hint of logic in what's going on.

"But you're not going to hand over the apartment to them." Iga doesn't stop tapping her foot, or smoking cigarettes. "It's absurd. 'They' are doing something that will send them to prison for a good number of years. People once tried bullying us like that when we were squatting. Bolted the door, chucked bottles full of petrol through the window. They all got six months when the police caught them. And this isn't some sort of squat. It's your apartment."

Gypsy merely shakes his head. In his opinion, nothing can be done. Nobody's going to go to jail because 'They' can do anything. To Gypsy, 'They' are financial freemasons. Owners of capital, main shareholders, owners of control packages.

Synods of anonymous billionaires hiding in the dark. People whose money he transfers from account to account as though picking air out of one cardboard box and putting it into another. Gypsy says that the old communist system's far from over in Poland. Capital remains in the same hands. It always has been in private hands. Once, the money had been kept in Swiss accounts. Then cable factories were bought, computer equipment imported and banks set up. But Gypsy claims it's the same people. It's 'Them'. He says all this without getting overexcited, which is something he usually does when spouting his theories. He's speaking quietly, barely opening his lips, slowly dragging on his cigarette, shrugging.

The second room on the left is Sebastian's. Sebastian is a bald, block-like mass, his name a joke. He weighs a hundred and twenty kilos. Is a metre ninety-five tall. Thirty-two years of age. His head and shoulders are covered with tiny scars; one, particularly large – a motorbike accident, he claims – runs from one ear, over his brow to the middle of his forehead. His face is coarse cut; the first thing to catch your eye is the huge, even line of his brows, but beneath it peer surprisingly expressive deep brown eyes that reveal every mood swing. When he falls into a rage, reined in by remnants of upbringing and awareness, the eyes become terrifying. Sebastian is an active fan of Cracovia FC and sometimes shows us photos of himself wearing tight jeans and a Fred Perry jacket, his face clad in a balaclava. I take his word for it because the other fifty men in the photos also wear balaclavas and Fred Perry jackets. And when he touches the screen with his finger to show us what's supposedly him pushing a plastic rubbish bin towards five policemen, his eyes glisten damply and he laughs so much I have to believe him.

When he's not being a security guard or an occasional debt collector, Sebastian does weights, lifting one hundred kilo barbells for two, three hours a day and working out diets for bodybuilders on the www.beefitup.pl forum. His room is neat with the neatness of a grandson living at his grandmother's.

Pastel-coloured walls. On the shelf, framed photos of him with a girl. Soft toys, flowers in flowerpots, Cracovia's ensign, a poster in a clip frame of some MMA contender who looks like an oiled, sinewy sack of meat with a head attached. Dumbbells and big tubs of powdered protein by the bed.

To Sebastian, 'They' are the police. Or Wisła FC fans. Or the united power of both. Sometimes he says this aloud, adding that he's joking, then returns to his previous theory, shouting that the whole thing is aimed at him. Threatens he'll kill them if needs be, crush them underfoot, rip their throats apart.

Sebastian is the calmest of us all – apart from brief moments when every single muscle, every individual ligament vibrates; at moments like these, he presses his fists into his eyes like binoculars and swallows huge gulps of air. While trying to control himself, he speaks quickly, swallows his syllables.

"You're not giving anything back to them. We're going to sit here until they come, and when they do, they're going to get the shit beaten out of them. They just try to come in and I'll throw them down the stairs one by one."

In the end, he simmers down, although it looks as if he's crushed the calmness into his head with his fists. He stretches and stands over us, hands in pockets.

"My handbag," says a voice that I don't instantly recognise. I turn in its direction and see Anna, Robert's girlfriend. She's squatting by the wall, smoking a cigarette with fast, shallow drags. Unshaken ash falls on her shoes. Robert is standing in the doorway looking at her as vacantly as Gypsy. By the look of him, he's not slept a wink.

Anna and Robert, Veronica's friends who'd come for a coffee right before we got locked in. One of them works, the other studies. Maybe they both work and study. I can't remember. All I know is that it's something to do with Spanish, because the last time Anna was here, she'd mainly talked about Spain, the Basques, flamenco and Sephardic music. To be honest, I don't know them – this is only the second, third or maybe fourth time they'd been here. Anna is shaking all over as though there was a little messed-up engine in her stomach. She's drumming her fingers on her knee and tapping her foot on the floor. Robert isn't paying her any attention, he just sits, turning a tin candle-coaster, which has assumed the shape of aluminium snot, over and over in his fingers. He looks like he's trying to be present, be in the here and now, but something, probably fear, freezes his muscles, makes him fold in on himself and shrink.

Anna suddenly breaks out into a cough. Controlling herself, she gestures apologetically at the cigarette.

"Why are you smoking?" asks Robert.

"It's my first," she says.

"Since when?" I ask, lighting another.

"First ever," she explains, choking again. Robert sits on the floor. They are now both sitting in the same position, on opposite sides of the room. He's looking at her as though wanting to say something but not knowing what.

"What handbag?" asks Iga, leaving the kitchen carrying two plates, one with rice and hotdogs, the other only rice.

"Someone stole my bag on the tram on the way here." Anna keeps choking over her cigarette, trying to inhale as shallowly as possible but without success. "All my things were in it: documents, phone, everything. Somebody – I don't know who – cut the strap with a knife. I didn't even notice."

"Your phone was in it?" I echo.

We'd all forgotten to ask these two whether they had a phone.

"Have you got yours?" I ask Robert, but he shakes his head.

"I left it in a taxi a few days ago," he says.

"Yes, phone, documents, everything, absolutely everything," repeats Anna, her voice breaking more and more, her words snapping in half, phrase by phrase.

Robert stands up, walks over to her and plucks the cigarette from her fingers, extinguishes it in the ashtray.

"Don't panic, Anna. Calm down. And don't smoke."

Anna starts to cry silently. I get up, take her by the hand and lead her to the bathroom.

"Come on, I'll touch up your make-up for you. It's smudged," I say and plunge both my hands into a box full of cosmetics. I feel an old pregnancy test beneath my hand. The cosmetics are rejects, used up – remains of foundation at the bottom, lumps of old powder, broken pencils. I pick up my make-up remover and a cotton pad, slowly wipe away the salt and old mascara from Anna's face. Try to smile.

Apart from rice, tea and hotdogs, we've also got cigarettes, which Papa gave us. We started with two cartons, now have less than one and a half. It would be much harder without them.

I want the girl to relax. I smile at her, but it doesn't help. Maybe I'm no good at faking sincere smiles. I rest one hand on her knee, and with gentle, short strokes, start to paint her eyelashes, tell her to look up, but she keeps blinking and staring vacantly into my eyes. It's like making-up a drunk guy.

"Anna," I say. "Anna, it'll be over soon."

"The question is *how*," she replies breathlessly.

"I'm sure it's going to be alright," I add and wipe away a new set of tears and mascara. An endless task.

"And what if they really *do* do something to us?" she asks.

"They're not going to do anything. Somebody will come and let us out. And a locksmith will come and cut the grating," I say.

There's a crash against the wall and the loud smack of something large against metal. I throw the mascara on the floor and run out to the landing. Everyone has jumped up and is standing in the doorway; I shove them aside and see a boy on the other side of the grating. He can't move. Sebastian, arms outstretched through the grating, is gripping his jacket and squashing him against the bars with all his strength. The boy is about eighteen, underweight like someone on speed, and visibly shaking.

"Tell your mates I'm going to kill them! I'll throw them all down the stairs. Tell them that, you piece of shit! That's the only reason I haven't put a knife in your guts yet, because you're to fucking go back and tell them," says Sebastian.

"Who is he? Sebastian!" I shout but instantly see the answer. Behind the boy, on the stairs, lies a thermal bag with the logo of a pizzeria; it's splashed with garlic sauce from a cracked container. The same logo is on his zip-up jacket.

"How did you get in?" I ask.

He can't speak. Sebastian is pressing him against the grating, hard, as though wanting to yank him to the other side. The bars dig so deeply into the boy's face it flattens it. I tap Sebastian on the shoulder. He grabs the boy with one hand and with the other catches him by the chin and bends his head back.

"As usual, by the stairs. The lift's not working. They're repairing it. I saw them on the way in."

"Who's repairing it?" I get close to him as though I were about to kiss him. Smell his cigarettes, chewing gum, deodorant from Carrefour, and the sweat of fear.

"Fucking hell, the people who repair lifts!" he screams. "Are you completely screwed up? Guys in overalls, with tools. They said the lift's going to be out of order until tomorrow."

I stretch and raise my arms. Realise that I've spent most of the day sitting in the armchair chain-smoking, in one position – the position of someone ready to jump up immediately and attack. I'm one enormous cramp.

"Tell your friends they're dead. Fuck you!! Cars are going to pick them up, their mothers packed into the boot, and they're going to fucking bury their mothers in the forest. You tell them that," growls Sebastian, like a raging beast.

This time I place my hand on his huge oval bald head as though checking if he has a fever.

"Let him go," I say.

"You must be crazy to think I'm going to let him go."

"He's only a pizza guy."

"Sure."

"Let go, Sebastian."

Sebastian's panting again, throbbing like an overheated machine, but he does what I say.

"Nobody here's ordered a pizza," I try to explain to the boy, but he's frantically looking for something in his pockets. Finally, he pulls out an order form and starts to read out loud:

"Apartment 12, 20 Mickiewicz Avenue. Four large pepperoni pizzas. Somebody ordered pizza here. They said you were shooting a film, a horror film, but I see it's even worse, bloody hell." The boy rattles out.

"Yes, that's here," I reply calmly, as though explaining to a retarded child. "But nobody here has ordered a pizza. There's no way we can phone. Our phones aren't working."

"You don't understand, nobody ordered pizza by phone. A woman came in this morning, just after we opened, ate something on the spot and ordered pizzas – to this address, this apartment, to be delivered now."

Iga and Veronica step out of the apartment.

"What did she look like?" asks Iga.

"Shooting a film? Who said we're shooting a film?" I ask.

"My God, some woman, okay? She was about forty. Dyed hair. Clearly looks after herself. I don't remember anything else… Glasses. I remember she wore glasses."

"What film?" I ask.

"I don't know!" yells the boy. "I don't fucking know what film! What's happening here, what's wrong with you all?"

For a moment, there's silence.

Sebastian spits through the bars at the pizza.

"We've got food," he says, then turns to me and adds: "They're probably spiked with something more than cheese and pepperoni that'd knock us out, damn it, so take the sodding pizzas and fuck off. Eat them yourself if you want."

"You're all fucked up," the boy sums up.

"Bugger off!" bellows Sebastian. "Sod off, out of sight. Here's two tenners, take those and fuck off."

"Wait," I say to the boy as peacefully as I can, wanting to

hold him back for a second. "Wait, you've got to do something for us, wait, please."

The boy hides the money in his pocket, grabs the pizzas, and, in one leap, lands on the mezzanine. But a moment later, he turns and walks up again. The bars are imprinted on his face and a metal leaf from the fin de siècle adornment has cut his nose; blood trickles down his face. He pulls something out of the thermal bag, slips it through the grating and drops it on the floor at my feet.

"The woman asked me to leave this here."

I pick up a typically girly purple-red bag speckled with blobs of coloured thread and sequins.

"Will you do something for us?" I ask the boy.

"Leave me alone. You're totally screwed up," he replies.

"Please?" I ask, more pleadingly. "Go to the police. Tell them that we've been locked in our apartment. Our phones have been stolen and the internet's been cut off. We've been shouting from the windows, but nobody can hear us. And tell those guys repairing the lift to come up. We want to talk to them. Please?"

"You're screwed up."

"I know that's how it looks." I look him in the eyes. "But I'm begging you. I can give you money. I'll give you two hundred złotys right now."

"You're screwed up."

"Two hundred złotys now and more when you come back," I say.

"You don't want that," he replies.

"Don't want what?" I ask.

"Those guys down there to come upstairs." The boy chucks the boxes of pizza at my feet and runs down the stairs very fast, so fast that for a moment I'm sure he's going to trip and somersault all the way down.

"My bag. You've got my bag." Anna's voice behind me sounds like glass cracking.

I hand her the bag. She grabs it for a brief moment then

immediately drops it on the floor, lowers her head and freezes like an appliance cut off from power. Iga picks the bag up and takes Anna by the arm.

Anna opens the bag. Starts to rummage inside.

"Anything there? What's in it?" I ask.

"It's not, it's not there... my phone's not there... only useless..." she says quietly to herself. Finally, she pulls something out. A crumpled piece of white paper. On it, in red ink, are the words:

WE'RE GOING TO MEET SOON.

"Go in, Anna," I say. "Go in."

She's looking at me. Reminds me of a frail animal. "Go in," I repeat, and she finally listens. Sebastian returns to the landing. He's shaking all over, as though he's been standing over a pneumatic drill for hours.

"We've got to get out of here." I turn to him, indicating the grating. "As quickly as possible. Then we can go to the police."

"Get out?" yells Sebastian, waving his arms. "And to what police? What the fuck for? We've got to wait for them here! They'll be here soon and then we'll fucking do them over!"

"No, Sebastian," I say, loud and clear. "No. They're not going to come unless we give in. They'll let us out when we let them know that I'm handing the apartment over to them."

"I don't understand," replies Sebastian.

"'They' have to come here to let us out," I reply.

"You're crazy." Iga has returned to the landing with a new cigarette. "You're crazy, woman, it's yours. We're going to help you defend what's yours."

They watch me, troubled, not understanding what I'm saying.

I have to inhale a bit more air, then slowly let it out. Several times. I explain further:

"It's my apartment and the decision's mine. We'll let them

45

know they can have it so that they'll let us out, and then we'll go straight to the police. We can't do anything stuck here. We already know it's not a joke, and since it's not a joke, it means they're capable of doing anything. I'm scared that they'll set fire to us, pump gas in or something. I'm scared."

"Agnieszka, wait," says Iga. "People are going to start looking for us soon. Somebody'll come, try to visit us, try to get in. Tomorrow morning. At the latest. I'm sure of it. Maybe we should all just calm down?"

"Listen, Iga, how often do you phone your mother?" I shake my head. "My daughter calls me twice a week. But she's twelve. Besides, she lives in Warsaw. Friends? They're all used to our phones being off for days, us not answering. People we know? Everyone we know in Cracow needs two weeks to sober up, let alone register that someone's missing."

"Our bosses," says Iga. "Someone at my uni. Someone at Gypsy's company."

"Iga, you just get kicked out if you miss uni or work. Nobody cares where you are."

"People at the Cat, Agnieszka."

"Everyone at the Cat who you talk to is here in this apartment with you." All this explaining is so exhausting I have to sit down.

"Agnieszka, we're in the town centre of a big city in Poland. This is going to end soon, it has to." Iga tries to sound positive.

"Exactly. We're in the centre of a big city in Poland," I reply.

Iga lights one cigarette from the other.

"It's not worth it," I say.

Everyone is silent, so I raise my arms to show I've said all I wanted to say.

"How do you want to let them know?" asks Iga.

"Fuck this shit." Sebastian turns and goes back into the apartment.

I stay outside. It's still painfully cold on the landing.

"I'll write it on the door," I answer.

I tell Iga to fetch some paper and felt-tip pens. She does.

We share them out. Each piece of paper is a letter. We get to work. Iga, Veronica and I sit on the floor. I give everyone some letters. We draw each letter's outline and meticulously fill it in.

Gypsy stares at his watch as though keeping time.

"I'd like to go to the cinema. Or a bar. Get fried," he breaks in.

"There's nothing on at this time anyway," I remind him, drawing the outline of the letter G.

"Then at least get drunk," says Gypsy. He finally climbs out of the armchair, picks up another piece of paper and, instantly guessing what the note's going to say, starts to draw the letter L. "Get so pissed I pass out on a bench in Planty at five in the afternoon."

When I finish filling in the E, Anna emerges from my room. Wrapped in my jumper, silent and calm.

"I've got some lorazepam if anyone wants some," she says, her voice flat and warm. I hand her a free felt tip and a piece of paper. It takes her three long seconds to react and take it.

"Draw a huge P," I tell her. It takes another few seconds for her to finally squat down and start to slowly, methodically draw a line.

"Can I have another cigarette?" she asks.

I pass one over to her, glancing at Robert, whose eyes are already closed. He's breathing too fast to be asleep; he simply can't look at anything anymore.

About four o'clock in the morning, the sign is ready. We carefully pick up our pieces of paper and go out to stick them on the door. Without looking at us, Gypsy says:

"We've let ourselves be pulled into some total idiocy. It'll be all over YouTube tomorrow."

I'm not listening to him. I'm going out to hang my pieces of paper according to my plan. 'They' are going to come in and we're going to get out. Then when we're out, we can do anything we want.

"We're going to get out," I state, sticking a straight, evenly filled P to the door. "And then we're going to come back," I add, sticking on a T. "And 'They' are going to get out." I stick on a U, then another U.

When we're done, the whole door of the Institute has got pieces of paper stuck to it. Six words, sixteen letters in all, on the same number of pieces of paper.

WE GIVE UP, LET US OUT.

The sign gives me strength, pours cheering warmth into me. Let 'Them' come. Let 'Them' have it. You can't simply take someone's apartment away from them.

For a moment, we stand on the landing without saying a word. Drink tap water. Then we go in, block the door with the mop handle, barricade it shut with the green sofa and close ourselves off in our rooms. We have to get some sleep, at least a little. I go to my room, the first on the right. It looks like a depot full of colourful objects just after a bomb attack. I wade my way through the rubbish scattered on the floor: clothes, bags, shoes, books. To bed, under the duvet, fully clothed, dirty. My face is starting to burn. Old make-up. Black follows me into the room, leaps onto the bed, curls up by my belly, but doesn't purr, constantly listening.

It's starting to get light outside. Slowly the whiteness in my room grows more intense. Birds start to sing; they're on the branches near my window. I imagine the first lot of people on their way to work and the last shift of factory and shop workers, those returning from parties and events, drunk students hanging on the arms of exotic guys making their way to hotels. Pissed Englishmen. The homeless. Municipal services and city cleaners. A whole lot of lucky, free people.

Veronica enters, opening the door gently, although nobody's yet asleep. Right up until our alarm clocks go off, the apartment's going to be filled with the sound of people trying to fall asleep: creaking springs, nervy gulps of water, doors opening quietly. Only at this moment, this brief and appalling moment, everyone's trying to even out their breath, to be momentarily still.

"Take a bath," she says.

"Yes, I should," I reply truthfully. "But I haven't got the energy."

"Everybody's already had a bath. The bathroom's free," Veronica says in the soft voice of a psychic reading tarot cards on some esoteric TV channel. I haven't the strength to say anything. Veronica understands, smiles. She always understands. I, too, smile at her.

Veronica shares a room with Iga. She was the last to move in, not really that long ago, a couple of months at most. She's a pale girl with a storm of red hair and is usually smiling. She wears odd clothes. Looks like a walking advertisement for The India Shop. She has a triangular face, narrow lips, wildly green eyes hidden behind horn-rimmed glasses. Veronica's gaze stops you short, giving you two choices: to quickly turn your head away or stare into her eyes for a few moments. Veronica hasn't got a boyfriend, doesn't go out much, hardly knows anybody – we in the Institute were the first people she met in Cracow. She works in a library and tops up her earnings working on the till at Cinema City in Cracow Plaza.

In Veronica's mind, 'They' don't exist in three-dimensional, tangible space. 'They' are like some kind of a shining, the invisible traces of past events. Without using such trite tricks as checking your lifeline, Veronica can tell you how long you're going to live, and she'll tell you to take some pills because she knows that you're going to get a sore throat in two weeks' time. To Veronica, 'They' are dead – former inhabitants who can't escape because they've got no bodily form endowed with arms and legs. They're locked in here like air trapped in an upturned glass. They're furious that they've crossed over to our tangible human dimension. Veronica's sure of it and is the calmest of us all.

That's why I got scared when Veronica used the word "strange". And that's why, when I recall how she said the words "Agnieszka, something strange has happened," I start doubting what's going to happen tomorrow; that we'll go to the police station and they'll help us get my apartment back, that we'll get out of the Institute at all. But I try to forget the word "strange", which I scrunch in my head like some needless piece of paper. We're going to get out. We're going to come back. We're going to win it back.

"Good night, Veronica," I say with great effort and turn onto my other side.

She leaves the room even more quietly than she'd entered. For a moment, she stands in the doorway and turns towards me.

"What do you think? Who are 'They'?" she asks.

"I don't know," I reply truthfully. "Does it matter?"

Because it doesn't matter. It's starting not to mean anything. Slowly I'm losing interest in who's locked us in the apartment and why. I'm more interested in thinking about how to stop myself from doing them permanent harm.

I blink my eyes. I'm trying to cool my brain so I can sleep for at least two or three hours. But I can't. Something occurs to me, a random thought; it's not going to let me fall asleep, it's going to scorch me like a hat left out in the midday sun. Maybe Veronica's approach is right. Maybe, in a certain sense, 'They' are a shining, a trace, a relic. But before the thought is clear, I start to fall asleep. Slowly, a heavy black eiderdown falls over my head. I surrender to it, lie beneath its weight, exhale, allow it to pour into my eyes, nose, ears.

Then another thought occurs. In a flash. Wakes me like a needle digging into my neck. I sit up in bed and breathe deeply. My heart's beating fast, I feel it as though another, smaller Agnieszka, hidden somewhere within me, is pounding me with her fists from within, as hard as she can.

"They said you were shooting a film," the pizza boy had said. "It'll be all over YouTube tomorrow," Gypsy said.

I run from my room, thump on Iga's door. Thump hard.

"Iga, Iga, get up. Get up!" I say. All I hear is the quiet moan of someone utterly exhausted, but I keep pounding. "Get up, we've got to search the apartment. We've got to search the apartment for cameras!" I shout.

* * *

Before my daughter told me that Thelma and Louise had gone to heaven, before we both lay down on the bed, spending the entire night prior to my leaving for Cracow wiping our noses, guzzling a nauseous amount of ice cream and watching *Mamma Mia!* and *Notting Hill*, before I got up at seven in the morning and made us breakfast – fried eggs for two even though a third person, my daughter's father, was asleep on the sofa – before I ran away a second time, for good, before all this had happened, a couple of weeks previously, the phone had rung. My mother.

"It's me." She cleared her throat. "Gran Vera's died."

I gripped the phone harder so as not to drop it and calmly replied:

"I'll call you back."

I sat down. I'd just been cooking some spaghetti sauce. For fifteen minutes, I'd stirred it vigorously to stop it from sticking to the bottom of the pan. Now I sat on the chair and watched it start to burn.

Her death, of course, hadn't come as a surprise – Gran Vera was ninety. As she herself had said, every day for the last twenty years she'd been over the moon to open her eyes and still see her bedroom ceiling and not a white-bearded man as large as the Palace of Culture – or something in that vein. *It's fine, really. She has, after all, lived a good, long life*, I tried to convince myself, breathing deeply. Meanwhile, the sauce started to give off a smell similar to motor oil.

Bullshit. I could tell myself that she'd had a decent, long life, had passed away surrounded by love, support and so on, but in reality, deep despair surged within me. Gushed into my mouth. Filled it as though someone had forced sand into it. Some people should never die. Gran Vera was one of them.

At every family gathering, Gran Vera had sat at the head of the table. When she was eighty, she had danced on the table with my father at my older sister's wedding, the same table she'd sat at a moment before, and when my dad's face grew crimson and was dripping with sweat, she'd told him:

"Work on your fitness, young man."

Gran knew everything about everybody. Little, if anything, was known about Gran Vera. She was a living mystery, unfathomable even to her own husband, who died around the time I was born. Grandad Wacław was a manager at some state enterprise. Gran treated her husband with kind-hearted tolerance, according to my mum. He was a docile, honest man, whose favourite things were his slippers, his book of crosswords and his armchair. Apparently, he met Vera at the actors' club, SPATiF, during the mid-fifties. Legends circulated about Gran Vera, who was over thirty even then. Rumour in Warsaw had it that Vera came from a line of rich Greek merchants or Vilnius nobility, that she'd spent the entire Second World War with some gypsies in Sweden or with a wealthy American Jew on a yacht.

Vera was a puzzle. Grandad Wacław managed to respect that. He didn't ask, because he knew that everybody we introduce into our lives carries with them the baggage of their past. "Why poke your nose into their rucksack if you can't put it down?" he would say. He didn't, for example, ask about the dark-haired man in thick-framed glasses who ran for a good half-mile behind the taxi that Gran Vera had climbed into at Grandad Wacław's invitation that evening at SPATiF. Only later, seeing a photograph in the newspaper, did he realise that the guy looked suspiciously like the writer Tyrmand.

All that was known was that before Gran Vera came to Warsaw and before she met Grandad Wacław in SPATiF, she'd lived, studied and worked in Cracow, where she'd been allocated an apartment in the newly constructed Nowa Huta. She sincerely loathed the apartment, just as she did the whole of Nowa Huta and communism in general. But the small apartment belonged to her right up to this day; my father rented it out to some students. When he took Gran Vera there once, she apparently spat on the doormat.

Gran Vera's manners belonged to the pre-war era. With steel consistency, she demanded the same from all those around her. If a man in a restaurant didn't stand as she approached the table, she demonstratively didn't speak to him for the whole evening. Yet, without blushing or vulgarity, she could tell jokes that turned everyone sitting at the table the colour of beetroot soup. I adored her. As she did me. One day, she said to me:

"Agnieszka, love, don't let any brute think you belong to him. They all think that if you go to bed with them, they can call you by some idiotically sweet name rather than your real one, slap you on the backside like a cow and not hold the door open for you. There's nothing more misguided, my dear."

The gran–granddaughter pattern is obvious. Up to a certain moment, more or less when the granddaughter is fifteen, the gran is dearest gran, and granddaughter dearest granddaughter. Then everything falls apart, becomes diluted, blurred, more and more people join the party called your life and slowly you start to forget those who were there at the very beginning. And Gran was the sort of person who, instead of patting you on the shoulder and reminding you of their existence, politely retreated to the kitchen, where she finished her glass of wine, washed the glass, extinguished her cigarette in the sink and finally left the apartment without a sound.

The last time I spoke to Gran Vera for more than fifteen minutes was when I returned to Ela's father so as to win Ela back. And because he loved me. With his whole stupid heart.

He's not a bad man, I'd kept repeating to myself. *It's his mother who's bad.*

"He opened the door, Gran, and said 'I've been waiting for you'," I said, and Gran Vera shook her head.

"And were you waiting for him?" she asked.

I didn't answer.

"I've got a child," I repeated. "The child's got a father, the child needs a family."

Gran looked at me with a distinct combination of love and distaste.

I'd really believed what I was saying then. I was in the process of resolving my new inner disposition. Its laws were simple. Life has to be normal. The child needs a family. A mum and a dad. The child can't go through her first years with a series of boyfriend-dads and then, at fourteen, cut words like "darkness" and "suicide" into her arms or inject drugs into her heel. Part of me didn't believe that I could have what would be considered a successful relationship with anyone anymore. I'd decided that it was better for Ela to witness the shit going on with her own father than with some stranger. But the truth is, I didn't ever want to lose her again.

"It's your life, darling, and you do what you want." Gran Vera took a sip of tea, pierced me with her eyes and added, "But that husband of yours…"

"He's not a bad man, Gran," I said. "It's his mother who's bad."

"That's even worse, darling. If he was a son of a bitch, it wouldn't be half as bad…" It was the first and only time she had used coarser words than "stone the crows". "But he's simply stupid. Stupid and, what's worse, weak."

"Weak," I repeated, not even trying to argue.

"Weak, because when they took little Ela, he didn't say a word, didn't lift a finger," she said.

"She's his daughter," I replied.

"You're a fool. You're such a fool. Agnieszka, love. Go now, we'll talk when I'm less worked up." Gran gave me a big hug. "They took your daughter away from you. Never forget that."

I gave her a kiss and left. That was the last time I saw her.

When I realised that, I sobbed so much that the neighbour upstairs phoned asking whether she should call the police or an ambulance.

I didn't have time to get dehydrated from crying, because my mother called again.

"When's the funeral?" I asked.

"In three days. But you have to come earlier."

"Earlier? Why?" I wiped my eyes with a hanky and swallowed my words.

"You've got to go to the solicitor. Gran's left the apartment in Cracow to you."

"The one in Nowa Huta?" I gulped, counted to four and added, "I don't want it. Gran hated it. You take it."

"You're mad," said my mother. "You've got a daughter. Besides, it's a different apartment."

"Different?" The worst possible state is to be in despair and irritated at the same time. My mother was capable of getting me there even without letting me know that someone's died. "Different? What the hell are you going on about?"

"A different one. Gran had another apartment. A hundred square metres in a tenement on Mickiewicz Avenue. She rented it out, no one knew about it. Everyone thought she'd sold it in '89 to pay off Uncle Staszek's debts when things didn't work out with his currency exchange bureau. But it turns out that she never did, so now it's yours."

"Mine," I repeated.

"Yes, yours," my mum confirmed.

"Why didn't anyone know about it?"

"Because that's Gran Vera for you."

I didn't say anything.

"Gran told me to tell you something before she died," added my mother.

"Oh, God, do you have to tell me these things over the phone?" Tears ran down my face again.

"She said: 'Tell Agnieszka that she's going to have to be very, very strong.'"

"I'll be there," I announced, hung up, rose and turned down the gas under the burnt sauce, soaked the frying pan in hot water and entered the room where Ela's father was lying on the sofa.

Ela's father went through a deep, inner change. From a Polish Lynch, he transmuted into the director of *Stars Look for Treasure*. He also did adverts and continued to work on the filming of subsequent episodes of *The Varsovians*, where the now balding Adrian told Basia to have genetic tests done since their previous child, little Jasio, had turned out to be a bastard from a short-lived relationship the slightly stale Basia had had with her boss, Jarek, who'd taken her on a romantic working weekend to Madeira where he'd vigorously screwed her in a hotel that looked suspiciously like the Ibis on Ostrobramska Street. Apart from that, the would-be Polish Lynch had – eighteen months ago – managed to film the comedy *Coolmen's Five Days*, the story of a secondary school's indoor hockey team who'd come across an international conspiracy whose members, commissioned by the Russian secret service, were trying to distil a brain-washing drug from a human spleen. *Coolmen's Five Days* ranked as one of the worst Polish films in twenty years.

For the first seven or eight years after I'd gone back to Ela's father, things were more or less fine. I forgave him for letting them take Ela away from me and for using it to coerce me into coming back. Things were fine insofar as "fine" means forcing every single muscle, joint and nerve in your body to pretend things were normal.

Be that as it may, I tolerated Ela's father's presence. I even liked it at times. We watched TV together, ate Mum's reheated *pierogi* and soup, read newspapers together, talked, mainly about our daughter, put her milk teeth into little plastic bags, mounted her pictures and first written letters in clip frames, stuck plasters over the cuts and grazes on her knees. We even exchanged jokes now and again. Sometimes laughed at them wholeheartedly. From time to time, I even went to bed with him. Who knows why, but I always needed two bottles of wine to do it, even though the whole thing took ten minutes at most. Once, we flew to Thailand together, where we argued merely fifteen times in ten days, and Ela caught a fever, which, thank God, turned out to be the flu and not malaria. Everything was fine, except that, day by day, the pots and pans grew heavier as though someone was adding tiny pieces of lead to them. Except that, day by day, the time between my hearing the alarm and getting up grew a few seconds longer. In a way, there's always an "except that". I bet that all the biggest personal tragedies in this shitty world begin with the words "except that".

But it was fine. Once again, as at the beginning, I liked him talking a lot to me; I listened with care and attention to the visions he described, the scripts he was going to film, his ardent tirades about a director's creativity, tutting over the commercial, plastic world that had lost its true spirit. I persuaded myself that it was good that he was talking because many husbands hardly talk to their wives. He still read books and still managed to pull me out for walks at five in the morning, took blurred photos of me lying naked in the bath. I was no longer fascinated but was pleased that he was doing something, that he was like a child imprisoned in a glass box who wants to smash its walls at any cost.

He tried. And since he tried, I tried. We were acting out the picture of the perfect family, like in some imaginary game. He changed the car wheels and mowed the communal lawn. He picked Ela up from school sometimes, attended parent–teacher meetings, went to the bank, repaired things in the house, bought me presents. All those normal things a guy does – a guy your mother considers a "decent man" – that make you start thinking of him in that way, even though you have no feelings for him.

He was trying, but beneath all this was silence, emptiness, hot air. And even deeper below, a scratching, burning conviction that really life was elsewhere, that I'd missed it, that I'd left it far behind at a crossroads at which I'd taken a wrong turn.

Ela went to pre-school. I spent my twenty-eighth birthday alone in the apartment, at the table, drinking three bottles of wine on the trot and listening to the radio where they played Polish rock, babbled talk and muzak from supermarkets. After the first bottle, it turned out that I remembered the words to "I Love You Like Ireland" by Kobranocka. After the second, I remembered the words to "Comet Nights" by Budka Suflera. Halfway through the third, my situation became as clear as a road sign. Apart from a little stability and Ela's father who, when he wasn't working, spent most of his time throwing dirty clothes around the apartment and staring at the TV, I didn't have anything. I didn't have any friends, because those I'd met at the party were still there, sadder and more tired by the year, or had disappeared somewhere into the abysses of London, Glasgow, Brussels or Amsterdam. I didn't have a meaningful occupation, couldn't do anything, didn't have a profession; all I knew how to do was burn soup, peel potatoes too thickly, inadequately wash floors and dishes. My daughter, when she was still in my belly, had catapulted me from my studies, which resulted in my not having drawn since, not even a map explaining how to get to the station. And I was permanently nailed to rags, pans and the gas cooker; I was a woman whose most intense conversations were with paediatricians, opticians and vendors at market stalls selling vegetables.

I had terrible scruples that I wasn't overwhelmingly happy. After all, I should have been. Because all was well. Because that's how things were supposed to be.

A colleague of Ela's father, a make-up artist, took me on set a few times. The normal make-up I did came out very well. For several months the job consisted of one phone call every two weeks. But one day, the make-up artist took me to the set of some cheap crime series like *Brigade Invincibles*, which was shelved after six episodes. It turned out that one of the make-up artists had been in a car crash in the city centre and was stuck there, hemmed in by police, a tow truck and a traffic jam a few kilometres long. A guy had to be made-up to look as if he'd been badly beaten by a couple of guys, bruises painted, a cut brow attached, a swelling on the lip formed. The other make-up artist gave me forty-five-second instructions because she herself had to make-up an actress as a Russian prostitute who'd fallen under a car. I panicked. I didn't know how to use silicone, powder, stickers, fake blood, how to form scabs out of pulp, draw grazes, make peeling skin out of a special substance. I improvised, concentrated and began to produce scratches, injuries, swellings and grazes from modelling materials. When I'd finished, everybody on the set looked at me, then at the actor, then at me again, and again at the actor until, finally, Ela's father's colleague said:

"You were supposed to make him up, Agnieszka, not beat him up."

Two months later, the phone was ringing every couple of days. After a year, I had to turn down half of the offers. Sometimes I earned nearly as much as Ela's father. Sometimes more when they took me in to cover for someone in a German war film. I'd thrust a métier into my hands. Started to live for it. Started to breathe through my hands, which magicked the most exquisite crushed and broken noses in the world, gun wounds, gouged eyes, knocked-out teeth, burns, acne and eczema. The SS soldiers who'd been turned into zombies and lived in darkness, whom I'd made up for some French B film through someone I'd known, won an award at an international horror film festival. I no longer waited, listened out, looked out for, no longer sat alone at the table, did the laundry or cooked. All day long, I moulded, stuck and painted, turning people into vampires, corpses, victims of car accidents. In the evenings, I played Scrabble, drank tea and watched romantic comedies on TV with my daughter. I'd detached myself from the rags; instead Ms Ałła appeared in our apartment every week in her enormous, black sunglasses and signet rings on her fingers like a rapping bishop and, while washing the floors, with the voice of a herald, told us not only the story of her life but that of the whole of Yalta from where she came. So the weeks went by as did the years of my life, measured by the marks of my daughter's height on the doorframe, her increasingly grown-up questions, her move up to junior school, her learning to read, write, sing, play the piano and speak English.

The years slowly passed in this new, relative routine, somewhat more bearable but in wait of something bad, not a happy end. As though I already sensed that I was waiting for the end, that over our heads, clocks measured out the time to our downfall. But I didn't think about it at the time. Didn't think about anything. Maybe that's why I recall this last period in which my daughter, my daughter's father and I coexisted in relative harmony, as the most peaceful time in my life to date.

But everything comes to an end.

* * *

The walls are deadly cold, the air so dry that, although we're all drinking water every few minutes, our mouths are constantly parched. Lack of sleep causes a tiny crack in reality felt by us all. Everything we see is overly vibrant, its acuity falsely turned up like taking a photograph using a flash at the end of a party. We want to sleep, but it's impossible. We wait. We bump against the walls, but softly like oil poured into water, semi-comatose, scrunched up, hungover even though we haven't been drinking. Someone gets up from the armchair, only for the next person to softly hit the seat. Someone goes to lie down for half an hour, only for somebody else to tell them to get up. We rarely speak to each other, as though every word we say could draw 'Them' a few centimetres closer to us.

We're waiting for Gypsy. He'll be back soon. He has to be. It's not as if the apartment has suddenly been severed from reality with a pair of enormous scissors and suspended in a vacuum like a bauble. It's still on earth, in Poland, in Cracow, on Mickiewicz Avenue, among people, streets, lights, cables, cars and trees.

We're sitting in front of the television in my room. White specks run across the screen, the sound is varied, crackles, but *The Towering Inferno* with Richard Chamberlain is on, which we'd most probably last seen as children on a television whose tubes were threatening to explode – the quality was identical.

We're trying to focus on the people leaping through the windows of the blazing building, but we keep interrupting each other with the same questions.

Why isn't he here yet?

Is he going to bring the police or admin?

Maybe he'll come during the night?

Maybe he's making a statement and they don't want to let him go yet?

Maybe no one believes him?

The minutes spill over like semi-congealed syrup. The crackling voices of the snowed-under actors seem to come from a broken, slowed-down tape. We don't even know whether it's us who's asking the questions or whether they come from the TV speakers. We feel as though time no longer exists; we look at our watches to make sure the second hands are working, unconvinced.

It's dark outside. Still silent on the landing. "Everything's going to be okay," we repeat in a whisper like a rosary. And then, "We're waiting for Gypsy. He'll be back soon."

About ten hours earlier, we'd searched for cameras. I'd torn everyone from their beds and told them to go through the whole apartment thoroughly. My expression had probably stopped anyone from trying to argue. So, we moved the beds, peered into wardrobes, threw all the contents of our drawers on the floor. We unscrewed the sockets, we studied the fridge carefully from all sides, the oven, washing machine, looked in the gas heaters. When we were done, the apartment resembled the scene of a police search.

In a situation like this, you look for a logical explanation otherwise you'd go mad. We looked for any rational lead whatsoever. Maybe this really is an experiment. Maybe we're on TV, maybe the whole of Poland is watching us right now.

We didn't find anything. A couple of long-lost trinkets, some money – nothing useful. Nobody was filming us. This wasn't a joke. Although maybe we'd just failed to find the cameras.

After the search, we sat on the floor, cross-legged.

Less than an hour later, Iga stood over me, lips pursed, dark circles blossoming under her eyes, shadows that hadn't been there in the morning when we'd all gone to our rooms to try to get some sleep. Her face didn't say "it's okay", didn't say "the grating's open". Instead there was something in her that I'd never noticed before. Iga was scared. Her lips were drawn, her eyes flitted, trying hard not to meet mine. I swallowed. Iga handed me a mug of tea as if she wanted to say, "That's the most I can do for you." I sat up and took a sip. Iga bit her lip.

"What's up?" I asked.

"Get up." She gestured listlessly with her arm.

This second time, I got up far more slowly. Took a long, long time opening the bedroom door, wanting to hold back what was inevitably waiting behind it. Gypsy and Sebastian were standing in the hall, also with circles under their eyes. Sebastian pointed to the grating. When I saw the door, I abruptly sat down as though someone had grabbed me by the arms and forced me down.

"Sons of bitches," I whispered and started to cry.

Iga came up to me, squatted and put her arm around me.

"I told you so," said Gypsy.

"Great, you won, so what?" Iga starts to shout and in her shouting are tears that have been waiting to get out. "Who the fuck cares that you said so?"

Gypsy shrugs. I put my arm around Iga, too. The crying

passes, or rather I feel myself gulping it down, choking, forcing it to the lower regions of my body.

"How's the girl? Anna?" I ask.

"I gave her some Xanax." Iga shows me a flat, half-empty blister pack of small pills, which she'd pulled out of her trouser pocket.

'They' know they can't let us out. For two reasons. Firstly, once on the outside, we could do anything to them; locked in here, we can't do anything. Secondly, letting us out would mean the end of the game.

'They' are going to keep us here until we've gone mad. Now I know. 'They' don't want this apartment. 'They' want nothing but a game, 'They' want that indescribable something that a cat wants as it tosses a live mouse with a broken spine from one paw to the other.

By the door lay our pieces of paper, torn down and crumpled. On the door is a sign, brushed downwards with white oil paint, the same writing as the sentences on the notes.

WE
DON'T
BELIE-
VE YOU

I sit on the floor and start staring at the letters as hard as if I was trying to erase them through sheer willpower. Gypsy hands me a cigarette. I light it. Take a sip of tea, which, in the unheated hallway, has instantly turned from very hot to the temperature of lukewarm beer. *WE DON'T BELIE- VE YOU*. I wonder whether the person who painted this sign purposely divided it into four parts: *WE DON'T BELIE- VE YOU*.

'They' have done it with a pun and play on a perverted heteronym. But I don't need the sign to know that 'They', whoever they are, wherever they are, are laughing. Chuckling like idiots watching YouTube videos of masturbating monkeys. Wherever 'They' are, whoever 'They' are, 'They' are having a really good time.

"Look at the lift," says Iga.

I look at the door but don't see anything.

"Walk up and take a good look," she urges.

I approach the old door and strain my eyes. Behind the dull glass, I see the dangling ends of cut cables.

"Those guys repairing the lift that the boy saw did a hell of a job," whispers Iga. "Hacked the cables."

I enter the apartment. Slam the door. Go to the bathroom. Look in the mirror. I look a hundred and ninety-eight, my face resembles an old leather sack into which someone has randomly packed muscles, nerves and bones.

I turn on the cold water. It flows in such a trickle, no pressure behind it, that it takes near to a minute to fill my palms. As though, hour by hour, the water valve was being tightened. I wash my face. It looks even worse. I take some cotton wool pads and make-up remover and cleanse it of its crust of old foundation, blotches of mascara, until a monster's physiognomy transforms into the face of a spent thirty-five-year-old woman, terrorised in her own home, with furrows like canyons in the place of expressive wrinkles. It's a sad sight, but familiar. I smile at it. It smiles back.

I leave the bathroom. The rest of them are standing in the hallway waiting for me to tell them what to do, now, later. I stand in front of them, clench as hard as I can everything that can be clenched within, so as not to wail again. I'm trying to think of something as fast as I can, beg myself to think of something, anything, but this plea for an idea merely fills my brain with pure air.

I turn away, pass them by, enter my room, sit on the bed again.

"Give me a minute," I ask, stroking Black, but they continue to stand in the hallway, continue to look at me as though saying: "It's your apartment, Agnieszka, it's your battlefield, you're the general, think of something."

"Please give me a minute," I repeat.

"But nobody's saying anything," says Sebastian.

I shake my head, try to indicate with my hand that I misheard; I know they didn't say anything. They don't have to. It's my apartment, I'm the leader. If I fall apart, then we can all slash our wrists or jump out of the window.

We can hear the hum of cars outside, the tinkling of trams, an ambulance siren. I don't believe what I hear. Have the impression that what's beyond the window is an illusion, a setting, a screen. That all these sounds are coming from an enormous speaker somewhere. I glance at the bed, the enormous bundle of crumpled sheets, clothes and our two cats tangled in all this chaos, and suddenly have an idea. Stupid and very dangerous, but still an idea. I leave the room, point to the window and say:

"Sheets."

They stare at me as though I'd spoken Latin, so I repeat, this time explaining:

"Sheets… Duvet covers… We can tie them together. Make them into a rope. Let it down through the window. One or two of us can climb down it and fetch the police."

Nobody contradicts me, nobody says it's an idiotic idea and could kill the ones going down, so I start tearing the covers off the duvets, pull old covers and tarps from thrift shops with pictures of Barbie and the New Kids On The Block on them out of the wardrobes. Everybody's momentarily surprised then instantly runs to their room, brings their bed linen and throws it on the communal pile in the middle of the floor. We work in a distracted euphoria like children who are preparing the biggest practical joke of their lives, snatch the materials from each other as we randomly try to tie two sheets until, finally, Iga says:

"Hold on, hold on. The terrycloth and old starched ones are no good. They'll tear. Give me those synthetic ones. Gypsy, yours are best, we'll tie them at this end, secure them to the radiator."

"Why mine?"

"Because you hardly ever wash them," answers Iga, stretching the material in her hands.

She's right, it's the fifth floor. If one of the sheets tears at something like the third floor, the consequences are obvious. Below, there's no lawn, no bushes, nothing other than the bare, sharp, hard pavement.

"Wait a minute," says Gypsy, "we've got to decide who's going. The fifth floor is pretty high. It might work once, but twice... twice is crazy. And then there's the question of what to do: do we enter the building and go to the neighbours, or—"

"Surely it's obvious what to do." Iga looks at him as if he is an idiot. "Bugger off to the police station on Królewska Street."

"I'm not going down." Sebastian shrugs, leans against the wall, pulls a squashed packet of chewing gum out of his pocket, takes one out and starts chewing. He's staring at Iga as though he were about to take the gum out and stick it onto her forehead.

"I'm too heavy," he says with an expression as blank as the floor. "Weigh too much."

"Yeah, you weigh too much," snorts Iga, tying more knots. "Okay then, I'll go."

"So do you." Sebastian ties a knot as hard as he can. "Weigh too much."

Iga doesn't say anything but looks at Sebastian with disgust as though he'd just shat himself. He simply smiles and sticks the gum to the doorframe. He approaches Iga, takes the twisted sheets out of her hands, unties them and ties them again, tightly pulls a triple knot with a few strong tugs.

"Give me the rest," he says.

Iga and I rip the rest of the sufficiently resistant sheets. Sebastian knots them together. After an hour, we have fifteen metres of rope.

"So, who's going?" Iga repeats the question.

"I'm scared of heights," Veronica announces, adjusting her glasses.

"I'll do it," I say.

"No, Agnieszka, I'll do it." Gypsy leans against the sill, and for the first time in two months, looks me in the eyes of his own free will.

Nobody objects. Me included. I want to go down but know I should stay. Have to stay. It's my apartment and these people are my friends. In a sense, they're my family; I brought them here and am responsible for them. The captain's always last to leave the ship.

"Are you sure?" I ask.

Gypsy nods.

"I'm light and used to do mountaineering," he replies. He stares at me as though he'd wanted to say something else but had suddenly changed his mind. Yet, after a while, he adds, scratching his head: "Surely you know I'm not going to desert you. That I'll be back. Surely you trust me, Agnieszka."

"I trust you," I say, automatically stretching my hand towards his shoulder again but immediately pulling it back and hiding it in my pocket. "Why shouldn't I?"

He looks at me a while as though I'd made a bad joke. Turns the corners of his lips up a little in a smile. Turns away from me and approaches the window.

"I'll be back in two hours max," he says.

We lower the rope through the window, tie the other end to the radiator pipe below the sill. Study the passers-by, but nobody reacts. Even if somebody notices the tied sheets and looks up, they immediately turn away, no doubt taking what we're doing as sloshed students playing stupid jokes. It's the norm, that's how it is with phoning the police. People in Poland don't phone the police when they hear somebody shouting for help, when they drive past a crashed car standing in a huge puddle of blood, petrol and shards of glass, or if they pass by somebody being continuously, steadily kicked in the head. People in Poland call the police when the neighbour below is holding a party.

The rope reaches the first-floor window.

"I'll manage," says Gypsy. "I'll just lower myself to the first-floor sill. From there I'll either go down to the ground-floor sill or simply jump. Everything should be fine."

"What do you mean 'lower' yourself?" asks Veronica. "I don't understand."

"It's easy." Gypsy looks out of the window. "Haven't you ever climbed out of a window on a sheet?"

"We should strengthen it more," I say, but Gypsy shakes his head.

"Strengthen it with what?" He shrugs. "Wait a minute."

He disappears into his room and returns with his ID and jacket. He puts the jacket on and slips the ID into a zipped inner pocket. He's already jumping onto the sill when Iga puts her hand on his shoulder, asks him to wait a minute. She leaves my room and returns with a cycling helmet. Gypsy bursts out laughing, but Iga doesn't smile, and this lack of a smile is sufficiently determined enough for him to get down and put the helmet on. He climbs onto the sill again, turns to us and squats, while we hold our breaths.

"I'll be back shortly. With the police," he says, then, perfectly still, takes a long look at us.

"Is there anything else you want to say? Last words of goodbye?" asks Iga.

"I hate you all and can't stand your presence any longer." He smiles bitterly.

We want to add something, but his legs are already in the air. He first holds on to the inner side of the window frame, then the sill, grabs the sheets and wraps his knees around them. I watch as the material next to my hands grows taut on the other side of the sill, against the window frame. We all take a deep breath. I adore him, but he and I – never, never would it have worked between us.

Gypsy says something, but we can't hear a word through the helmet and the noise in the street.

He begins to slide down, little by little, and we stop

breathing. He's going slowly, steadily, first loosening his grip and slipping a little, then gripping again. When he reaches the first knot, his legs are halfway down the fourth-floor window. He pauses a moment. Doesn't look down. We watch. Gypsy grows smaller with each move but isn't yet small enough for us to release the air from our lungs, not small enough to land safely if the rope snaps.

This goes on, and on, and on, and on. When Gyspy grabs the third-floor sill, I turn away. Turn away and watch the fabric out of the corner of my eye. It's getting tauter against the metal ridge of the sill. I look down. Gypsy's between the third and second floor.

Sebastian yells something like "You're making it, you bastard!" I automatically put my hand over his mouth as though any sound we make might tear the sheets and kill him.

Nobody in the street pays Gypsy the slightest attention, perhaps apart from a couple of people at the bus stop on the other side of the street who point at him.

"Hey!" Iga shouts.

Again, I block her mouth with my hand.

And at that moment, Gypsy loosens his grip and, scraping his hands and knees against the sheet, falls a whole floor. A fraction of a second.

And then the fabric grows taut again, and we hear a snap, it's the sheet snapping, tearing right next to my hand, on the ridge of the sill; only a quarter of its thickness is now holding.

I look at Iga, but it's like looking into a mirror, she's gawping like me, then Sebastian screams his head off:

"Get on the fucking sill! On the sill!"

And then the sheet snaps completely, the fabric rope falls, and I press my hands into my eyes as hard as I can. I'd never have torn them away again if Sebastian hadn't called:

"It's okay! Are you going to get down?"

Gypsy stands glued to the window on the first floor, holding the internet cable running from the roof with one hand

and, as if nothing has happened, waves to us with the other – the hand red as if plunged into snow for half a day.

"You're hardcore, mate!" Sebastian chuckles. "Fucking hardcore."

Gypsy waves again, removes the helmet and chucks it on the pavement. He squats on the sill and, resting his legs against the wall, continues to descend, then leans his elbows on the sill and, finally grabbing it with his hands, dangles off like a film hero on the edge of an abyss. A few seconds later, his feet carefully find the ground-floor sill. When he jumps down, it feels as if all this – his descent, standing at the window – has lasted all day. We hear the slap of his shoes against the pavement as he lands. Several people turn towards him. He loses his balance momentarily, squats, and then a moment later, he's up. He takes the helmet under his arm and yells something to us; we can barely hear what.

"I'll be back shortly," breaks through the hum of passing cars.

Finally, we let the air out of our lungs and breathe in air from the outside, mostly fresh with a delicate hint of smog. It tells us everything's going to be fine. This bad horror film will break off as quickly as it started. We're shortly going to step onto the landing, then the street, walk to town to eat a good dinner, then take ourselves off to Kazimierz for a coffee. Then after the coffee, we'll stay in Kazimierz and knock it back in a bar until we're out cold; it doesn't matter what bar as long as we get a three-day hangover. Meanwhile, completely smashed, I'll call my daughter several times. Then I'll pack and go to her in Warsaw.

Everything's going to be fine.

Gypsy turns right and runs ahead, cuts across the pedestrian crossing, runs along Krakowski Park. We can still see him for a short while as he passes the people at the bus stop, but then he leaps over the wall between the park and the pavement and completely disappears from view.

And now, ten hours later, he's still not back. *The Towering Inferno* has nearly finished. Veronica, Anna and I sit on my sofa without saying a word. We keep drinking water, but still our mouths are completely dry. The walls might be cold, but I'm so hot that I'd be more than willing to strip my skin off if it would help. Anna and Veronica sit wrapped in blankets, warming up even more beneath the cats curled up on their stomachs. Robert, meanwhile, is lying in Gypsy's room and only leaves it to take a leak.

"Barricade the door carefully, Sebastian," says Iga. "We've got to get some sleep."

"Sleep?" Iga's suggestion is just as absurd as the idea of drinking a crate of champagne. "Now? And what about Gypsy?"

"You wait up for him, Sebastian. I've just got to get some sleep," she pleads.

Sebastian nods and returns to what he's been doing for the last hour – sharpening all the kitchen knives on an old leather belt.

I switch channels. On Polsat, I can just make out *Aliens* through the snow and hum, but it doesn't matter what they're showing, white noise would be enough; I just need to watch something, something that moves, a collection of dynamic dots.

"And you, Veronica? Do you want some?" asks Iga. She stretches her clasped hand towards Veronica and shows her the contents – four halved Xanax pills.

Veronica shakes her head.

"You said we've got to be on the ball," I remind her.

"We're long past that." She shrugs. "And I've got to get some sleep. Just got to."

She's right. I long for sleep more than anything in the world. I'd told her I'd slept, but it hadn't been proper sleep, only lethargy perforated by awakenings.

"You take a half too, sis." Iga tries to smile. "It'll be alright. When you wake up, Gypsy will be here."

I try to smile at her, then swallow the pill without water. When I wake up, Gypsy will be here.

* * *

Ela's father and I went out to dinner. We were celebrating my success in creating artificial wounds and the start of the *Coolmen's Five Days* production, which, according to the producer, was going to be a hit not only in Poland but even Canada, the RSA and Jupiter. Ela's father couldn't sit still, wriggled in his chair like a little boy with a new PlayStation. I really and wholeheartedly believed in his success. I wasn't interested in the film, I was interested in him.

I wanted him to become an adult in his own mind. I wanted him to make enough money to finally make his film about the blue corridor. In the brief moments between his gunfire of monologues about the bright future and more bottles of dry table wine, the fact that Ela's father was still with me meant little more than just Ela having a father.

I didn't love Ela's father. There was no deep bond. I observed him from the side, studied him like a stranger. I wondered what had got into me at the time that made me leave the club with him and prompted me to be with him. But now it was too late, now we had a daughter, now I had no rational reason to end our collaboration other than my feelings. So, in the belief that all that feelings did was ruin everything and thus shouldn't be given much importance, I simply wanted us to be together and I wanted it to work.`

"Sure, the film's commercial. Very commercial," said Ela's father, as though justifying himself. "But it's going to be a hit. The producer predicts a box office attendance of something like one and a half million. And then, you know, I'm going to be free to do what I want. I'm going to be able to…"

Blue room. Silhouette, a light, hypnotic music, scream were the last things I wanted to remember.

"I've already got the script. It's called *Confined Woman*." He leaned over the table and, knocking the carafe of wine onto the floor, kissed me on the cheek.

"I'd like to read it," I lied.

"I'll give you the next version." He tried to smile mysteriously, succeeded even.

I remember that when we got home, we had sex, and I remember I liked the Polish Lynch as I fell asleep. In the morning, he made us breakfast, which was inedible because he even managed to burn the tea, but I still liked him.

And I liked him for as long as they were shooting the film. The next six months were like a hot and smooth béchamel sauce. Peaceful and safe. Everything worked. Ela went to school. We did homework with her. We visited friends. Organised family dinners.

That's how it was until, two weeks after its premiere, *Coolmen's Five Days* stopped showing in cinemas. I'd just come home after twelve hours of making-up prisoners of war on the set of a series about Westerplatte and was scouring an ovenproof dish from a hideously burnt pie when Ela's father phoned the producer and asked:

"What's going on, why aren't they showing it anymore?"

"Because about nine hundred people went to see it," came the voice at the other end of the line. "Because all the papers say it's a load of shit, full stop. Every single one. Read them."

"What now?" asked Ela's father, his voice like that of a panicking officer who's sent his battalion to certain death and now has to report to his general.

"What now? What's now is that I've fucked three million because you couldn't fucking direct a film," said the producer, a fat, incessantly belching guy who, whenever I saw him, always had a starving little Pekingese under his arm.

Ela's father froze.

"It's you who fucking got me into it," announced Ela's father in a tone I'd never heard before, cold and icy. "I wanted to do my own stuff."

"Then go and do it," retorted the producer.

"We've got an agreement," said Ela's father.

"We didn't agree that I'd lose three million."

Ela's father hung up and sat on the chair and, as he'd seen in so many films, hid his face in his hands. I wiped my forehead with a hand clad in a rubber glove.

"The film's really fallen through," he said and, shrugging, added, "It was a mistake. I made a mistake."

"You didn't make a mistake. You did a good job," I consoled him.

"It was a mistake to have fucking started it," said Ela's father.

"You've just got to do your own thing, darling," I added and, with all the tenderness I could muster, I laid my hand in its rubber glove on his head.

Ela's father wept, and I finally realised that I had two children.

He still tried to submit all sorts of applications and documents to get more money for his film. Sent the script to various financing commissions and institutes. They kept him in suspense for weeks, which he spent fidgeting in the armchair and compulsively checking his emails. Finally, an old school friend phoned him, a guy who'd had some success in the form of two romantic comedies shot in IKEA with titles like *Life is a Piece of Cake* or *Love to Madness*. He'd received the script about the blue corridor and the scream and wasn't at all happy at having to play the good pal offering advice.

"Listen, old man. I'd ease up in your shoes. It's... well, you know... I'd... well... Don't take this the wrong way, but... Oh, fuck it... I talked to David at the gala. It's too big a risk, you know... You should, well, fucking polish it up," he said. "You know, even if you get there, remember that you're a good craftsman now. Okay, *Coolmen*... but it's the producer's fault, everybody knows that, old man. But if you do this, it'll be your own fault."

"Maybe I should give it to somebody to rewrite?" asked Ela's father.

"Look, there's already one Lynch and, well, he's Lynch!" replied Ela's father's friend.

When you love someone who's just experienced a great setback, perhaps one of the biggest setbacks in their life, you should lay them in a horizontal position, drink with them and hug them, repeating over and over again that it's not true, that they're still going to get a chance and that everything's going to be okay. Yet I couldn't even look at him. I was angry, and it made me feel terrible. But I couldn't look on as he craved support, moped around the kitchen snivelling and, to mark his great failure, started his days with a bottle of wine. He repulsed me as though he were covered in mould. What's more, I found myself a little repulsive.

I put Ela in the car and we drove to the woods, drank fizzy pop and ate cakes, tried in vain to fly a kite and take in a stray cat the size of a toy bulldozer, also in vain. We then went to a pizzeria with plastic seats and plastic plants, where they served huge pizzas as thick as old sleeping bags.

Meanwhile, Ela's father drank. That is, he'd always drank, but when it turned out that he wasn't ever going to leave *The Varsovians* serial, Biedronki adverts and the *European Omnibus* game show, that the temporary work he'd been doing for ten years was indeed for life, that his name was never going to find itself in the thick book with the words *Great Directors* embossed on it, his alcoholic hobby stepped up a gear.

Ela's father became a drunk.

It's not that he suddenly started throwing dinner plates at the walls or leaping at us with his claws, trying to force the door open with an axe at four o'clock in the morning or the gate of the secured estate with his car. Something else happened. After his bottle of wine for breakfast, he plunged his glazed eyes into the TV or computer screen, sipping vodka on ice. The slight indigestion that he'd always had after drinking neat vodka passed after a couple of days. He took a shine to it. He was out of it, absent and drunk, spent entire days like that, unless he had a shoot. At three, four in the morning, he crashed on the bed or fell asleep in the armchair. He didn't yell, didn't say anything; he stopped talking, stopped reacting.

He phoned only his mother. And a few friends I didn't know. He came back in the early hours, collapsed on the bed fully clothed, so I threw him off onto the floor and covered him with a blanket.

When I tried to talk to him about it, he waved it off. When I proposed he get some therapy, he yelled at me. So I suggested he cut down or limit himself. He retorted that he knew how much he could take and drank as much as he could take, and could I kindly please fucking leave him alone because he needs support and I'm not giving him any.

"I've got to keep this family together," I replied coldly.

"Nobody's asking you to," he riposted, gripping the armchair, partly because he was surprised by his own insolence and partly because he nearly lost his balance.

I could have slapped him, but I let him be.

It was a typical story, played out in dozens of Polish homes.

As time went by, the sound of him opening the door reminded me more and more of polystyrene being dragged along glass. When I needed to say something to him, even if it was some simple communication like "get up", "move up", "I've made some dinner", it felt increasingly like my mouth was full of coarse breadcrumbs.

On some nights, at first, then every other night and finally every night, when I lay next to him under the duvet, I had to make sure that no part of my body was touching any part of his. I'd discovered that Ela's father had happily fucked his colleague, the make-up artist to whom I was indebted for getting me work, when they were shooting an advert for some make-up in Tenerife. I took it with indifference, didn't bear him a grudge. I didn't have the slightest desire for him to even breathe in my direction. I bought my own duvet.

When Ela's father started to drink, he stopped pretending

that he was my husband and that I was his wife. In a word, we stopped pretending to be a family. When Ela's father realised that he'd lived his whole life mistakenly convinced of his own worth, he stopped trying. Stopped doing anything. Once in a while, he went to work, but less and less frequently. He didn't open the door, even for the postman. He was out of it, unconscious, unfamiliar and terribly pitiful, so pitiful that I didn't even have the strength to shout at him.

He was sure nothing else was ever going to happen to him. And I myself was becoming certain that nothing else was going to happen to us.

Besides, for ten years, ever since I'd gone back to him, I'd hoped that he'd finally become a strong person. He was pretty good at pretending to be strong, laughing at small setbacks and temporary lulls, turning somebody's sneers into a joke and once even punching somebody in the face – somebody smaller than him, in fact – a camera operator who'd groped me on set. But you can't count on people changing. My husband hid in a room, weeping quietly, slept in his clothes and totally neglected his family, all because somebody had made it impossible for him to shoot a film about a woman screaming in a corridor.

This was far worse than him shagging some idiot. Besides, one night I found his script behind the bookshelf. I read twenty pages and put it back. I was glad he hadn't shot it.

There was no point in continuing with this charade. Ela's father hardly spoke to me. I was spending my life in a nice big apartment with a young daughter and a drunk stranger. So when Gran Vera died, and I was given her apartment, I just needed two weeks to pack my things up, re-register and go back to Cracow to sort out all the formalities with the solicitor. Those two weeks passed with him yelling that I was a vile, heartless, loose woman.

"I've also needed support a few times over the years," I replied quietly, tersely.

"I love you." He started snivelling and crying like an

old woman. I didn't even look in his direction. "You're the meaning in my life," he whined and I covered my ears.

"Please understand," I said. "You're the lack of meaning in mine."

"I'll stop drinking. You're right. I'll go get some help," he said.

"That's good. Good for you. But as far as we're concerned, it's not going to change anything," I replied.

"You're despicable. You're a whore!" he screamed.

"Calm down. Dignity – the most important thing is dignity," I tried to remind him.

When Ela's father had stopped yelling and whining and sought solace in his vodka again, calls started coming from his mother.

"Don't even try to take Ela with you," said my mother-in-law. "We know what you're like. We'll take her away from you straight away. You're a drug addict and a drunk. You're crazy. You think I don't know, but I do."

"The law in Poland sides with the mother." It was the one sentence I could manage to force through the wall I'd erected to hold back all the screams and oaths whirling around in my mouth.

"In our family, the law's on *our* side," retorted my mother-in-law, "because our family is on the side of the law."

Ela's father's father knew everybody and could work miracles, as though he had magical buttons at his fingertips to speed up or slow down time. With the help of his telephone directory, he could get people back their driving licences, get property locked by bailiffs, free those who'd been arrested. He specialised in alimonies.

"You're going to end up in a loony bin and you'll never see her again," said Ela's father's mother, "so watch it. Ela stays with her father. You do what you like. We don't care what happens to you. You wound him round your little finger and landed him with a child. You go to court and you'll never see Ela again. Try the same trick as before. Try it, really. Try it."

I didn't interrupt her. She liked talking. She really had a great talent for loud, long oration. Like Hitler.

"It's because of you, this whole situation with the film," she continued. "How could the poor man do anything sensible with a monster like you around? It's simply impossible. I know what happened. Everything was on his shoulders – his home, his child – because you didn't lift a finger, didn't do a thing. You never supported him. It's a good thing that you're leaving. When he took you back, it was the worst day of my life; I prayed for him not to do it." And then she started to cry. "How can you do this to my baby?" she moaned. "How can you make him suffer so much?"

"Oh, shut up," I said.

"We'll take the little one away from you the same as before," she said.

"Shut up," I said again. "Just fucking stop."

"You take the child with you and we'll destroy your life. We really will. You won't be the first. You don't even know what we can do. They'll take away all your parental rights. Legally incapacitate you. You think things like that don't happen," she spewed out, long and loud, then added more quietly, "I knew from the very start that all you could offer him was suffering and heartache."

"Goodbye," I said and hung up, then threw the phone at the wall. I knew the woman was capable of doing all she said.

"We'll soon be together." I consoled my daughter as she lay in bed and I removed *Mamma Mia!* from the drive and flung DVDs across the room, searching for *Bridget Jones's Diary*. My daughter nodded. I'd bought her more ice cream. "I've got to go," I said for what must have been the hundredth time that evening, more to myself than to her, as usual. "You know that if I take you now, Gran will come to fetch you and we'll never see each other again."

"I told you, Mum, please, let's do it – let's run away somewhere." She dipped her spoon in the ice cream carton, sobbing.

"We will, but I've got to get things ready. It's a plan we've got to have together, the two of us. It has to be our supersecret, our secret plan, yours and mine, okay?" I kissed her on the cheek.

Ela nodded. I couldn't tell her that her Gran had already taken her away from me once or scare her by saying that she'd do it again and then I'd probably never see her again. It might have made Ela do something rash. It could have spoiled my plan.

"We'll live together," I continued with great difficulty, as though I was spitting razor blades. "For the time being, you're going to stay with Dad. You'll call me every day and tell me what Dad's doing, how school's going, how you are. You're going to be good to Dad and Gran. From time to time, I'll come for the weekend and we'll spend time together."

"And then?" asked my daughter.

"Then… then we'll go to Cracow and stay there forever, or we'll go to a totally different place," I said.

The longer I spoke, the more I realised that I was giving her my word. A word I had to keep.

"But why so far? Why Cracow and not just another part of Warsaw?" asked my daughter.

"Because I've got a super apartment there. And we're soon going to live in it together." I lay on the bed again and loaded a spoonful of now lukewarm chocolate slush into my mouth.

"Gran Vera's old apartment?" She moved closer to me.

"Yes, Gran Vera's old apartment. It's got an incredible history. I can tell you about it if you like. But it's a bit scary."

"What?" My daughter sat up.

"Yes, it's a bit horrific." I smiled and scratched her head. "Well, something very strange happened there once."

My daughter became all ears, even though it was four in the morning and I needed to catch a train in three hours. I wanted us to finally stop sobbing like two butchered goats, so I started to tell her what the solicitor and her friend, the estate agent, had told me. I started to tell her the strange and funny story about the apartment I was going to move into the following day.

And, finally, my daughter stopped crying.

* * *

When I open my eyes, it's dark. The Xanax, I suspect. I've slept through the day. The first question that flashes through my mind, as loud and clear as the adverts in a cinema, is *Where's Gypsy?* After a split second, more follow: *Is he back? When did he get back? Are we still locked in? Why didn't anyone wake me if he's back? And if he isn't, where is he?*

I rub my eyes. Feel like I've been shaken out of an anaesthetic. The apartment is completely silent. I switch on the lamp and get out of bed. Walk to the window. My heart sinks and then, in a fraction of a second, bounces back into my throat.

"Iga!" I yell. "Iga! Iga!"

Iga rushes to my room.

"What's up?" she asks. "What's happened? Why's it so dark?"

"They've bricked up the windows." I speak quietly, slowly, as though I don't believe it myself.

"What? How? Bricked up?" asks Iga.

"I've no idea." I still speak quietly. "I've no idea."

Instead of the street and Krakowski Park, instead of trees appearing opposite, straight rows of white bricks loom at our windows. I slap myself in the face, once, twice, three times. Pray that this is a dream, that I'll immediately wake up. Still imprisoned in the Institute, but with open windows. I slap myself a fourth time, and a fifth, hard. The bricks don't disappear, are still in the windows. White, separated by strips of grey mortar.

The rows of bricks dance momentarily in front of my eyes. I close my eyes, open them again: the bricks are still again.

Very briefly, I want to laugh, but I stop myself at the last moment and bite my tongue, hard.

"I don't understand why we didn't wake up! Or how they could have done it, because they must have come up here on some, fuck it, I don't know, platform or something. I can't understand it," says Iga. She doesn't know what to do with her hands. Keeps alternating between touching her face and compulsively searching for something in her pockets. She approaches Sebastian and hits him on the shoulder several times. At first, Sebastian doesn't react, then finally pushes her away. I grab Iga's hand.

"I fell asleep for a moment, okay? For fuck's sake!" he hollers.

"Fell asleep? You fell asleep?!" Iga raises her voice. "What do you mean you fell asleep?"

"Just like you fucking fell asleep because you got stoned!" Sebastian shouts back.

"You took pills too?" Iga shouts, getting louder with every word.

"Stop screaming! Stop bloody screaming!" Now I, too, am yelling. For a moment, they fall silent. I leave my room and inspect the whole apartment. It's the same everywhere. Bricks in all the windows. As though what I'd imagined would happen really has happened, as though someone has ripped the Institute away from this street, this building, and thrown it into a black vacuum, sentenced it, with us inside, to endless drifting.

Maybe we're dead, I think fleetingly, *and we're in purgatory. Maybe it's some sort of afterlife.*

My head is spinning. I close my eyes. I need to rest against something, grope the wall with my hands. Lean on it. Breathe deeply. I must be alive, blood still flows through me; a corpse doesn't get dizzy, grey lines don't dance in front of a corpse's eyes, a corpse doesn't bite its tongue to stop itself laughing hysterically. Or maybe I did laugh but nobody noticed.

"Sebastian," I say. "You must have heard something. You must have. 'They' couldn't have done this without making a noise."

"But they did," replies Robert, emerging from the bathroom.

He looks a little better than yesterday. But only a little. He leans against the doorframe. "They must have come in and put us all to sleep." He approaches the walled-up window and stares at the bricks for a while. "Concrete," he states, as though it made any difference.

"What do you mean come in? Put us to sleep?" Questions tumble from me of their own accord, asked by some other Agnieszka concealed in my stomach.

"It could be done in a couple of hours, probably. If you've got everything ready," he answers obliquely.

I notice that he's calm – strangely calm.

"What do you mean they put us to sleep?" I repeat, raising my voice.

"You don't know what time it is, what day it is, how long you've been asleep…" he replies.

For a moment, we say nothing. I look at my watch. It says one o'clock. I don't know if it's one in the morning or one in the afternoon. I'm filled with panic, filled with dread.

"There must be several of them," states Robert, and he shuts himself in the bathroom again.

I return to my room and sit on the bed. I feel powerless in my body. I have the impression that my bones are weak and dissolved, my muscles wet pieces of string.

"They must have seen Gypsy," says Iga. "Shit. They must've seen him. Maybe they were standing at the bus stop. Saw him get out and caught him straight away, round the corner. They've got him. I want to leave! I don't want any more of this!" She sits next to me and starts to sob violently; the crying jerks her body as if she were being systematically punched in the jaw. She's exploding. I, too, am on the verge of exploding. I feel everything tear away from me: first my clothes, then my fingers, feet and hands, legs and arms, then my internal organs, liver, lungs, heart – every part of my body falls one by one into a bottomless, black well and the last to fall is going to be my head, then I suddenly realise something.

"Hold on." I look around. "Hold on, hold on."

Veronica comes in, spreading her arms. Looks at us as though, apart from the bricked-up windows, there is something else we hadn't noticed.

"The cats have gone," says Veronica.

"Exactly." I look around. "The cats aren't here. They've disappeared."

I leap from my bed. Walk the length and breadth of the apartment. Peer into the kitchen, the bathroom, every room. Black and White are nowhere to be seen. I search for them for long minutes, calling them and, though it's idiotic, ring their toy bell balls. I scatter leftover hotdogs in the corners.

They're not here, our cats aren't here, somebody's taken them.

I return to my room. Look at Veronica, my eyes searching hers for an explanation as to why our cats have disappeared, why the windows have been bricked up, imploring her to tell us why all this is happening. But she only glances at me and her feet in turn, as though trying to calm us down by cooling the air with her steely eyes.

"They're not here," she repeats yet again, without stirring a fraction of an inch. "I told you."

"Finkiel," I say. "We have to knock on Finkiel's door again."

"But we hammered on it on Sunday evening." Iga wipes her nose and face. "She's not there, just as there's nobody else in the building."

"No," I reply. "We've got to try again. The cats. She hates our cats."

"This wasn't done by one old woman," remarks Robert from the bathroom.

"She hates our cats," I repeat, trying to cling on to what remains of my sanity.

"It's not her, the woman's old," repeats Robert, and this time emerges from the bathroom.

He's so calm, I think. *So strangely calm.*

Sebastian, on the other hand, is not in the least bit calm.

"Why didn't we think of it before, damn it? It's her, it's that old whore – that's why she's not opening the door!" shouts Sebastian as he runs out onto the landing.

We run after him. The landing looks a bit different and a bit askew. Maybe it's the same, but I can't fully describe it. There's something different about it, something doesn't add up. We pass the locked grating and lift. Stand in front of Mrs Finkiel's door. Knock. Pound. Kick. Knock. No response.

"Mrs Finkiel!" I scream, knocking harder and harder.

No answer. Nobody opens. I put my ear to the door. It would take a long time to pick up any sound from behind the old pre-war door. I block one ear and press the other right into the wood while trying to breathe as quietly as possible. But we can't hear anything. No movement, scraping of furniture.

Mrs Finkiel is our nearest neighbour. It's possible that she got locked in her apartment like us. She must know something about what's been going on over the last seventy-two hours. Either she'll open or we'll break down the door.

Mrs Finkiel lives with her husband, Mr Finkiel, but the man is, to all intents and purposes, totally immaterial – from what we know, he's had several strokes and has been sick for a long time. His life seems to consist mainly of watching the test card on television or paint peel off the walls, whereas Mrs Finkiel has a far greater number of active interests. Phoning the police, for example, if somebody's running a bath after ten in the evening.

"They could have slipped out when I was barricading

the door." Sebastian rubs his sticky eyes. "I could have missed them."

"You can't miss them, they're enormous," I say, putting my ear to the door.

"So? They've fucking evaporated?" Sebastian's voice bounces off every corner of the stairwell. "They've somehow fucked off, and that's it. We haven't got any grub, so they went in search. Or that old whore grabbed them for her soup."

Black, who is older and fatter, had gone missing before. He'd sneaked out of the apartment and wandered all the way down to the cellar. We heard him when we were in the yard, growling and meowing because he couldn't get out. We didn't have our own key, so I went to Mrs Finkiel for hers. I knocked. She opened after two minutes. A combination of smells hit me as though Mrs Finkiel's apartment secretly contained a number of different places: milk bar, old hospital corridor, antique dealer, taxidermist's workshop. Nowhere did I see any ornaments, artificial flowers, framed photographs. The walls were bare, splattered here and there with greasy stains. Old, scratched lino covered the floor. From one room jutted the corner of a colour TV. I also saw a hand, the hand of an old man, dangling limply from the armrest of an armchair. The hand was still; for a brief moment, the thought crossed my mind that Mrs Finkiel might be keeping a mummified corpse in her apartment.

From what I could hear, the sitcom *Clan* was on the TV. The volume was turned up to maximum; the speakers crackled, and the actors sounded like they were speaking through a megaphone at a procession. I squinted. Felt there was something missing. I'd seen many an old woman's apartment, and this one was in some way incomplete.

"What?" Mrs Finkiel had asked that time and Mr Finkiel, watching the TV, emitted a throaty groan.

"I wanted to ask for the key to the cellar," I said and automatically curtsied like a little girl at a school performance.

I wanted to be nice to her, because I didn't know yet that it was pointless being nice to her.

"Why?" asked Mrs Finkiel, not looking me in the eyes but at my lips, as though there was something on them. I touched my face automatically, to check if anything was there.

"My cat's gone in there," I replied.

"No," said Mrs Finkiel. "I'm not giving you the key."

I leaned against the doorframe and sighed. Mrs Finkiel, draped in a torn pink dressing gown, its pockets stuffed with foil packs of pills, kept observing my mouth with the attention of a retired dentist. Her greasy hair was slicked back into a tangled bun and her eyeballs, protruding from her wrinkled skin, pierced right through me. I glanced once more at the corridor behind her. Now I knew what was missing. There were no crosses, no images or statues of Our Lady, no holy pictures. No K+M+B on the door to show that a priest had visited. Mrs Finkiel, unlike most of her peers, didn't have any religious accessories in her apartment. That's when I noticed there were no calendars, framed photographs or crystal vases on the shelves of her glazed cabinets, either.

"Why?" I asked, finding it harder and harder to breathe evenly. "I'll bring it straight back."

"Because I'm not giving you anything," growled Mrs Finkiel. Almost without breathing, she added, "Get out of here. Scram. Those shitty cats of yours stink and make a noise. I'd throw them into the cellar myself if I saw them or out of the window to stop them meowing and howling. Go back to that brothel of yours; go on, clear off."

I remember that I froze. I've come across enough sanctimonious, demented, nasty old bags to know how to talk to them, but Mrs Finkiel showed me that you can always learn something new. I inhaled a good quantity of air and tried to hiss out as politely as I could:

"Mrs Finkiel, we don't have to speak like this."

Mrs Finkiel took two steps towards me and, supporting

herself on a crutch with a trembling arm, gathered all her strength and brought her face up to mine. Her breath smelt old and carried a peculiar yet oddly familiar odour. To avoid her eyes, I peered into the corridor again. Next to the coat rack, overgrown with old coats, stood the case of a large string instrument, a cello or double bass. Resin. Mrs Finkiel smelled of resin.

"Don't bother me again about your cats. Or anything else," said Mrs Finkiel. She pushed me lightly and I retreated two steps. She slammed the door.

I stood in front of it for a while, just as I was doing now, trying to listen for any sounds, but everything was muffled by the noise from the TV. And just like now, I couldn't hear any shuffling, grunting or the tapping of a crutch. Mrs Finkiel must have known that I was standing in front of the door. Just as I was about to turn away, I heard:

"You should have stayed with your daughter and not gone whoring."

It was as though someone had thrown me against the door. I grabbed the doorknob. I later thanked all the powers that be that the old woman had already slammed it shut. If she hadn't, I'd have torn the crutch from her and beat her wrinkled head with it until it turned to pulp.

I hadn't asked myself at the time how the old witch knew about Ela. It had seemed obvious – evil old women know everything.

Now, with my face pressed against the old, flaking door, I try to convince myself that an eighty-year-old woman who needs a crutch even at home wouldn't be able to close the heavy stair grating or cut the phone and internet cables. I repeat to myself: *Don't kill her as soon as she opens the door. Don't do it. Even if it is Mrs Finkiel who's poisoned your cats. Even if it's her, leaning on her crutch, with her snake eyes, who supervised the bricking up of your windows.*

I put my ear back to the door. Nothing. I look at my flatmates.

*If she opens the door, just ask if everything's alright,
apologise for disturbing her, and ask if she's seen our cats,*
I think.

"Don't be scared, Mrs Finkiel!" I shout, banging my hand
on the door.

"Open up, you old whore!" booms Sebastian. I thump his
meaty arm. He clutches where I hit him and looks at me with
the eyes of a dog who's been smacked on the head with a leash
for no reason. "It's her, Hat. It's that old slut."

"Listen." I turn to them. "Robert's right. Maybe it really
isn't her. She can barely walk. I only want to see if she's still
alive, if she knows anything. They sometimes don't leave
their apartment for weeks on end."

"It's her." Iga moves me and Sebastian away from the door
and kicks the letterbox. "Fuck it, Aga, when all this started,
the old hag somehow packed her bags and went on holiday.
Like everybody else in the building by the look of things."

"It could have been her at the pizza place," adds Sebastian.
"The old cunt."

"She can barely make it to the corner shop. The pizza place
is at the end of Karmelicka Street," says Veronica.

"Tell me again," I ask, eyeing everyone, "without working
yourselves up: who saw her last? Before we got locked in."

After Mrs Finkiel refused to give me the cellar key the
first time Black disappeared I went down to Mr Banicki, the
neighbour below. Moving in a dignified manner in a fleece
tracksuit, the retired neurosurgeon had invited me in as usual
and offered me some tea. He said it might take him a while to
find the key, so I had the choice of either hanging around at
his door or going in and "savouring a cigarette".

Our conversation, as usual, had been pleasant enough.
Mr Banicki's wife had just left for a spa break and he, as he
described it, "relished the sacred peace". While searching for
the key, he talked about his sons, who were living in England;
his house by the Masurian Lakes; his Volkswagen Passat,
which kept breaking down. Between telling me all this and

looking for the key, Mr Banicki kept eyeing me up and down as usual but tried to do so discretely – he was a well-bred gentleman. So well-bred that, when I asked him about Mrs Finkiel, he refused to comment extensively and merely said:

"My wife and I once considered poisoning her."

When we finally got down to the cellar, Black was meowing in pain, his body jammed between the wall and an old, peeling sofa bed. Sebastian had to move the sofa aside while I picked him up. He was traumatised, covered in shit and so hungry that when I took him in my arms, he immediately bit my finger. His meowing and growling could be heard throughout the whole building. Now, standing on the landing in front of Mrs Finkiel's door, we heard nothing.

"I saw her about a week ago," Veronica finally says, without taking her eyes off the floor, as though there was something there only she could see.

"And what?" I ask.

"Same as always," she answers indifferently. "I was coming home, and she was hobbling towards the lift. I said hello and she didn't reply. As usual."

"Right." Sebastian pushes me gently aside and studies the door carefully.

"What are you going to do?" I ask.

He's concentrating so hard he doesn't hear me. He turns to Iga and says:

"Give me a hairpin."

"Sebastian, what are you going to do?" I repeat.

"What we all want to do," he replies, staring at the two locks – one old and thick, with a heavy steel key no doubt, the other a very ordinary Polish Yeti. "Find out what the shit's going on. Iga, hairpin."

"Please and thank you." Iga hands him one.

"We used to sneak into houses in Kazimierz when I was a kid." Sticking out his tongue and, with a concentration that contrasts comically with his size and voice, Sebastian carefully slips the wire into the Yeti lock. "At about three in the afternoon, teatime. The woman would usually be cooking and the man reading or nodding off in front of the TV after working all day. We'd open the front door, grope the coats in the hallway and leg it."

"I don't think I want to go in. I don't think I do," Veronica mutters under her breath.

"We'd think up all these fucking amazing contests." Sebastian turns the hairpin in the lock, left and right, waiting for the moment he gains control over the lock. "The others only did houses where the doors were open. I did them with the doors locked. A guy called Wacław taught me. He'd been locked up half his life. Robbed more screws than you've had hot dinners."

I wouldn't have suspected Sebastian of having fingers capable of moving and working individually. I'd thought they could only operate together, clenched in a fist. Nor did I suspect that he could be so focused and scrupulous.

"Seeing as you can open this door, why didn't you open the lock on the grating?" I ask.

"No chance. The bars are too fucking close together. I can't squeeze my hand through. Besides, I've never opened one like that in my life, it's some sort of pre-war piece of shit. Don't you think I thought of that? Okay, hold on, if the big one's locked, we're fucked; we'll have to kick the door in," he says, constantly poking the tip of his tongue out. "But if this... yep... got it..."

The clank of a lock turning. When Sebastian opens the door, we all hold our breath.

The corridor is as I remember. The coat rack spilling over with clothes, moth-eaten coats, polyester jackets from the Polish Red Cross, woollen Sunday-best overcoats. Beneath it, piles of assorted shoes – worn-down, fake-leather slippers, flip-flops, rubber moon boots for bad weather. On a table next to the wall stands a lone glass of unfinished tea, a teabag drifting limply inside. Just as I remember, there are no ornaments, no photographs, no framed pictures, Jesuses

91

or Our Ladies hanging on the walls. There are bottles of medicine and half-empty blister packs of pills. A peculiar smell hangs in the air, a mixture of old, arduously conserved bodies, cheap soap and hair spray, damp and mould. But there are no souvenirs, no photographs of children, no calendars, holy pictures. *Strange, for an apartment belonging to an old couple*, I think once again.

We step into the corridor, switch on the light, and close the door behind us. The layout is exactly the same as that of the Institute – two rooms to the left, two to the right, a bathroom, and beyond that a kitchen. It's a mirror image. Forty years ago, the Institute must have looked identical.

"Mrs Finkiel," I say. "Mrs Finkiel, are you in?"

We're answered by nothing but a dull, low hum spilling out in a dense wave across the floor, as though one of the rooms was entirely taken up by an enormous old generator.

"It's an old fridge. Russian probably. My gran used to have one. It made the exact same noise," says Iga.

"Then maybe there's some grub around." Sebastian heads towards the kitchen. "I don't know whether you've noticed, but we don't have any left."

"Wait." I grab him by the am. "You and Iga check the kitchen and bathroom. Veronica and I will take the bedrooms."

Robert and Anna stand at the threshold, utterly still. They haven't got the strength or courage to go any further. I understand. Anna is shaking a little, her body gripped by a strange tremor. She can't move for fear. Doesn't even look at her boyfriend, Robert, while he in turn doesn't try to comfort her. He, too, stands still as though groggy from some heavy medication.

Maybe it's odd that the rest of us are not behaving like them, that despite everything we're still moving, still searching, shouting – but perhaps we all still have something that keeps us going, something greater than the fear. For me, it's Ela. It's Ela who reminds me that after each nightmare comes an awakening. That every house, every cage, every trap has a way in and a way out. That every situation comes to an end.

Veronica is standing next to me. She is listening in, trying to become one with the apartment, to hear what, according to her, is hidden within the walls. To start talking to this something. Ask this something for clemency and in return help it to get out, escape – that something, after all, doesn't want to be here, that something is imprisoned here. Veronica inhabits the world of ghosts.

Nobody took Veronica seriously when she made a strange movement over her plate and told me not to leave the house at four in the afternoon one day. Nor did we take her seriously two days later when we found out that some stoned moron had driven his vamped-up Ford into some people on the zebra crossing on Plac Inwalidów at exactly ten minutes past four.

We thought Veronica was mad when Iga told her the dream in which she was being followed down the street by a blurry, black and white figure against a coloured background. "Gucek wants to talk to you," Veronica had said.

Gucek was Iga's boyfriend from when she was a teenager and she'd left home and lived in a squat with forty other punks. Gucek was eighteen, smoked heroin, wrote abysmal poems about endlessly high towers and walls that disappeared into the cosmos ("and every brick in the wall is you"), kept rats – two but wanted more – and had started a punk band called Mayor's Last Obstruction. Iga had told Gucek she loved him and that her period was late. A couple of days later, Gucek jumped out of a window on the seventh floor, and Iga went to Germany for a few days.

She'd never talked about Gucek or what had happened. Not to her mother. Not her other boyfriends. Not me. Nobody. Especially not Veronica. Veronica was a stranger who'd answered our "Room to Let" ad.

From what Iga said, it seemed that Gucek had had a fixation

with black and white films. When watching TV, he'd fiddle with the contrast until the image lost its colour.

"Makes no sense otherwise," he'd say.

The figure in the dream whom Veronica called Gucek was black and white, even though everything else was in colour.

There was another incident. One morning, I returned from my shift at the Cat with a bottle of vodka magnanimously given to us by comatose Papa. Four or five of us sat in the kitchen knocking it back to spite ourselves, because the anticipated hangover might otherwise have been too light. We opened the windows wide to allow all the sounds and colours of dawn inside and we drank until below us, in the street, well-groomed people marched to church, parents led screaming children for a walk to Krakowski Park or Błonie, and Brits, knocked out by vodka like us, slowly dragged themselves to Karmelicka Street for breakfast and a hair of the dog. There were many mornings like this, but on this particular one, trashed after two drinks, the usually teetotal Veronica, who'd been living in the Institute for about two weeks, propped her head on her hands to stop it gravitating all the way to the table and said:

"It's bliss living with you guys. Such a shame something bad's going to happen to us."

I soon forgot the comment but today remembered her words.

"There's nobody here," says Veronica. "The apartment's empty."

"Good. We've got to open the windows," I urge. "We've got to open the windows, make another rope and climb down it. We'll tie all these coats together, and there must be some blankets somewhere, there must—"

"It's probably the middle of the night," Iga interrupts. "I think it's night time."

"Shouldn't we go further in?" I ask. "Or are we going to just hang around in the corridor?"

"How do you know there's nobody here?" Iga turns towards Veronica.

"I just know," she replies.

"We'll stay by the door," says Robert, finally putting his arm around Anna. Anna nods silently, without changing her expression.

Sebastian is already making his way forward. Robert turns and locks the door from the inside.

"Anna's scared," he says, hugging his girlfriend into his chest. She, in response, closes her eyes, and two huge tears trickle down her face.

I nod to them and wave to Veronica. I enter the first room on the left – the room corresponding to Gypsy's in the Institute. We switch on the light. There's nobody there. It's not a large room, a living space of no more than a few metres.

"No," I whisper. "No. Fuck, no."

The window is bricked up.

Of course it is. We couldn't just step out of our apartment, enter the one next door and leave when 'They' had gone to so much trouble to make sure we couldn't escape.

The room is so small I can barely stretch my arms. On one side is a plywood wall unit that takes up the entire wall and is practically empty. Apart from dust, all it contains is a small display of photographs stuck to the inner side of the glass.

The photographs are black and white, posed, with motionless figures staring at the camera lens with both amusing stateliness and troubled confusion. Old people, children, young women with backcombed hair and heavy make-up, all standing against a background of trees and dilapidated fences. I bring my face close to the photographs, trying to find Mrs Finkiel, but Veronica edges me away from the cabinet and says:

"Come on, let's move on."

We go to the second room on the left. It is larger but also dark. The windows are bricked up in here too. On the right-hand side of the room stands a battered, bare divan, and next to it a wardrobe. I slip my hand between the wardrobe and the wall, feel for a socket and switch on the light.

The whole wall above the bed is covered by an enormous and hideous painting. Someone, the person who had painted it, had tried – despite having no knowledge of proportions – to depict its essence, meaning a man on a horse. But all that remained were grey-purple outlines, the original colours now impossible to make out. The man has horns or is wearing a horned helmet on his head, and he holds a long object to his eye with one hand and a weighing scale in the other.

"What's he holding?" I ask myself out loud, and Veronica replies:

"A telescope."

"Hold on," I urge. "Hold on." I return to the first room on the left.

Veronica follows me.

"What are you doing? What's the matter?" she asks.

"Hold on," I repeat.

"Don't touch. It's not yours. You'll be cursed. Don't touch," she says. I study one of the photographs. It's a retouched portrait photograph of a man with a neatly trimmed moustache, a strong square jawline and resolute little eyes set beneath narrow brows.

"Look, Veronica." I point to a badge pinned to the man's wide lapel. "It's the same, look."

The badge adorning the man's jacket shows a man with a telescope riding a horse. And suddenly, in a brief flash of déjà-vu, I know I've seen this image somewhere before. And in the same place, on the lapel of a jacket.

"Come on," says Veronica. "That's not so important now. Come on."

She places her palm on my back. I can feel her hand shaking.

The next room we enter, the second on the right, is probably the Finkiels' bedroom. There are two single beds, each with a bedside table. On one – presumably Mrs Finkiel's

– there are crosswords, more bagged medicine, a silver spoon and some illegible notes, probably a shopping list; on the other, nothing but a glass of water. On a chest of drawers are several books: Sienkiewicz's *Trilogy*, an encyclopaedia, some crumpled crime novels and a number of short novels about the Second World War from the Biblioteka Żółtego Tygrysa series.

The apartment's like a tomb, a cold and ugly grave. I'm beginning to understand why Mrs Finkiel screamed at me through the door. I'd scream non-stop if I lived in a place like this.

"There's nothing here," growls Sebastian from the depths of the apartment. We quickly walk down the corridor, though we haven't yet checked the room on the right, and burst into what ought to be the kitchen. I switch on the light. It's just as dead and ascetic as the rest of the apartment, devoid of any furniture other than one wooden cupboard, a couple of chairs and a fridge. Not even the trace of a plant. No cookbooks. The chipped, miserable mugs by the sink look like they belonged to a canteen three decades ago. The walls are the piss-like colour of faded bile. Sebastian looks twice as large as usual, like a giant against a backdrop of dwarf furniture.

"Aha, a tin. Two tins. And tomato paste. And pasta. There's going to be some munch," he says and loads the contents of the fridge into a shabby carrier bag decorated with a picture of a bowl of citrus fruits. He picks up various items, unscrews the lids, opens and sniffs. What's gone off, he returns to the fridge.

"Agnieszka, come and look at this." I hear a whisper behind my back. It's Iga.

I follow her down the corridor and she points to a pale blue light pouring through the glazed panes in the door of the second room on the right. Ten seconds ago, it hadn't been there. A pain shoots behind my ribs. I hold my breath.

It was the room where Mr Finkiel had been watching *Clan* the last time I'd been here.

"A screen," whispers Veronica. "Someone's switched on the TV."

Sebastian rushes out into the corridor and approaches the door. He presses the handle.

"It's locked from the inside," he says. "Shall I blast the fucking shit out of the damned door?"

Yes, Sebastian, you do that, you blast the fucking shit out of the damned door, I want to say. I want to go in, see where the blue glow is coming from and destroy it, but suddenly I forget about what might be in the room and say nothing, because when I turn to ask Robert how Anna's doing, I realise there's nobody there.

"Robert!" I shout. "Anna!"

I inspect every room except the one that's locked. Sebastian drops his bag of stolen fridge contents and darts to the front door. Presses the handle.

"It's locked," he says. "Double locked. Someone's locked the other lock from the outside."

The door of the room with the TV is still closed; the blue-grey glow floods the empty hallway.

"What?" I ask.

"The front door – it's locked," he repeats, wrenching the handle as hard as he can.

"Finkiel, you old whore!" yells Iga. I run to the door, try to open it too, but it's as though someone has rammed a heavy chest against the door and barricaded it shut. Sebastian waves me out of the way and kicks the door with all his might, but all he accomplishes is a dent in the brown leather padding.

Somebody – Robert? Anna? someone else? – has locked us in Mrs Finkiel's apartment.

"Open up! Open up, you cunt!" screams Iga.

We hear something behind the door. Footsteps. Shuffling. A metal clank, then the distant, muffled sound of a key being inserted on the other side of the landing, of a key being turned, a slam, then muted footsteps growing fainter as they descend, as though someone has put carpet slippers over their shoes.

Someone had opened the door to the Institute with a key. Someone had entered.

We begin to push and kick the door with all our strength. Sebastian retreats to the kitchen. There's the sound of cutlery crashing to the floor, plates smashing. After a while, Sebastian returns carrying two kitchen knives with heavy wooden handles; one he grips tightly, the other he hands to Iga. The landing is quiet.

We bang on the door as hard as we can. We want to tear the door from its hinges. And then, as though all the elements of the house are being controlled by a supernatural force, the blue glow disappears from the hallway, and the front door opens with momentum, almost breaking my nose.

"Robert! Anna!" we call, running out onto the empty landing. Iga shakes the metal grating. It's locked, as before. I press the lift button violently. Nothing happens. Robert and Anna are nowhere to be seen.

"We're going back to the Institute," states Iga. "Can you relock it?"

"What the fuck for?" Sebastian turns and disappears back inside Mrs Finkiel's apartment. He comes back with the old, torn plastic bag stuffed with stolen food.

"I locked the door. I locked it." I repeat the sentence aloud like some mantra at a tai chi class, in the vein of "I'm a ball of light". "I locked it."

I had locked the door of the Institute. Both locks – top and bottom. The top, which requires a fat, conical key, and the bottom, a Yeti, like the Finkiels'. Air enters my body through my nose but takes three times as long to get to my lungs. I locked both locks.

"Are you sure?" asks Iga, but I'm sure. I gently push the door. It falls wide open.

A divan lies at the other end of the hallway, overturned, as does the table and the sofa, an ashtray; strewn everywhere are clothes, torn newspapers, receipts and the recipes that had decorated our kitchen.

Something's written on the wall in red oil paint. So fresh that oily streams trickle down the wall to the floor. I put my hand to my mouth to stop myself from screaming. Iga and Sebastian come closer.

WE'VE GOT OUR OWN KEYS.

Veronica emits a brief, broken scream as though her voice were a device that someone had momentarily turned on, then off, then on again.

A second, smaller note, as though an afterthought, says:

TO OUR APARTMENT.

"Anna! Robert! Anna!" I shout, but nobody replies; there's no sound, no murmur, nothing.

Suddenly, I step onto something soft and squelchy. I shudder at the thought of what it might be and I look down at a carrier bag similar to the one in which Sebastian had brought Finkiels' food. I open it and press my hand to my mouth even harder. A scream wants to escape, violently, but if it did, it would destroy my vocal cords.

Iga leans over my shoulder, then turns her face away instantly. Inside the bag are Black and White. Tongues lolling. Chopped to pieces. Paws, heads and tails methodically and sharply severed from their bodies. Bellies slashed open so that individual entrails and strings of intestines swim in a slush of blood, fur and shit.

Somebody has done this slowly and scrupulously. Without batting an eyelid. Then thrown them back into the carrier bag and mixed them up like soup.

And then, silently and suddenly, the light goes out.

* * *

The estate agent was called Marta. Marta, a woman who was the opposite of me in so many ways that we could have appeared together in a silly comedy. She'd been invited – without my knowledge or permission – by the solicitor who was dealing with all the legal matters concerned with the apartment. I went straight from the train to the meeting. In enormous baggy trousers, a jacket, three fleeces, a hat and five hastily tied shawls despite it being late August and quite pleasant October weather, I shuffled down Planty after a sleepless night and four Irish coffees drunk alone in the kitchen over an entire American series about a murdered girl and an alcoholic detective.

The solicitor was waiting for me by the Bagatela Theatre. We made our way to an apartment that I knew absolutely nothing about. I'd never been there, but I planned to move in as soon as I could. I nodded, pretending to listen, as she described the various formalities, claims, payments and taxes involved. Her monologue continued once we were in the Institute, walking through the empty, unfurnished spaces, touching dirty, dull walls, and looking at the cold bathroom with its square bath covered in yellow stains and chipped pink tiles. I peered into every bare room. I rubbed the mouldy curtains, tapped the windowpanes, pressed the door handles. As if making sure that it was all real.

When I first walked into the Institute, it smelled of old age, rust, rotten wood, reeking pipes – as though the windows hadn't been opened for years. The apartment, like my life, needed an overhaul.

"You're convinced that you want to move in in a week's time?" asked the solicitor, and I nodded, squatting on the floor, feeling the parquet beneath me, digging dirt with my fingernail from between the boards of a floor that needed sanding. I didn't really have a choice. I needed to leave. "The apartment's in need of repair. And the repairs are going to take longer than three days, you understand." The solicitor hovered over me as I examined the texture of the brownish stains on the bathroom wall. Finally, she noticed that her pertinent comments and rhetorical questions washed over me. "We've got a lot of documents that need signing. Maybe we can do that somewhere else. Let me buy you a coffee," she said, looking around the apartment with unease.

Despite the excitement, I was faint with exhaustion, so a coffee sounded good. It was then, as we were leaving the apartment, that I noticed the sign on the entryphone: "The Institute". I asked the solicitor about it on our way to the tram stop. She had no idea what it meant and why Gran Vera's name wasn't there. We got on the tram and went to a café on Bracka Street, one that belonged to a well-known Polish singer who also lived on the street and whose songs about rain on Bracka Street always turned my stomach.

The atmosphere in the café was just as stale as the one in the songs. A surprise arranged by the solicitor awaited me there: Marta. Marta had tightly pinned back, chestnut-dyed hair, glossed, shiny skin, which in the artificial light resembled rubber, a pair of optical lenses set in a brown frame, and a beige, seemingly asymmetrical suit. We were the same age, but Marta was somewhere else entirely. I wasn't even very sure which planet she came from. Marta ordered green tea. I asked for an enormous black americano.

"This is the ideal time, you know. Market prices are up, but a lot of people are still interested. Mainly English, not particularly well-informed, who came here for a friend's stag night, for example, and… you understand. Prices are going up and then it'll take a year for me to sell your apartment. Or two. And meanwhile, prices will fall, you understand."

It was as though they hadn't noticed the way I looked at them.

"And once the apartment's refurbished, it can be let and you'll get a steady income. It'll be let immediately, of course, for a good sum, too," said Marta, pleased with herself, slurping little teaspoonfuls of green tea.

A seriously anaemic waiter brought the solicitor a tart and Marta a salad.

"I take it Marta's your friend," I said to the solicitor, who I think was called Ola. She nodded. Ola and Marta must have studied together. Both must have got top marks in everything. Must have had crushes on their lecturers.

"Yes, Marta and I know each other…"

"And because you're friends, I understand that you sometimes throw Marta a tasty morsel," I said. The caffeine had started to have an effect, and these women had already raised my blood pressure to such an extent that I didn't need any more.

"You know, inheriting real estate is lucky, but it brings with it a lot of problems. We find solutions. You could make a lot of money, not have to worry about anything. Surely that's more than you could ask for, don't you agree?" Ola, the solicitor, asked rhetorically and drank her sparkling water with lemon.

"As far as I know, you live in Warsaw with your husband and daughter." Marta drank another tiny amount of green tea.

I finished my coffee in two gulps.

"I live where I live." I smiled and turned to the solicitor. "You know, I've only just seen the apartment and we're already talking about selling it. I don't intend to sell anything."

The solicitor evaded my eyes and seemed to follow a fly, visible only to her, buzzing around the café.

Marta adjusted her glasses and took another sip of tea.

"An apartment like that, in such a spot… You'll pay for the refurbishment, that's true, but after it's done, you can sell it. For about one and a half million at the moment," she said.

"Thank you very much for your help. I'll manage," I replied. I was trying so hard to be polite that I started to sweat. Talking to them brought up bile.

"I understand you've got the keys." I smiled at the solicitor. "And all the documents to sign."

"The full set will be ready tomorrow," she said quietly.

Suddenly, I realised that I was speaking loudly and that half of the customers were looking at us with unabashed curiosity.

"I was going to go back to Warsaw today, after the funeral. I don't even have anywhere to stay," I replied.

"Alright, I'll try to get them ready for today." The solicitor nodded.

I noticed that her hands had started to shake a little. She pulled out a pile of papers from a crammed plastic folder, then a pen and bunch of keys from her bag. Marta watched her abrupt, nervous movements, stony-faced, eyes half-closed.

"Would you like to come out for a smoke?" she asked.

I couldn't stand her from first glance, but I wanted a smoke even more. I agreed.

We stood outside the Cracovian singer's café. The rain on Bracka Street really had started to fall; it was like a bad joke. Marta offered me a thin Davidoff.

"I have a client willing to give you even more for the apartment," she announced.

"Please," I said. "It's out of the question. Firstly, it's an investment for my child. And secondly, I'm at a point in my life—"

"Two and a half million." Her expression didn't even change. "That's how much he's prepared to pay. That's way above the market price."

I didn't react.

"The client can pay in cash. Opportunities like this hardly ever come around," she said, unyielding and with such force that it seemed she wanted to press every word into my skull. "You'd be mad not to take it."

"Why? Why would he pay that much?" I asked out of curiosity.

"When people are rich and sentimental, well... I'm sure you can understand," she replied.

"Please thank him for the very nice offer," I said.

"Please consider it," she added and extinguished her cigarette. She smoked even faster and more greedily than me.

I looked at the solicitor through the café window. She was studying the documents spread out on the table. She looked troubled and nervous. Marta opened the door and let me in first.

"My business card," said Marta, putting down the card on my side of the table. She started to pack her phone and purse into her bag. Her salad remained untouched. Meantime, the solicitor, forgetting about the documents, gobbled up her tart as though she'd not eaten for two weeks.

"I'll have the full set in three hours. Could you come to my office in Salvator?" Ola pleaded, pointing to the papers.

I looked through the certificate of ownership, the inheritance documents, tenement administration forms. Marta was already on her feet, clutching her handbag. But then, as though remembering something, she sat down again.

"You know what, Mrs Celińska, there's an interesting story about your apartment," she said, glancing at the phone she'd taken out of her bag.

"That someone wants to give three million for it?" I asked.

"Your grandmother has owned this apartment since the fifties," Marta stated, ignoring my weak joke and not even looking in my direction. "But she never really moved in."

"That's no big deal; when Gran met my grandfather, she lived with him in Warsaw until she died."

"But do you know why?" Marta smiled as though she was about to announce that my gran had been spying for the CIA in President Bierut's time.

"Because she was his wife and he came from Warsaw?" I asked. This woman was seriously starting to get on my nerves.

"You know, this apartment, as well as the entire tenement, used to belong to a man called Antoni Waraszyl. This Antoni Waraszyl transferred the apartment to your grandmother in the fifties."

"That doesn't mean anything to me," I replied, my patience now wearing thin. Maybe if I said nothing, she would just drivel on for five minutes and finally leave.

She didn't say anything, merely smiled and looked at her friend the solicitor, who had finished eating her tart and was nervously wiping her mouth. Seeing this smile, the solicitor turned her eyes away with what looked to me like fear.

"I take it that some son or grandson of Mr Waraszyl wants to retrieve what supposedly belongs to them? That by selling the apartment, I'm really ridding myself of an even greater problem?"

"You know, if the client was a member of Mr Waraszyl's family, he'd probably take any other possible means to retrieve the apartment. Buying would be the last resort. But anyway, please listen to me," she said as she put the phone aside and looked me in the eyes. Her gaze was below freezing point.

"I am listening. How do you know all this?" I craved another cigarette.

"You don't even want to know how many real estate registers I've read in my life," she replied.

"Please carry on, but bear in mind that I won't sell, even for ten million."

"We'll see what you say to ten million…" She smiled. Her smile was as fake as if two invisible fingers were pulling up her cheeks.

"Great, you're lightening up with the jokes. Relax," I said.

"Anyway, that's just the beginning of the story. In the forties, after the war, your grandmother was Mr Waraszyl's wife. In fact, she remained his wife until she died. The marriage was never annulled. You know, finding all the documents was a pain, but it turned out that your grandmother's marriage to your grandfather was, shall we say, invalid."

"What did you say?" I hissed, taking another gulp of yet another coffee. It crossed my mind that the young harpy had made all this up just to keep me talking.

"That is, it's valid in God's eyes, but not legally. Your grandmother and Mr Waraszyl had a civil wedding, you understand, which was never invalidated. We were searching for documents to check if the apartment had been transferred to your grandmother by Mr Waraszyl after the alleged divorce as part of dividing the possessions and so on. Your grandmother, according to the documents, asked Mr Waraszyl for a divorce in 1953, you understand, but he officially refused, by letter. This letter was among the property documents. Your grandmother left for Warsaw and was later married to your grandfather in church. Mr Waraszyl, despite the fact that she'd left him, gave her the apartment. Did he want to ensure her future? I don't know. What's interesting is that he must have known a great number of important people. He somehow managed to see to it that nobody was allocated the apartment, which was practically impossible at the time. It was so important to him that your grandmother should live there, you understand, that he must have bribed the entire city along with the Wawel Dragon to see to it that the apartment remained empty and waited for her until she changed her mind."

I was becoming so annoyed, so furious, that the contents of my stomach were boiling over. In her need to persuade me to sell the apartment and get a hefty commission, she'd started to solve one of the greatest mysteries of our family – Gran Vera's past – with the stoic, blasé calm of a corporate tin god.

She noticed but didn't react.

The solicitor, Ola, looked in the other direction; all that was needed was for her to start whistling.

"The most interesting part's still to come," Marta announced. "You see, your grandmother didn't want the apartment, and for the next thirty years, she tried as hard as she could to get rid of it. She tried to sell it, but, you know, it was communism, things like the market and ownership officially didn't exist, so you couldn't just sell. Masses of formalities. She could, of course, have tried to donate it to the housing co-operative and even tried, at one point—"

"And why didn't that work?"

"You know…" Marta smiled. "I got drawn into the case. It was like a crime mystery. I came across this going through the documents at the client's request."

"The one with the two and a half million?" I asked.

She ignored the question.

"Perhaps your grandmother didn't, at first, donate the apartment to the co-operative because her new husband, your grandfather, or someone else from the family vetoed it. Here one can only guess," she continued quite calmly. "But later, at least this is what the documents suggest, by finding a loophole – inadequate standards, some fictitious damage – Mr Waraszyl made it impossible."

"Who was this Mr Waraszyl?" I asked. The worst thing was that I was beginning to believe the story myself. That the mystery of Gran Vera's secret life was being solved in front of my eyes by this walking advert for Swiss loans. I was beginning to get drawn in, and this made me hate her even more. *She's turning me into a little kid who's being accosted at the school gate*, I thought.

"You know, that, in fact, is the biggest mystery. He was a man with no clear responsibilities, no formal position. He was a member of the Party, but he didn't play a role in the committee. Made some profits, ran Hotel Cracovia for a while, but really, he was a nobody, you understand. Yet he must have been some sort of grey eminence, pulling the strings behind the scenes, because what he did was practically impossible."

"Did anyone ever live in the apartment?" I asked.

"This is where it gets interesting again. The apartment was finally allocated, but the family moved out after a month. Of their own free will. Nobody knows why. Things like that didn't happen in those days. Getting accommodation was, on the whole, like catching God by the ankles. Then a distant relative of your grandmother lived there, some niece. That didn't last long either, maybe six months. The niece had an accident. I visited the archives to find out what had happened to her, you know, and found a mention in the *Polish Daily*. It turns out she fell out of the window of this very apartment. Straight onto the pavement, on Mickiewicz Avenue. In broad daylight."

I blinked. I felt like I'd just woken up from a nap. What she had just said got through to me, and I began to laugh, genuinely, wholeheartedly.

"It's incredible how stubborn you are." Laughing, I asked for yet another coffee. I tried to compose myself – my laughter was so loud that the customers in the café were starting to look at me again.

"I don't understand," said Marta, though there was not the slightest sign of confusion or any feelings at all on her face. I believed she really didn't understand.

"What's your commission? Twenty percent? For half a million, I'd be able to invent a whole lot of stories too." I laughed again.

The waiter brought me another coffee.

Marta didn't react. Ola continued to pretend that she was looking at something else. Marta opened her bag and started to extract some photocopies, then spread them out on the table. She arranged them evenly in front of her, in ordered rows, as though playing patience. Copies of articles from the local press over the last few decades. The headlines screamed:

TRAGEDY ON MICKIEWICZ AVENUE.

UNEXPLAINED GAS POISONING.

CURSED APARTMENT.

OLD MAN'S SUICIDE.

It was enough to skim my eyes over the extracts in bold type and the photos to see that they were all about 20 Mickiewicz Avenue, apartment 12.

"Every apartment here has its story," said Marta.

"Exactly," I retorted.

"But none so interesting as this one, you know." Marta shook her head.

I vowed to myself that if she said "you know" or "you understand" one more time, I'd dig a fork into her artery.

"Do you really think I'll get scared and agree to sell?" I said. "You're quite something."

"This is interesting," she said, pointing to one photocopied extract. Judging by the font and layout, it was an opposition paper from the seventies. The headline read:

ANOTHER FATAL ASSAULT ON OPPOSITION ACTIVIST.

"Let me guess, he was assaulted in my apartment?"

"Not quite," she said. "Darek Kusiak. It was in '77. Sometime in September. It wasn't as loud as the Pyjas case. Maybe because Kusiak wasn't a student. He was just a guy who worked in a galvanising plant in Huta. He'd somehow wangled himself into the opposition and distributed leaflets for them. One day, he was found dead on a bench in Krakowski Park. The keys to your apartment in his pocket."

"How come?" I asked. I took a large gulp of my coffee even though my heart was beating much too fast already.

"It turned out that your grandmother had opened the apartment to the opposition. They ran a printing press, collated samizdat, held meetings. They left after Kusiak's death. But the case was investigated again after '89 by the public prosecutor's office and it suddenly turned out that politics had nothing to do with it, that yes, the boy had helped the oppositionists, they knew and trusted him, but only for about two months. Kusiak wasn't under any surveillance; he wasn't of interest to anyone, didn't even have a case file. Somebody had simply beaten him up. It was completely unrelated. But, due to Kusiak's death, the militia learned that the opposition were printing and hiding in your grandmother's apartment, you understand, and the oppositionists thought that it was the militia who killed the boy, so they left practically the next day."

"My grandmother was never involved with the opposition. She wasn't really interested in politics," I said. The coffee was finished; it was time to part ways. Nobody had ever tried to force me into something with so much impertinence before. By the end of the meeting, I knew I wasn't going to sell the apartment even for a billion dollars, even if I was starving to death.

"In that case, it might have been another way of trying to get rid of the apartment." Marta shrugged. "I don't know. There are indications in the documents of her efforts to transfer the apartment into yet another person's name."

"I really admire your efforts," I said, gazing at the evenly arranged photocopies.

"And you say I'm stubborn. It's you who is stubborn," she retorted.

Her voice seemed to come, not from her larynx, but from a speaker located somewhere on her body.

"Perhaps you could email me the rest of the story." I looked meaningfully at my watch, then at Ola. "I've still got a few things to sort out."

"The apartment belongs to you as of today." Marta, too, glanced at hers. "They're just interesting titbits. I'm not going to use them to force you into a deal."

"Good." I smiled.

"I'm in a hurry, too." She got up, slid the photocopies into her bag, which she slung over her shoulder, smiled her fake smile at her friend, shook my hand and made her way to the exit.

I was sure that she'd turn around at the door and say something else. People like that always keep trying, right to the very end.

"You know what's interesting?" She turned, of course. "Antoni Waraszyl died in '88. Two years later, your grandmother had hundreds of opportunities to sell the apartment. Got masses of offers. But she didn't take up any of them. Communism fell and her view on the matter changed completely."

"My grandmother was wise. She understood that times had changed, that nobody was going to hand accommodation out to anyone." I shrugged.

"It could be that." She smiled again.

Now I remembered something.

"Do you have any idea what 'The Institute' means? On the entryphone?"

"No idea!" She spread her arms. "Lots of things happened in that apartment, as I told you. But that sign is terribly old. It's probably been there ever since the entryphone was installed. Since the sixties. You've got my business card, haven't you?"

I nodded. Marta left. She walked briskly. I heard her heels tapping on the pavement for some time.

Ola was still pale, her lips pursed; she drummed her nails nervously on the table. She tried to say something, but I pre-empted her by raising my hand.

"It's all too absurd for me to be really mad at you. Don't worry," I said.

"Shall we go to my office?" she asked.

She was still scared, but I realised it wasn't me she was scared of. She was scared of someone, or something, entirely different. I had no idea what.

* * *

The candle around which we're sitting came from the supermarket and is called Almond Breeze. It gives off a faintly nauseous scent similar to that of a toilet freshener, which has nothing to do with almonds or breeze. But that doesn't matter. Almond Breeze and its five friends in the multipack we found in a drawer are our only supply of light. 'They' have cut off our power. We don't know how 'They' did it. There was no short circuit; the fuses are in place and functioning. So, what's left are lighters and these candles, which cast our giant shadows on the wall. 'They' have left traces – shattered objects, ripped clothing. I found my favourite jacket torn in half. Torn as though somebody exceptionally strong had picked it up and simply ripped it like a sheet of paper. Books torn apart, scrunched-up documents, contracts and tax forms, trampled DVDs. I found my old cork board – which I'd rooted out from behind the wardrobe when I moved out of Ela's father's – crushed. The photograph of me and Ela pulled out of a smashed frame, ripped up. The candle picks the scattered remnants of our home out of the darkness. We huddle around it. It feels as though we've been bombed, buried in a basement beneath rubble.

"Why didn't you mention it before?" Iga speaks slowly, quietly. She is sharing one of the last cigarettes with me. They're nearly all gone. The tea, rice and Xanax are already finished.

I hope they're not going to cut off the water.

"I don't know. I didn't want to think about it," I reply truthfully, and Iga just nods.

I'd give anything to get drunk now. To drink some beer, a bottle of wine, half a litre of vodka. I'd be happy with moonshine, any old cheap plonk. Amol or eau de cologne. Any alcohol, fuck it.

"You think it's him then, the guy with the two and a half million? The one who wanted to buy the apartment?" asks Iga, and I shrug. I don't care who 'They' are. What matters is our helplessness. Their complete upper hand. We're like animals in a slaughterhouse. Rats in a laboratory. Anything could happen at any moment and there's nothing we can do about it.

At any moment, we might die. Somebody who chops a cat to pieces and leaves it in a carrier bag for the owner to find won't hesitate to hurt a human being.

"And you'd have two and a half mill," Sebastian says from the kitchen. "Instead of what's happening right now. You'd have a nice house near Warsaw, a good car. Run a business."

Again, I shrug.

"Reasonable people don't think in terms of what ifs," I say. "It can drive you mad."

"That's soon to come," chuckles Sebastian. "Soon we'll all be totally fucking nuts."

"Do you think they're going to kill us?" asks Iga, to no one in particular.

The question's cropped up many times since we returned to the apartment. First through tears, then calmer, quieter. Each time, the answer is "I don't know." Because nobody knows what's going to happen next.

'They' could come in with cake, candles and party hats and shout, "Surprise, happy birthday!" Or 'They' could pump gas in through the door, set us alight, put us to sleep, then come with saws, pliers and knives and start to cut us to pieces, like they did to our cats.

Anything can happen, and we won't be able to do anything about it.

The candle flickers and I pick out the edge of the carrier bag with the cats in it in the corner of the hallway. We haven't decided what to do with it yet, so we've shoved it into a cardboard box. We covered their bodies with sawdust and the remainder of their cat litter, to hold back the stench for a while. The apartment's getting colder and colder, as though 'They' were gradually turning down the heating. Maybe soon the cats' corpses will freeze.

Sebastian suggests we burn them in a huge bonfire on the landing. That maybe starting a fire is a good idea anyway. Iga agrees. She says 'They' must be in the building with us and we should smoke them out; that when it starts burning, the fire brigade will come and we'll finally get out.

I don't think I've gone mad yet, because I know how ridiculous the idea is.

I feel myself shaking from the inside; I'm being tugged around by something coming from within my belly. I feel as though I'm dangling over an abyss and holding onto a thick, coarse rope. That's why we keep whispering to each other, to convince each other that we've not yet gone mad. Perhaps that's why I told them the whole story about the solicitor. Not to explain anything but simply for the sake of speaking. Perhaps it's something to do with the people she mentioned, perhaps not; perhaps it's the descendants of my grandmother's former husband, or perhaps the ghosts of young boys from the opposition who fled from here terrified by the death of their aide?

But from where I stand, it's not important. When somebody holds a gun to your head, you don't ask for their ID.

Apart from our voices, all we can hear are the sounds of the apartment. The creaking of the floors, the hum of pipes. The quiet purr somewhere beneath the floorboards.

If I had two and a half million złotys now, I'd give them all away just to hear the sounds of the street, to know that day still continues out there, that there are normal people going to work, people walking to the park to recharge their batteries; I'd give them all to know that, outside, truth, life and the world still exist.

I imagine that it's my favourite sort of weather outside: blood-freezing, healing frost, blue sky like on a postcard from a surf camp, snow crunching underfoot like crumbled polystyrene. I imagine it, but I can't check. Not even a single ray of light can get through the bricked-up windows. If I had it, I'd give two and a half million złotys for a ray of light.

Robert and Anna. They're nowhere to be found. We try to talk about what's happened to them, where they could be, but our questions just lead us round in circles.

"Maybe they ran out when 'They' opened the gate. Maybe 'They' let them out, maybe they're not important to 'Them', because they don't live here," I say.

"Ran out? Got out, like Gypsy? And haven't come back either? If they got out, why didn't they go to the police?" asks Iga.

"They just wanted to get out of here. They were sick with fear."

"I just don't feel anything." Veronica is looking nervously around the room like a cat observing a laser beam projected on the wall. "I don't know what's happened to them. I've got no idea. I'd sense it if something bad was happening. Or something good."

"Give us a break with all that mumbo jumbo, please." Iga hides her face in her hands. "But if you really do have magical powers, then use your telepathy and summon the lift. Get those bricks to fuck off from the windows."

Veronica doesn't respond. She nervously starts cleaning her glasses.

"Do you know Robert and Anna well?" I ask.

"No." She shrugs, and now she's staring at something hidden in the dark somewhere behind me. "I knew Robert at college. A bit. We talked sometimes."

"So why did they come here on Sunday? And last Sunday, too?"

Veronica shrugs again, nervously, as though she wants to say "I don't know", but then decides that we won't believe her anyway, so she gestures with what's partially a shrug and partially a plea to leave her in peace.

"They came to see the clairvoyant." Sebastian's voice reaches us from behind the wall.

Veronica raises her head as though trying to bring the ceiling down on her through sheer willpower. She avoids us with her eyes. Sebastian steps out of the kitchen and says:

"Veronica was telling them whether the kid was going to be okay. Tell them, Veronica." He quickly returns to the kitchen, lighting his way with a small torch attached to his keys. There, the cooker still working, he continues cooking the pasta he stole from Mrs Finkiel's.

"Kid? What kid?" I ask Veronica, who shakes her head and says:

"She's pregnant. Let's not talk about it. It won't change

anything." She stares at me for a moment, then pulls her head up again. "She's not here and we don't know where she is."

"Jesus Christ." I let my breath go.

"I told them there might be some problems," continues Veronica. "That's what came up. I wasn't going to lie to them. I told them to go and see a doctor. But the doctor didn't see anything. Didn't want to hear of it, said it was a con, that I wanted to extort money from them. She insisted on coming again. And this time I said I didn't want any money."

"What problems?" I ask.

"You get paid for it?" Iga grills.

"The child might be ill." Veronica finally focuses her eyes on one point: the door of the small, unused toilet. "In my opinion, it's something to do with the head. Some sort of blockage, a lack of something. Air or blood, I'm not sure. An obstruction. I don't know, I'm not a doctor. I just put my hand on her belly and I could tell that something wasn't right."

The argument over the cigarettes. That's why Robert didn't want Anna to smoke. Sometimes we're all blind fools.

I have to tell myself that somebody let them out. That in blind terror, they took the opportunity of the grating being open and went straight home, that they'll live long and happy lives.

The dish that Sebastian's trying to concoct reeks like a sack of dirty socks. But I don't care. It reminds me that I'm still alive. I imagine that we're at some sort of survival camp, that this is all a game. A strange version of some stalking game. That the tools we've laid out next to us – a hammer beside Sebastian, a knife beside Iga, a screwdriver, sharpened with a file, next to me, scissors next to Veronica – are only props meant to add to the atmosphere, to immerse us deeper in the game.

"Wait. Wait, Iga," I say and look round at everyone. "Don't we have anything from the Cat? Have we checked everywhere? Is there definitely nothing? No vodka stashed away for somebody's birthday? Nothing?"

I'm answered by silence and shaking heads.

"Old wine?" I ask again, as though repeating the question would conjure up a bottle of wine. "Flat beer? Amol?"

"I can take a look, Aga, but there really is nothing, we've drunk it all." Iga gets up and tiptoes to the kitchen, lighting her way with the small pocket torch attached to her keyring.

I follow her. Sebastian loads a mushy sauce onto the pasta and shoves a plate in my hands. Iga searches the drawers again, the fridges, baskets, any hiding place she can think of, but everything's empty, everything's finished.

"Thank you," I say as I put a piece of pasta mush in my mouth. It tastes foul, like a reheated pudding of meat and fat. But it's hot. It's carbs, it will fill us up.

"I did a course in cooking but didn't pay much attention," he explains, as though justifying the pasta mush he's prepared. I forgive him, but Iga protests:

"I'm not eating this."

"Why?" Sebastian is baffled. He looks at the contents of his plate. Then at the contents of Iga's. Sticks the plate under her nose.

"I don't eat meat. You know that, Seba," Iga answers calmly, gently pushing the plate away.

"There's nothing else," Sebastian says after holding the plate under her nose for a while. "There's nothing else to eat."

"I know there isn't," replies Iga.

"Shove all that leftist diet crap up your arse!" Sebastian explodes and forces Iga's plate up under her nose as though he's going to decapitate her with it. "Eat it and stop fucking around."

Iga shakes her head.

Sebastian is starting to pant. He doesn't know what to do with himself. He's the sort of person who, when he comes across any resistance, usually belts it until the resistance is felled, and that's what he'd like to do now, but he can't. He's confused. He puts the plate aside.

"So, it doesn't suit you?" He raises his voice. "It doesn't *suit* you?"

"No, it doesn't suit me," Iga replies calmly. "I'm a vegan, Sebastian. Which means I don't eat meat and don't drink milk."

Sebastian stares at her, turns and puts the plate on the table. He takes a couple of deep breaths, grabs the plate again and takes it out into the hallway, then returns, stands in the doorway, takes another deep breath and says to Iga:

"You're all fucked up. When we get out of here, you can get back to your filthy mates. But right now, we're stuck here together."

"Let's just not talk, Sebastian, we're too different," Iga states and turns away.

"How are we fucking different?"

Iga turns towards him.

"Civilised-wise," she says, still calmly, quietly.

Sebastian scratches his head. Looks at her blankly, coldly. He's breathing more rapidly now, more forcefully. I'm starting to feel scared.

"Just what I think, too. Fuck you," he replies after a while. "I'm a good guy. And you're a fucking slut. Lesbo."

"Sebastian, what did you say?" she asks.

"Stop it, Iga," I plead.

"Your head's fucking screwed up. You think you know it all when you know fuck all. You think you can build a better fucking world full of fucking poofters, Arabs, sodding filthy pigs, where no one eats meat except for embryos. Fucking great world. And cunts, stupid bitches like you, who come from good homes, whose daddies are always there to help them out, leftist cunts who give their arse and think they'll build a world just for kicks and it'll be great because they've read about it in fucking Jewish TVN papers."

Iga doesn't say anything; her face is drawn into a mask of fury. She turns and goes back to the kitchen. She returns to the hallway with a different plate of plain pasta and some tomato paste.

"You know shit all about me, Sebastian, shit all, where I've been, who I am," she says, sitting cross-legged and placing the plate on her knees.

"What d'you mean, I don't know?" Sebastian loads the last forkful of pasta into his mouth. "I know everything. I'm not one of those idiots who says they hate lesbos then jerks off when they watch two sluts doing it on the internet. I think it's vile. Perverse."

"Sebastian, I'm not interested in your views. I'm really not interested," Iga assures him.

"When I see bitches acting the way you do, I want to fuck them up," Sebastian adds. "I want to get up and trash them."

"Stop, Sebastian, for fuck's sake, shut up!" I scream, thumping my fist hard on the table.

"You moron," says Iga.

"Moron?"

"Yes, dickhead. You're a thick fucking Nazi."

"Stop it, both of you!"

"Nazi? You're calling me a Nazi?"

"Yes, a thick, fucking Nazi. It's not me who yells 'We'll do with you what Hitler did to the Jews, at the stadium."

"Fuck you, you lesbo scab."

Iga gets up and approaches Sebastian. He, too, gets up. I want to say "stop it" again, but it's pointless. I walk up to Iga and pull her away from Sebastian.

"Stop it, please, have you both lost it?" I push Sebastian in the opposite direction, but he's taken root on the floor. He's not looking at me – he's looking through me at Iga, and he's smiling. I've seen that smile of his outside the Cat when clueless victims reel towards him, yelling at the top of their voices, so drunk they think they can shout anything they like. When he knows he's going to fuck somebody up. With no repercussions.

"And you know what else fucking annoys me?"

"Sebastian, stop it," I repeat, louder.

"Chicks who think they know everything because they gave their arse to some junkie in a band."

"Sebastian," I plead.

"If I knocked you up, I'd throw myself out of the window, too," he says.

Iga whacks Sebastian in the face. I freeze mid-move, intending to pull Sebastian away from Iga. The sound is loud, so sudden it feels as though I got hit in the face myself.

The smile transforms into a grimace – Sebastian has become an enraged but focused beast. *Nothing's going to stop him now*, I think.

"You touch me," says Iga. "You just touch me."

Sebastian takes a step forward. And another. For each step he takes, Iga takes one backwards. Sebastian leans over her face and pulls her up close. I glance at Veronica, but she's not registered any of this; she's still staring at the toilet door.

I'm just about to scream when Sebastian starts to grin again and says: "Just kidding! Surely you weren't taken in, eh?"

"What?" Iga shakes her head, not understanding. "What?"

"I was joking. I couldn't give a shit what you eat."

But his smile doesn't leave his face as he walks away from Iga, retreats to the wall, sits and pulls a packet of cigarettes out of his pocket. He takes one out, puts it in his mouth, then throws the packet at her.

For a moment, we sit in silence. Veronica continues to stare at the door to the unused toilet as though willing her eyes to transform it into a way out.

Sebastian is still smiling his shifty smile. Suddenly he gets up, runs towards Iga and slaps her on the face several times.

Iga yells. Sebastian yanks her up by her fleece and hits her against the wall.

"Slut!" he roars. "Fucking slut!"

"Stop!" I scream. "Stop!"

But Sebastian throws Iga against the door to my room. She protects her face with her hand as her back smashes through the glass, which scatters across the floor in thick, sharp pieces.

"Stop!" I screech.

Veronica crumples into a corner, hides her head in her

hands. Sebastian is standing in the middle of the hallway, panting, raising his arms then lowering them. Iga squats among the shattered glass by the door. I see only the outline of her body as she hugs her knees to her chest. She grabs her head, trying to hide as much of her body as possible.

I stand, run up to Sebastian, try to grab him, stop him, but he pushes me aside and says:

"I didn't want to be here. Didn't want to be in this fucking apartment. I didn't want to live with you, you stupid whores."

He pushes me so hard I fall to the floor. He runs to the kitchen and comes back with the plate of meaty pasta mush and a fork, leans over Iga, puts the plate in her hands and, wrapping his arm around her head, says:

"Now, you're going to eat this all up, you hear? Lovely, yummy food. Eat it, bitch."

He grips her black fringe as hard as he can with one hand, and with the other he uses the fork to force the food into her mouth, smearing it all over her face. I run up to him and start pounding my fists on his head and shoulders, but he's lost it, doesn't react.

"Stupid whores," he says. "You got what you wanted. I didn't want to be here."

I grab the plate, take a swing and hit him on the head with all my might. The plate breaks against his skull. Sebastian grasps his head, moves away from Iga and leans against the wall, heaving. He doesn't say anything. Looks down. Iga slowly gets to her feet, shakes bits of glass off her clothes to the floor. Picks up the closest towel from the floor and slowly wipes her face.

"Calm down," I plead, not really knowing what else to say.

Iga, panting heavily, picks the scissors up from the floor.

"Iga, no," I say. "Don't, Iga."

Iga, scissors tightly grasped, turns towards Sebastian. I run to her, catch her hand, but she frees herself from my grip with one tug, pushes me away, approaches Sebastian and quietly and slowly says: "Well, come on. Come on, you son of a bitch."

Sebastian turns to her, still heaving: "You come here."

This isn't Sebastian, I think. *Sebastian's a good man, it's the situation, he's the first to crack, somebody had to crack first. Sebastian injects something before going to the gym, I don't know what, probably some growth hormones for horses. He's big and aggressive. Gets carried away. He's the first to crack.*

"You come here," he repeats.

Iga walks in his direction, displays the scissors, then hides them in her pocket. I can't see Sebastian's face, but I know that smile's still there.

I always assume that people are good. That's my starting point. I'm stupid, I'm a stupid person. Maybe that's why everything's the way it is. People I know have to be good because I'm good. Bad people are among those I don't know. An idiotic error in logic I've made throughout my entire life.

They're standing face to face.

Suddenly, we hear a shout. A muffled but audible scream. A woman's scream. *It's Anna*, goes through my mind. *It's Anna.* The scream isn't coming from our apartment. It's coming from the other side of the stairwell. Mrs Finkiel's apartment.

Just then, I remember the locked door with the blue light. The room we didn't enter. As though somebody didn't want us to go in. As though what was in there wasn't ready yet.

"Come on," I yell to Sebastian. "Come on! Move!"

For a moment, Sebastian stands, motionless, then his expression changes, as though somebody is steering him with a remote control. He follows me, the screwdriver in his hand.

"Stay in the apartment!" I shout to Iga and Veronica.

Sebastian and I run across the landing towards Mrs Finkiel's door. It's wide open. We go in. The blue glow pours through the patterned glass onto the hallway floor again. A steely, cold gleam. There's another quiet hum, not the one from the fridge. This sound is like an instrument; every now and then it changes tone. Like an orchestra tuning. Like what's left of a used, worn tape. I know the scene from somewhere, have already seen this moment.

I see a movement, momentarily, at the other end of the corridor. A shift in the air. A black figure. It makes a slow gesture, moving its arm up and down by its side. It is hidden, deep in darkness.

I don't even know whether I see it or only guess that it's there.

The figure starts to scream, loud, as though it is standing right next to me, screaming into my ear. But it's still at the end of the hallway, and now it slowly moves its arm as though sending a command to something or somebody standing behind me. The scream changes into a modulated, fluid sound, ever higher, squealing like cut glass.

"Hey!" shouts Sebastian.

I turn towards him and his hand catches hold of my cheek.

"Stop it," he hisses. "Have you gone mad?"

I shake my head; I don't understand what he means.

"Don't scream your guts out, for fuck's sake," he says. He walks to the room with the blue glow. Signals me to follow him. There's no figure at the end of the hallway. I repeat: *there's no figure at the end of the hallway.*

Sebastian hands me the screwdriver. He's just about to open the door when we hear another scream behind it, short, broken, as though someone has just removed their hand from somebody's mouth. Then there's a quiet, pleading request:

"No, please. My father... my father, he'll give you some money. Please, he'll give you money."

I press the door handle. The door is unlocked. I push it. Tumble in. Sebastian is right behind me.

The room drenched in blue is just as stale as the rest of Mrs Finkiel's apartment. One heavy, old sideboard from the fifties, on its glazed shelves a single crystal plateau and a few glasses in wicker holders. A small table. Two armchairs.

Heavy curtains concealing the window and an unwashed carpet alive with moths.

There's nobody in the room. The blue glow is coming from the switched-on television set. As are the screams.

We squat in front of the screen, on which we can see a well-lit room with a low ceiling.

I think I shout "Oh, God!" and cover my mouth with my hand. I think.

On the screen, we can see two chairs. Anna is tied to one, to the other, Robert. Their arms are tied behind the backrests, their legs tied together at the ankles. Anna is yelling, her back arched against the chair, trying to lean back as though someone is walking towards her. Robert, on the other hand, is slumped forward. Black liquid is running from his head.

"Oh, God," I moan through clenched lips.

"Shut up," hisses Sebastian, touching the screen. "What is this? Where's it coming from?"

A man steps into frame. He is dressed all in black, a balaclava over his head, a knife in his hand. The man walks up to Anna.

"Don't, please don't, please don't do it. I'm begging you, I'm having a baby, I'm having a baby! Don't do it, please..." Anna coughs all this up in spasms. She looks terrified.

The man raises the knife, approaches her and grabs her by the throat. Anna screams, the man takes a swing, and then, suddenly, the TV switches to another channel and we see the Institute hallway. There's no one there.

"What the fuck is this?" asks Sebastian. He walks around the TV table, peers beneath it, but there's no video player; there's only one cable coming from the TV and disappearing into the wall.

"So that's where the camera is," I say to Sebastian. "That's where they put the camera, on the ceiling in the hallway."

"But there's nothing there. We searched the entire apartment. All of it," he replies.

"Then explain this to me, for fuck's sake, explain this!" I answer, tapping my finger against the screen.

The channel switches again. The television shows us – me and Sebastian – as if the camera were attached to the wall behind us. I turn around but see nothing.

"What's going on? It must be under the plaster. What is all this?" I ask.

"Wait," he replies.

"There must be some other circuit here," I state.

He runs his finger around the place on the wall where the cable disappears. Then he stands up, shuffles to the wall unit. It doesn't cover the whole wall. Between its edge and the corner of the room is a good two-metre gap.

He then examines the unit, holding his breath, and tries to move it. Clenching his jaw, he puts his whole weight behind it. The wall unit is massive. Sebastian tries again. I join him, try to help. Hold my breath, clench my teeth.

I turn towards the screen. Now we can see the stairwell, the locked grating, the cut lift cables. We lean on the wall unit again. It's starting to budge. The wood slowly starts to scrape the floor. We put all our strength into it. I don't ask why we're doing this. I trust him.

"You're not so bad," he says, panting.

Suddenly, the unit stops resisting and slides right up to the wall, and we momentarily lose our balance. Only once we've regained it do we see that there's a door behind the wall unit. An unpainted, dirty door with one handle.

I look at Sebastian. Sebastian looks at me. From the wall, just next to the doorframe, the white cable resurfaces, then disappears between the door and floor.

I look at Sebastian again. Sebastian presses the handle. The door is unlocked.

Behind the door are stairs going up, into darkness. We hear the hum of a machine, a scraping and the sound of footsteps. Darkness, like an enormous black throat, and a penetrating chill hits us from the unheated room. I feel for the light switch.

After a while comes a pale yellow glow from a single bulb, too weak to light the large, low, empty room.

This room shouldn't be here, I think.

We close the door behind us. The walls of the room are yellowish, dirty, smeared. The far end of it is completely drowned in darkness. We press our eyes into this darkness and see something move. A sound like a quiet coughing up of phlegm.

I scream and instinctively lean against the wall. My back senses something hard, and at that moment, a white, hospital-like glare explodes in front of our eyes: fluorescent strip lights along the length of the ceiling have been turned on. I cover my eyes; when I open them, Sebastian is already halfway across the room. There are two overturned chairs, a small digital camera on a tripod and a metal door on the far wall.

Robert and Anna are tied to the chairs. I go numb, don't feel anything.

Anna is dead, lying on her side in a thick deep-scarlet puddle, as though she tried to curl up at the last moment in spite of the restraints. Her mouth is half-open. Her eyes are glassy and surprised like a doll's. I don't know why, but the colour doesn't seem quite right. The blood looks too much like concentrated syrup; the colour needs working on.

Robert's throat has been slit. His blood looks more real than Anna's. He's covered in it, from the neck down. It's fresh. He lies on the floor next to the chair, still tied to it. Doesn't seem to have resisted. It looks as though he died quickly.

Sebastian stands next to me. I don't know what state he's in. He's breathing heavily, deeply. Maybe he's scared. Or maybe something's switched off in him, like it has in me.

I automatically place my hand on Robert's forehead, then stand up. I don't really know what to do. I feel I should perform some gesture, an incantation or something, but I don't know any, or maybe I do but can't remember.

I point out the metal door to Sebastian, then make my

way to it and start to run my hand over it. There's no handle, no opening. Perhaps it can only be opened from the other side. The metal is the same colour as the walls – a dirty yellow cream.

Sebastian very gently moves me aside, kicks the door as hard as he can, then kicks it again, but the only effect is a sound that makes me cover my ears: a mighty yet non-resonant gong.

He keeps kicking the door as if in a trance: with the side of his foot, the sole, the tip, with one leg then the other. He stops, grabs the large camera with its tripod and flings it against the door as though it weighs merely half a kilo. The tripod cracks in two. He runs up to it, picks up the camera and throws it again in the opposite direction, far, with superhuman strength, and it shatters into several pieces.

"Enough," I said. "Let's go back." I gesture with my hand.

We make our way back down the stairs. I notice that he's limping, moving slowly, holding on to his leg.

"You must have sprained your ankle," I say, then squat and pull up his trouser leg. His ankle is swelling in front of my eyes.

"It's nothing," he says. I want to take him by the arm, but he shakes his head. "And what about them?" he asks.

"What about them?" I repeat.

"Their bodies. We've got to do something with the bodies," he says, nodding up towards the secret room.

"There's nothing we can do right now. Come on."

I touch his shoulder gently, but he jumps back as though electrocuted.

"We've got to do something, got to," he repeats. I can see he's had enough.

As we cross the doorway back into the room with the TV, I turn towards the screen, and think I scream something again, but I no longer know what.

I can see the stairwell on the screen, the grating, torn lift cables and door to the Institute. And there now, on the landing, stands a black figure in a balaclava. Behind it, another figure, also in a black balaclava, locks the grating. And then we see the first figure open the door to the Institute and enter.

I hear Veronica scream and Iga swear.

Seconds later, as though roused from a stupor, Sebastian and I cover the distance between us and the Institute. Everything that's happening seems distanced, removed, as though I am watching myself in a bad film. *A bad film directed by Ela's father,* crosses my mind. *Silhouette, scream, blue light.*

We burst into the Institute. The first person I see is Iga. She's kneeling, kneeling in shards of glass, shaking with effort, holding somebody by the neck. Somebody dressed in black and wearing a balaclava. The person I saw on the screen. The person is wailing in pain. The handle of the heavy sewing scissors is protruding from their thigh. Blood runs down the leg.

"I heard somebody open the grating," says Iga. "So I stood by the door. He didn't see me. I struck blindly, as hard as I could."

Veronica doesn't say a word, just sobs and shakes her head. She's taken off her glasses, tears run down her cheeks.

I crouch over the person in the black balaclava. The person is howling and breathing heavily, presses his hand to the wound. Blood seeps between his fingers.

"Who are you, you son of a bitch?" I ask him, clutching the scissors in his thigh. Suddenly, I'm calm. Suddenly, I'm warm. As though I were slowly falling down an enormous abyss yet convinced that I was going to die. "Who are you?" I ask once more. Calmly. Or so I believe.

He shakes his head, wants to struggle, lash out, but knows he can't. The blood seeps slowly, bright red. The scissors haven't severed any major artery. Probably. But even so, one abrupt move would do it.

"Right, you motherfucker," says Sebastian, moving me gently aside and leaning over him. He wants to move Iga aside, too, but she punches him in the shoulder. So he leaves her there, crouches and punches him in the face, once, hard, without even taking a swing, as though wanting to hammer in a nail. We hear one loud crunch, like a packet of crisps being scrunched up.

Veronica looks on, now standing at the side, lighting us with Almond Breeze. A scene from some medieval surgical operation.

I tear off the balaclava. The man catches his breath, choking. Tries to breath through the mouth. Still doesn't say anything.

"What the fuck?" I yell, instinctively drawing back, almost knocking Veronica over.

"It's Gypsy," I say, looking around at them all, my eyes pleading them to say it's not him. But they can't, because beneath the balaclava is Gypsy's face, his eyes wide open and something like squashed fruit in the place of a nose. "You must have broken his nose, Sebastian."

"I never liked the bastard," says Sebastian and hits him again, even harder.

* * *

I slipped out at dawn, like a thief. The taxi driver just needed one look at me to cotton on to what was happening, so he let me smoke all the way to the station.

In running away, I realised two things. Firstly, never, absolutely never in my life had I decided to change anything; secondly, now, having made my first decision about a real change, I didn't feel a thing. As though the anticipation of change is harder to bear than change itself.

When I ran away from Ela's father for the first time, I didn't get far. I knew only one place. Moving back to my parents, to their house in Rembertów, wasn't much of a change. I landed back in my old room, which, when I'd lived with my parents, had only served as a place to regain consciousness every few days. I was surprised that something like "my room" in my house still existed.

When I found myself there with Ela, I spent more time in the room than ever before. At night, I squatted on the divan watching TV, surrounded by what now looked like a cheap set in a TV serial about my past life: books, posters, boxes full of old make-up and cassettes, postcards and handmade T-shirts – the useless and faded objects of a stranger.

Ela played on the floor with my old teddy bear, which at her age I called Beggar. Sometimes I picked her up and told her stories, went downstairs with her and made her porridge or sandwiches, or sometimes simply handed her over to my mother and watched TV until I fell asleep. From time to time, I smoked grass, which I bought from some kids on the estate. I smoked it in the loo, blowing out of the window. My mum pretended she didn't notice.

That wasn't a change. A step backwards isn't change. A step backwards is a step backwards.

Mum found me a job working in a nursery, but I turned it down. I only had patience for my own child.

I stayed at home. To contribute to the bills and buy food and things for my daughter, I decorated shop windows, worked on simple graphic commissions. Then I met a guy somewhere, whose face I can't remember anymore. He didn't mind my life being in pieces with an added bonus in the shape of a small child. Then I met another. I deleted all of them from my phone after two, three weeks. They never came to my home. None of them met my daughter.

In this way, six months went by. Then one day, my husband's parents, with his unspoken consent, took Ela away from me. My mum suddenly had to go to her sister's for some reason. I had to go into town to sort something out, I can't remember what – probably to sign some shitty agreement for some shitty commission that paid five złotys. I left Ela with my cousin Daria, who was at home with her own new baby. When I returned, Ela wasn't there.

"Her gran took her," said Daria, standing in the doorway with the expression of a dopey fish and wearing an over-stretched tracksuit. She'd never been too bright, to put it mildly.

"You mean my mum?" I spluttered, rummaging in my bag for my phone to call my mother and reproach her for taking Ela without telling me.

"No." Daria's expression didn't change. "No, not your mum. Your mother-in-law. She said you'd arranged for her to take Ela to the zoo."

My heart and stomach were flooded with a corrosive substance. Then I turned ice cold.

"No," I whispered. "No, we hadn't arranged anything."

"Well, that's what she said," replied my moron of a cousin, and it took all my strength not to grab her stupid, pale head covered in old dye and smash it against the doorframe.

I rushed away without even saying goodbye. Pulled out my phone. The evil old witch picked up on the first ring.

"Ela's fine," a croak at the end of the line informed me.

"Give me back my daughter!" I yelled. People in the street were looking at me. "Give me back my daughter!"

"She's fine," she repeated. "You've no right to her. You think we don't know what you've been doing. We hired a private eye to follow you. We know everything. Drugs. Whoring. You've no chance in court. You're a hopeless wife, a slut, a terrible mother."

"Give me back my daughter!" I yelled again, as hard as I could. My hoarse throat seemed to spit blood over my phone.

"She's fine," she repeated and hung up.

Ela's father came in the evening. Alone. I was sitting at home having consulted a lawyer my parents knew (who, knowing who my father-in-law was, informed me that I didn't stand a chance), numb from grass, wine and tranquillisers. I didn't let him in even though he rang for half an hour. He came again the next day. And the next.

"You bring Ela, and I'll let you in," I said through the door.

"You're not going to see her unless you let me in," he replied. "I'm coming one last time tomorrow."

The following day, when he entered, I ran up to him, and with all the strength I could muster, I slapped him so hard on the jaw that his head fell back and bounced off the door. He reeled.

"Give me back my daughter!" I yelled.

"Agnieszka, let's talk," he stammered, holding his jaw. "Nothing's happened to our daughter. She's fine. Please, let's talk."

I slapped him again in the same place. He tried to grab me by the hand but was too slow.

"Give me back my daughter, you prick!"

"Nothing has happened. Nothing has happened between us. You had no reason to do this. No reason to take Ela and run," he said, rubbing his jaw.

He left. I stood in the hallway, frozen stiff, shivering, exhausted. He returned a moment later with a huge basket of flowers. Stood it on the kitchen table.

"I love you," he declared, standing at a safe distance. "I love you and want us to be a family. Let's talk. I don't even know what happened. I don't even know why you've done this."

"Your parents have taken my daughter away from me." It was only the moisture on my lips that made me realise I was howling. "Your parents took my daughter away from me, and you're to give her back. Give her back to me right now."

He looked like he wanted to come closer and touch me, but instead he took a step backwards and left. I put the flowers in the bin.

This went on for a month. Every day for a month, I found a basket of flowers outside the door, and every day for a month, I lived on a cocktail of wine and tranquillisers, damaging my liver, and every day for a month, my mother-in-law informed me in the same tone of voice that, "Ela's fine."

Once, they let me see her in the park. They stood at a distance, with pursed lips, piercing me with police eyes, watching me hug Ela so hard that it was only later that I realised I could have hurt her, that something could have snapped in her beautiful, tiny body.

I talked to everyone. My mother, Gran Vera, my father, cousins. I didn't have the slightest chance of getting Ela back. The private eyes had photos of me with four different guys, had taken shots of me in some shitty gateway in Praga buying awful grass, and had got hold of my prescriptions for the psychotropic drugs I had started taking in order to sleep, eat, wash and excrete after Ela was abducted. I had the official stamped certificate of a junkie, a slut and a terrible mother.

Yet Ela's father came every day with flowers.

In the end, I gave in and went back. I rang the bell, one bag in my hand with all my things packed into it. He opened the door. He wasn't surprised; he stood there and said "I've been waiting for you," and looked on blankly as I hugged my daughter, as I showered her with trillions of kisses, as I wiped my tears against her, as I let go of her for a moment just so as to hug her again, as I cuddled her close as though wanting to rub her into me, attach her permanently to my breast, stomach, skin, as I repeated her name ten, fifty, a thousand times.

I went back to him and I stayed. Later, things were calm and relatively normal. Later, we started to simulate a so-called "normal" life. We simulated it so well that, for a while, I almost believed it was real. Almost began to like it. All the while repeating to myself that a child needs a family.

I repeated many things to myself to chase away the thought of defeat. Of being cornered. The thought that in leaving Ela's father, I would also lose Ela. Unless I ran away with her in the middle of the night to the far end of the world.

Climbing out of the taxi in front of the Institute, I was sure I was soon going to do just that. I was sure that moving to Cracow was only the beginning of a plan. I gripped the bunch of keys in my hand like a talisman, ran my finger over the entryphone, wiped the layer of dust from the plate by my number. The sign "The Institute" became clearer.

I'd take her from him, put him off his guard. And perhaps sell the apartment later and take the two and a half million. Then we'd run away.

I talked to my daughter on the phone regularly, for half an hour. I always called her mobile, always at eight in the evening.

"You probably don't care what Dad's up to," said Ela over the phone. "But he's drinking a lot now, a lot. And he sleeps a lot and sometimes cries, quietly, but I see the water running from his eyes."

"That's sad, darling. I want to cry, too," I answered.

"When am I going to be able to come and see you, Mum?" asked my daughter.

"When I finish redecorating," I said, wondering if there was a small muscle in the tear ducts that could be tensed by sheer willpower to stop the flow.

"Okay, Mum, I love you," said my daughter.

"Good night, darling, sleep well," I answered and hung up.

You have to put them off their guard, I kept repeating to myself. *You have to be careful though; this time it's you who has to do the abducting.*

A few days later, the redecorating was, indeed, finished. I'd done the bathroom – tiles, loo, bath, a finishing coat on the walls, painted them, sanded the floors. But really, it was two moustachioed, constantly tired men who did it, starting their day with five beers and a miniature bottle of flavoured vodka each. Whenever I tried to force them to tell me what they were actually doing at any given moment, they looked at me as if I were a monkey with two heads.

But, in the end, they got the job done, and I learned not to look at the places where things were a bit crooked or coming away a little.

I bought a huge unvarnished brown table for the kitchen. Changed the chandeliers, bought plastic and plywood furniture from IKEA, bought a few standing and table lamps, changed some of the sockets, took all the old, worn carpets and curtains to the rubbish dump.

Once I'd finished, the apartment no longer looked or smelt like a hospice, the walls weren't corpse-grey, but something was still not right.

The apartment somehow wasn't mine. It was too big. Too empty. I bounced off the walls, unable to sit anywhere for long, to lie down, watch a film, write an email, read a book. I had a strange feeling that I wouldn't be there for long. That I'd furnished it for somebody else. That all this was some sort of experiment, a transitional stage. That this space wasn't home and there was no sense in trying to turn it into one.

"The redecorating's done, darling," I told my daughter on the phone that evening.

"So I can come, Mum?" She screamed with joy at the other end.

"In a while, darling," I replied. "We have to wait a bit. But not long."

"What for? Father's not talking to me. He only asks about homework. And if I like what he's cooked for dinner." My daughter's voice was already breaking.

"And do you?"

"Do you like coal?" asked my daughter, and I briefly laughed.

"Just a little longer, darling, a little longer," I said.

"When?" questioned Ela, demanding a firm date.

But I couldn't give her a date. Although I'd have given anything to be able to tell her she could come tomorrow.

I choked out some questions about school, English and karate, and my daughter choked out the answers. When we ended the conversation, I lay on my IKEA mattress and cried. I cried for about two hours, then fell asleep, exhausted.

"I take it you've left," said Ela's father over the phone, when he finally called.

"I have," I replied.

"I've started therapy. I'm getting a grip on myself. Finishing the script," he said, but none of it interested me.

"I want Ela to come and see me," I informed him. "And I don't want her anywhere near your mother."

"No chance," he said quietly, phlegmatically. It felt like somebody had punched me in the throat.

"She's my daughter," I whispered.

"You made a choice," he retorted. "You want to see her, then come to Warsaw. You want to live with her, you come back."

I said nothing. Couldn't say what I wanted to say, meaning *I'll kill you, you prick*.

"You made a choice. You knew what you were doing, Agnieszka," he concluded.

Once the apartment had been redecorated, I realised a couple of other things, such as I didn't have a job and I didn't know anybody here. I had to change this in order to not go mad and die of hunger.

I found a temporary post in Cracow television, creating bruises and streams of blood for *Police Intervention*, the only TV programme still being shot in Cracow. Then I got a job at a drama festival, which I think was called *Kantor's Genotype*, and created school uniforms out of cellophane for a student's interpretation of *Dead Class*, the action for which the twenty-something-year-old director had decided to set in space. I still didn't know anyone, even though – in spite of everything – I wanted to, more and more as the days went by. But most people limited themselves to a "hi", especially when they were fed the information that I'd come from Warsaw, where, what was worse, I'd lived all my life.

From time to time, I talked to my neighbour, Dr Banicki, by the stairwell or in his apartment when he invited me in.

"Did you know my grandmother?" I asked one day when I realised that I ought to stay longer than a few minutes so he didn't think I was rude. I also thought I might be able to learn something about the place in which my failure as a wife had interned me.

"Oh, not very well, not very well at all." Mr Banicki shook his head. "You know, nobody's lived there for a long time."

"And the Institute?" I asked. "What does it mean, why is that on the entryphone?"

"Ah!" He waved it away, turning his eyes away from me for a moment. "That was some nonsense. There was some sort of sect here for a couple of months."

"Sect?" I repeated, wondering whether I'd heard right.

"Sect." Mr Banicki smiled and dug his warm doctor's eyes into my cleavage. "Some company like Amway or Rainbow Vacuum Cleaners or something. They had an office here for a while, in the nineties, but it soon went bankrupt. No shortage of bankruptcies at the time."

"And the company was called Institute?"

"It seemed to be, the institute of something or other... They sold toothpaste, I think..."

"But apparently, the name was there before. In the sixties even," I said, recalling what Marta had said.

"Maybe it was? Maybe the company got its name from the sign?" mused Doctor Banicki, gazing through the window and directing his question at the air. Then, unexpectedly, he said, "Please forgive me, but I have to lie down. But do please come tomorrow."

That had to suffice me as an answer. I didn't see the other neighbours often. Sometimes I had the impression that this part of the tenement was practically deserted. Sometimes a sleepy, scared student would flit past me on the staircase – I never knew whether it was the same person each time or several look-alikes. A mysterious family lived on the first floor, who, according to Doctor Banicki, never left their apartment. They'd been allocated it in the sixties and were now scared of being evicted. On the second floor lived, I believe, a young married couple with a baby, at least that's what I imagined when I saw a buggy outside the door. And there was Mrs Finkiel who, if she ever replied to my "good morning", made it sound like a cross between an African curse and phlegm being brought up.

I was alone. This loneliness grated on me and was becoming unbearable. I wanted to meet someone, talk to someone, even just to avoid sobbing all night thinking about my daughter. To find some peace, stop myself going mad.

For a week, I held back from going to one of the thousands of bars alone. *Normal people don't do things like that*, I thought. *People who go to bars alone are alcoholics who are too embarrassed to drink to the mirror.*

Then, one evening, I noticed that I was talking to myself more and more as I paced the empty apartment, made soups and sandwiches for myself, cleaned, read, played Scrabble on the internet and awkwardly performed asanas I'd once picked up somewhere: *Agnieszka, you idiot, you forgot to buy the toilet paper again*; *Agnieszka, the washing's going to rot in the machine again*; *Agnieszka, one more cigarette, another tea and it's bed, okay?* And I realised that I wanted to talk to another human being so much – even the girl at the supermarket checkout or the tram driver – that I had to go out, hear a voice other than my own.

It was a crazily warm yet fresh evening. I walked down Karmelicka Street wearing no make-up, in a colourful, light blouse, tracksuit and trainers. Swarms of people passed me; everyone seemed happier and more normal than me. The first bar I entered turned out to be the Ugly Cat on Sławkowska Street.

Sometimes I wonder whether if I'd entered any other bar, I'd have stayed there. Perhaps I wasn't as desperate as I thought I was; perhaps it was simply that the Ugly Cat had and has something homely about it. It is the cosy home of lunatics.

When I stepped inside, into the first, colourfully painted room shrouded in smoke, all the men were standing up, shouting, "Shame!", "Shame!" and "Go, Papa!", "Go, Papa!"

The subject of the cheering was a forty-something guy with a heavily furrowed face, scarce, long hair, dressed in a washed-out hoodie. He was standing on a stool behind the bar, fully focused, using a roller to cover a TV – attached by a boom to the ceiling – with white oil paint. Half of the screen was already layered with a white shell; all that was visible was the double chin and suited torso of a sports commentator saying, "Wisła's defeat is shameful. The defence's criminal mistakes can only be put down to…"

The men in the room were whistling, clapping, raising their glasses of beer so dramatically that most of the contents ended up over their heads. I walked up to the bar, pushing my way through the chaos, and asked the barmaid, a chubby girl with dyed hair, what was going on. I ordered a beer with lemon and pointed to Papa, who was determinedly rolling another layer of paint over the screen.

"They lost the derby," said the girl, pouring my beer.

"Who did?" I asked dimly, watching as Papa, having finished painting over the still switched-on TV, jumped off the ladder, climbed onto the bar and raised his arms triumphantly, thick white paint dripping from the roller and tin onto the bar.

"Fuck the lot of you, you useless bunch of wankers!" Papa started shouting.

The customers quickly pitched in, thumping the tables.

"Where are you from?" the girl behind the bar asked. She had a pleasant, slightly hoarse but strong voice. Human.

"Żoliborz," I said. I looked at her meaningfully. She smiled.

"Okay. What would you like?" she asked.

"I just want to get drunk," I explained.

"A large vodka sour," she responded, nodding, understanding. "You've really never been here?" she said over her shoulder as she made my drink.

Before I could answer, Papa leapt off the bar, handed the paint and roller to another barman, walked over to the other end of the bar and approached a well-sopped, fat and heavily made-up woman sitting at a table by the window. He knelt in front of her, kissed her hand and whispered:

"Queen of the night, it's time to dance the dance of victory. Our hearts are always the hearts of victors."

"Fuck off, Papa," retorted the woman, leaning her chair back precariously.

"Hop onto the bar, dear queen, and I'll notch you one on tab, and your tab's huge," spluttered Papa.

"Papa, give me a fucking break," moaned the woman.

"Huge and beautiful, like your arse," groaned Papa, who clearly felt some sort of strong, erotic fascination for the woman.

When I saw the woman give in and jump onto the bar, start dancing to the song "Papa Dance" turned up loud, I downed my vodka in one go. When I saw half the room instantly join in, and the woman's body – already spilling out of her tight blouse – turn into an undulating sea of white blancmange, I looked at the barmaid.

"I'm Iga. Another?" she asked, and I nodded.

Iga smiled, then shouted to Papa to stop fucking making an idiot of himself because the Lech beer was finished, and the barrels needed fetching.

I spent the rest of the evening dancing with strangers and talking to Iga across the bar, talking about anything and everything. I told her the entire saga of my apartment and my daughter and my, to all intents and purposes, now ex-husband; told her about my fear, my escape, how I'd wasted my whole life maintaining false, toxic appearances.

I felt at home, looked after. Iga kept sliding more vodkas my way, which I drank between dancing and talking, and I talked in at least five different languages and everything was great until some fifty-something British guy grabbed me roughly by the bum.

I automatically turned and slapped him in the gob; he probably wanted to slap me back, but suddenly, from amid the hive of drunk people dancing, an enormous bald giant emerged with a thick, strong line of brows above his eyes, wearing a jacket with the name Banda written on it. When the Brit yanked my hat off against my will, the giant grabbed him by the armpit, twisted his arm, forced him into a squat and dragged him in the direction of the door, which he opened with his free hand. He let go of the Brit and, as though we were in a silent movie, gave him a hefty kick up the arse.

"Call Sebastian next time," he said, pointing at his chest.

"Sebastian," I repeated.

"Or Seba, if you like," the giant clarified, and he returned to the gate. Towards morning, there was only me and Iga, another barman nicknamed Hangover, Papa swaying on his feet, Sebastian and Yogi, still rooted at their tables.

I was barely conscious, but still talking. Iga was talking, too. Sometimes we spoke at the same time. We laughed like two idiots. I had a best friend again and it was a good feeling, a feeling I'd last had when I was about sixteen.

"Get your daughter down here, sis, she must be really brilliant. You're brilliant, so she must be brilliant, too." Iga was pouring us yet more drinks, at the same time trying to aim the dishes into the dishwasher and the money into the cashbox.

"I'd give my mother's heart for a woman like you, Hat," declared Papa, leaning against the bar.

"I need to drop anchor here." I spread my arms out, almost tripping. "I haven't got anything. Haven't even got a job. Painting those bruises on TVN for twenty złotys isn't a job. I've got to get something. Give Ela something."

"Be a barmaid here." Iga smiled. "Papa, give Aga a job. Look, Aga's great, fucking great."

"Fucking great," repeated Hangover, then fell asleep.

Papa lay on the bar. I began to laugh. I was really enjoying all this.

"Stay," repeated Iga. "What have you got to lose? Ever been a barmaid?"

"I'm too old," I replied.

"The hell you are," retorted Iga. "You've got to give it a go. It's miserable, but it's a laugh. Isn't it, Papa?"

Papa raised himself, supported his elbows on the bar and whispered, reeking of stale vodka:

"Listen, Hat. Let me tell you something, and don't take it bad. You going to take it bad?"

I shook my head, trying gently to move away.

"I'd give my mother's heart for a woman like you."

And that's how, at the age of thirty-five, I became a barmaid. It rejuvenated me inwardly by about fifteen years. At least that's what I thought over the first two weeks. At least that's how I played it. Maybe it was unwise, strange and extremely unhealthy. Maybe I was making up for something, something I'd lost. Maybe at the deepest layer of my character, I was an irresponsible idiot. But Iga was right – it was a laugh. There were lots of people. Loud music all the time. I was constantly at least a bit drunk. I needed this like I needed air. I needed not to think.

Now I only cried a little in the mornings, when I woke up with a hangover.

My best friend, Iga, moved in, of course, after a week. For the past two years, she'd been renting a twenty-square-metre broom cupboard near Radio Cracow, half of which was taken up by a table and the other half by books. She moved in without a second thought; all I asked her for was to contribute to the gas bill. When she moved in, we talked again for days on end. Non-stop. I loved talking to her.

We spoke about Iga's flights from home, about a boyfriend whom she'd got out of drugs and sleeping on park benches and who was now the managing director of a metal company, about another boyfriend whom she still couldn't stop loving even though everything had dried up between them, about her mother, a professor at a private Catholic college, about friends, about my daughter, about bad choices.

One evening, Sebastian, our bodyguard, came to work with

a different expression on his face than usual. His brows were drawn, lips downturned. He slouched as though somebody had placed something heavy on his back. It took us a couple of hours to grasp that he was just sad. When we asked what was wrong, he said that his fiancée had thrown him out of the house and he didn't have anywhere to live, that he didn't want to go back to his parents, who lived with his brother in a Nowa Huta apartment the size of a large bath.

Of course, Sebastian moved in. He took the smallest room, repaired the electricity on the first day, screwed together the already wonky furniture from IKEA and insulated the windows.

Everything was still great, and I'd have carried on feeling good if it wasn't for my daughter's questions. I was still calling her as often as I could, and Ela kept asking when she could come. I kept trying to work out what to do. And I quickly realised that, really, I didn't have a clue.

I met a few guys, of course. Some left in the morning; others stayed longer, for a few nights, but they always left in the end. Some were younger, some were older, some were my age. Some were intelligent, others stupid. Good looking and less so. There was no rhyme or reason for them leaving, no pattern or regularity.

I didn't talk to them much. I was an adult and didn't want to hurt anyone. It was enough that, beneath this happy charade at being a student, I should be unhappy.

One day, however, a guy appeared at the Cat who had a week's stubble, was slim, had unwashed shoulder-length brown hair, dirty trainers and a good, fitted jacket. He was both worn and fresh. He'd come with another man who talked to him a lot, but he only smiled politely as though not wanting to disappoint him.

"Do you take cards?" he asked, leaning over the bar. He didn't look like the owner of his own voice. His voice was strong, melodious and rough, gave him height and gave him breadth in the shoulders. I fancied him when he spoke, really fancied him, and it was a strange feeling because I hadn't really fancied any man for about ten years.

Iga noticed and laughed.

"Credit cards?" he asked.

"No, we don't," she replied.

"It's my card," he said, pulling his ID out of his wallet. "Really."

"I believe you." Iga laughed again. "But the terminal's dead. Give him a tab." Iga turned to me. "You'll go to a cashpoint, won't you? Otherwise, we'll be paying for you."

He nodded. At first glance, his eyes, hidden behind horn-rimmed glasses, looked like a pair of broken headlights. But, in fact, they revealed shrewdness and sharpness. They contained little knives. These knives cut through reality. He wasn't stupid, I could see that.

"I'd like a straight vodka on the rocks, then, please, and one with lemon for my friend."

Iga handed him two vodkas, one with lemon, the other only ice.

"Thank you," he said.

"No problem," I replied. I felt like a teenager, nervous and embarrassed. And to all intents and purposes, I was an adolescent. An overgrown adolescent.

The place wasn't busy. That was still to come. The sharp, good-looking guy's friend was still talking to him, but he wasn't listening. Instead, he was smiling at me, which annoyed me even more. Iga stood nearby, laughing out loud. The man finished his vodka and peered into his wallet again.

"I think I'll go to that cashpoint now after all," he announced.

"I think my colleague's going to accompany you." Iga nodded at me.

"You don't trust me." He smiled.

"No, we don't, not a bit," said Iga.

That evening, we didn't return to the Cat. To be honest, I don't remember where we went. He was called Jacek and everything about him was intriguing. Or perhaps that's how I wanted it to be. He was like a book with a twist on each page. He told me about his work and about how he made a lot of money as a stocks and shares analyst and employee of an investment fund, about the three degree courses he'd done, and that he'd spent two years in the United States, six months of which he was homeless, three in jail, that he'd tried peyote in the Arizona desert and that it wasn't anything really special. He told me how he'd had his driving licence confiscated twice, how his concerned teachers had phoned his parents when he was ten because he'd compiled a set of historical errors in Bolesław Prus's *Pharaoh*.

We went for an excellent dinner, then to his place. Then, in the early hours of the morning, we had sex under the walls of Wawel Castle, which made me feel ashamed.

The following day, he visited me at my apartment. We watched TV. Jacek dubbed every programme and advert quietly and idiotically; I nearly split my sides laughing. Then we had sex again. Later, he got up, went to the shop and made Viennese eggs for breakfast. Halfway through preparing breakfast, he announced that he'd also like to make some coffee. I told him truthfully that the espresso machine wasn't working. He got in a taxi, went to the market square and twenty minutes later arrived with a new one.

While Jacek was making the first coffee, Sebastian knocked on my door and asked:

"I know that we all like to have fun, Hat, but did you have to bring a gypsy like this home?"

Jacek, returning from the kitchen, passed him in the doorway and stretched out his hand.

"Sebastian," said Sebastian.

"Gypsy," responded Jacek.

"Come here, Gypsy." I called him into the room and closed the door, and when we finished making love, the eggs and coffee were long cold. Gypsy binned the cold ones and made some more.

Two weeks later, I told him to move in. Into a separate room, of course.

"You're regressing more and more," noticed Iga.

"I've fallen a bit in love with this guy," I countered and shrugged. "Besides, one room's still empty."

"And he hasn't got his own place?" asked Iga.

"I've no idea," I answered truthfully.

He arrived at the Institute with a laptop, a rucksack of clothes and one cardboard box. He put them down in the empty room, took a taxi to IKEA and returned two hours later with a mattress, bed linen and a few enormous cushions.

"Is that it?" I asked, when he'd put the cardboard box in the corner, laid the linen on the mattress, the laptop on the linen, stood with his arms crossed and looked at the room like it was a furnished home.

"Yes, that's it," he replied.

I don't know how long it lasted, maybe thirty days, maybe less, maybe a little longer. Days when I called my daughter to make sure she was alright, while she got further away from me. I don't even know how far. A step? A kilometre? An entire galaxy? But they were also days when I fell asleep and woke up with Gypsy, went for walks with him. We read books together and I listened to what he said – and he talked a lot, really a lot, and he knew a lot.

For about thirty days, still exiled, still in a colourful simulation of student life, still on a different planet from my daughter, it didn't even occur to me that I might hurt him. What's more, one day, maybe while washing dishes, or maybe lying in the bath, it crossed my mind that Gypsy might possibly hurt me.

After thirty or maybe sixty days of this charming relationship, talking, listening, watching and strolling, a problem arose. For Gypsy, this was it. This was just what he wanted, what he'd been waiting for. The Agnieszka he saw, the fake Agnieszka, the Agnieszka who was painted pink, Agnieszka pretending to be a fun-loving student of the Academy of Fine Arts, was the Agnieszka he'd fallen in love with. When I sensed this for the first time, I shuddered, and when I felt myself shuddering, I realised that, for me, it was over.

But it wasn't real. The real Agnieszka wept looking at photographs on her phone when nobody saw, photographs from an outing to the zoo.

"All this isn't real, Gypsy," the real Agnieszka said one day, the one whom Gypsy was seeing for the first time. The real Agnieszka had furrows and crow's feet, downturned lips; the real Agnieszka walked slowly, slouching a little, had to catch hold of the wall from time to time; the real Agnieszka could have been fifty-something, not thirty-something. "It's all a fairy tale."

"I don't understand," said Gypsy.

"It's all going to end soon, which is why we should enjoy it all the more." I smiled.

"I don't understand, Agnieszka," he repeated. "Don't talk in riddles."

"What I'm trying to say," I put my hand over his heart, "is that we're having a great time."

"Exactly," he whispered, but his face tensed a fraction. "Exactly. We're having a great time."

"I'm only doing this so I don't have to think about what I've really got to do," I whispered clumsily, totally incoherently.

"Isn't that why people have a good time?" he remarked lucidly.

I got up and went to the kitchen for a bottle of horribly over-sweet wine and poured us each a tumbler since all the wine glasses had been smashed by Black, who I'd adopted from a shelter two weeks earlier, and White, who Gypsy had given me as Black's companion.

"You're a distraction for me, Gypsy," I said.

"I don't mind you having a child," he forced out. "I'd like it to be our... well, you know."

"No chance." I shook my head.

"What do you mean, no chance? There's always a chance! What do you want me to do?" he stammered.

Our conversations about trifles were effortless. Long and continuous, like extended interviews. Conversations about

148

important things, however, were a different story, as they are with most people.

"Move out," I declared. "Best to do it now. I'm very sorry." I was sorry. I pitied him. But mostly, I felt awkward.

He put on his shirt, took his wine and knocked it back in one go.

"I'm going to my room," he said, trying not to look at me.

"I'm really sorry," I whispered.

"No need." He nodded. "I understand everything. But I don't want to move out."

"What?" I asked.

"It's alright, I've got my own room. Really. I understand, but tenants get a month's notice," he explained.

I was transfixed, mouth agape.

"And don't let's talk about there being no agreement, or unlawful use or whatever. Let's just not talk about it. These splits don't have to be so ugly," he said.

I quietly hissed a curse.

"Let's just agree like civilised human beings. I've got to find something. Something suitable; I can't just live anywhere," he stated. He smiled as brazenly as he could and closed the door.

I sat on my bed, rested my head on my hand and picked up the phone. Four missed calls from my daughter.

* * *

I'm not scared. My insides have turned into asphalt. My heart is beating regularly, my breath is steady. I'm not scared. I'm going to get out of here soon. Maybe I'll be scared when I'm out. But that doesn't frighten me.

"Funny how you've dug it into me. Torn the artery but not fully," Gypsy says calmly. "Gives me something like twenty minutes."

"It's you." I point to him.

149

He shakes his head. "Whether it's me or not," he replies, "doesn't matter."

"You're sick," I whisper, because I've lost the ability to talk out loud. "You're sick. You locked us in and you killed Robert and Anna. All because you wanted to get back at me for breaking up with you. You're sick, Gypsy. Or Jacek. Or whatever your name is."

Gypsy shakes his head. He pulls himself onto his elbows, trying to get up. Blood drains from his thigh; there's already a large black stain on the floor. Yet none of us do anything. Nobody's trying to stem the bleeding. We stand over him, calm, and let him die.

I'm trying not to think about how terrible this is.

After a while, he falls back on the floor. We stand over him in a circle. Stare down at him without a word.

His nose is shattered and turns his face into a brownish, bloated splodge on a white background, with stuck-on eyes and the black hole of a mouth, through which he breathes heavily, speaks slowly. I move closer to him.

"I don't even know what your real name is," I say. "I've never seen your ID."

"And how many people's ID have you seen?" he remarks, spitting phlegm out.

"What's your name?" I demand.

"Jacek."

"Where are you from?"

"The Institute," he answers after a pause, first taking a deep breath.

Sebastian stands behind him, grabs him by the hair and yanks his head back. "Talk, or I'll fucking kill you!" he yells.

"What do you want me to say?" asks Gypsy.

"Who's helping you?"

"Do I look as if anybody's helping me?" Gypsy smiles.

Gypsy making a joke as he lies dying on the floor makes me feel terribly cold for a moment. But I'm still calm, still not scared.

He's the one who's betrayed us. He's the one who's done all this to us.

"I'll fucking kill you!" growls Sebastian.

"You've already killed me," he says quietly, coldly. "Remember? The guy in Olsza, three years ago. No big deal, eh, Sebastian?"

Sebastian freezes. He drops the knife for a moment, then jumps at Gypsy and starts shaking him.

"I've never fucking killed anyone!" he yells. "Never fucking killed anyone!"

"November 2007." Gypsy smiles. "You tried to enter a housing estate and beat up a couple of Wisła fans. You were attacked as soon as you got out of the car. Later, when you came round, there was this guy at the bus stop. A broken pane of glass next to him. You got all upset that he'd smashed the glass."

"Shut up!" he screams. "Shut that fucking gob!"

"A quick knife in the lung. You didn't even think. There were no witnesses. You ran a long way. Threw the knife into the Vistula."

"Shut up!" roars Sebastian, like a savage beast. "Shut your fucking face!"

"He died pretty quickly, Sebastian." Gypsy smiles again. "His name was David Malinowski. He was seventeen and studying to be a mechanic, liked to play Pro Evolution Soccer. He died twenty minutes later in the ambulance. You didn't know."

Silence. Sebastian stands over him, heaving.

"Who the hell are you?" he asks.

"My name's Jacek, also known as Gypsy. I'm from the Institute," he replies, drops his head limply for a moment, then raises it again.

Silence.

"What were you planning to do next? Kill us too? Like Anna and Robert? Maim us? What were you planning to do?" I ask, hearing my voice, aware that it's muted, muffled, has a strange tone. It could easily belong to somebody else entirely.

Even if I wanted to shout, I couldn't. It was as if somebody had sealed my throat. As if something had dried up inside.

"You'll see," he replies.

"And all this because of us?" I ask, composed.

"You overrate yourself, Agnieszka." He shakes his head. "But don't worry. It's natural to think yourself important, valued."

"You insisted on being the one to go down the rope on purpose," I say, struggling not to trample over him.

"Ten points for perceptiveness," he retorts, clearly annoyed.

I'm waiting for him to say something else.

"You killed them," I repeat. When I'd first said the word "killed", I felt something, a cold shudder, like a brief epileptic fit. But now the word "killed" leaves my mouth like any other. It's neutral. Doesn't phase me at all.

"I know you feel hard done by, but everybody in the world is hard done by, people are conned every day, imprisoned every day, so I've no idea why you feel so special," he says. He pauses, catches his breath to gather his strength. He's very weak. He really might die at any moment.

It might seem terrible that we're not trying to save him. That we have, in fact, killed him by not helping him. I think about this perfectly calmly – that it might seem terrible to somebody. Something's switched off in my brain and it really doesn't frighten me.

"Were those people important to you in any way?" he asks. "Would they have been important to anyone?"

"They were expecting a baby," says Veronica.

"The kid would have been a cabbage for the rest of its life," he replies slowly, coughing at the same time. "And the guy, Robert, would probably have ended up a total alkie. Started beating her. Would probably have worked as a bodyguard or on a checkout. She'd sit at home with a degree, no experience. Spanish. She only took the course because her rich friend did the same. She'd never even been to Spain. They'd never have gone. Wouldn't even be able to get a mortgage. The child would have dribbled in its wheelchair while he threw bottles and beat her when the parents were out. Because they'd be living with his parents, or her parents, or in some sad bedsit rented for a thousand złotys. He already had the beginnings of neurosis. Had already been diagnosed with extreme aggression by a psychologist at junior school. Did you hear about how they met? She was drunk at a friend's party. She'd only slept with one guy. He hadn't had a girlfriend since secondary school. When they were alone, it was a disaster. He had to sit in the bathroom for fifteen minutes to stand his semi-fertile prick to attention with his hand. But in the morning, they both knew that if they didn't have each other, then who would have them? Back to the point, do you think they were important to anyone?"

"Shut up! Don't say another word! Go on and die! Just shut up!" shouts Veronica, every word clattering like an old bike on a cobbled street. Then suddenly she leans over him. I grab her arm.

"But you didn't tell them anything. Why are you getting so worked up?" Gypsy turns towards her. "The doctor detected everything. Cerebral ischemia. They knew everything. They came to see you for comfort. And you lied to them, that second time. You didn't know whether the kid was healthy or sick. You had no idea."

"I'm not a liar," replies Veronica. "I never deceived anyone."

"You don't have any special powers, you idiot," he continues calmly. "You're just trying to make yourself seem interesting, but you're actually as interesting as a ream of paper."

"You don't know anything about me. You've no idea," Veronica counterattacks. She's become hysterical, quickly trying to catch her breath as she speaks. "You know fuck all."

"There are people who tell everyone they've got cancer," he replies slowly, trying again to raise himself into a half-sitting position, "to get attention. There are people who, I don't know, people who say they speak to ghosts. It's a bit sad being a cashier in a cinema, isn't it? Having tried and failed four times to get into film school?"

Veronica retreats to the corner. She is crying soundlessly.

"But it's even more sad knowing that you're never going to be important to anyone." Gypsy breathes out. "People try to deal with it at whatever cost. They simply used to start a family in the past. They simply used to set up a family in the past."

I've had enough. I stand over him and take his face in my hand, squeeze it like a soft leather pouch. I lean over and stare into his eyes, which are slowly growing empty as sleep and death approach, dilute and condense his gaze. It's as though the white hum of a television was reflecting in his eye sockets.

"You're calm, Agnieszka." He smiles. "You've just found two corpses, yet you're so calm."

"Fuck off," I reply.

"There are going to be more," he says.

"There are. Yours," I retort.

"No." He smiles. "Not only mine."

"He really is going to die soon," Iga throws in.

"Let him die," I say, or maybe it's the somebody else hidden in my stomach.

Iga walks up to him, puts her hand next to his wound, squeezes.

"We can't, we can't," she repeats, then goes to the bathroom. She returns with a towel and tries to tie a tourniquet at his groin.

"Iga, they want to kill us all," I say, but she, still repeating "we can't, we can't", squeezes the towel even tighter around his leg. "We can, Iga," I add, but I don't hold her back. I let her do what she wants.

I know we can. I've realised that you can kill somebody, that sometimes you have to kill somebody before they kill you. I realised that earlier, when we'd found the secret door in the Finkiels' apartment, the door concealed behind the wall unit.

"Agnieszka." Gypsy's speech is slower and slower, weaker and weaker. Despite Iga's towel tourniquet, the puddle beneath him is growing larger and darker. "You know, it's not about you at all, but – incidentally – I really did grow fond of you." He has to concentrate hard to finish the sentence.

"What's that supposed to mean, 'incidentally'?" I ask. "Incidentally, man, what are you talking about?"

"Reach into my jacket, the left pocket." He nods. "I've got some fags."

I don't react. I look at the others.

"Take one." He smiles. "Take one, all of you."

I move towards him, but Sebastian signals to me with his hand not to move. He squats at Gypsy's side and carefully extracts the cigarettes from his pocket. The packet is wrapped in foil. He throws it to me, I catch and open it, pull one out and smoke my first cigarette in twenty-four hours, but it feels like the first in my life; the smoke is a soft, bitter eiderdown, soothing. It tastes so good.

I blow it in Gypsy's face.

"What do you mean 'incidentally'?" I repeat.

"Incidentally, when I met you, I grew fond of you," he repeats.

"Incidentally?" I force myself to raise my voice. It takes a great effort, as much effort as if I suddenly had to lie down and do five push ups.

"Tell us who you are, you son of a bitch! Tell us who's helping you, tell us what's going on. Tell us, for fuck's sake, tell us now!" Screaming, Iga leaps up suddenly. "Tell us or I'll tear the tourniquet off!"

"It won't make any difference," replies Gypsy.

Sebastian is silent, rolling his eyes, now. He walks up to my door and punches the doorframe as hard as he can. I look deep into his eyes. I know Gypsy was right. Sebastian did kill that guy.

He punches the wall and stands up, panting. *Control yourself a bit longer, Sebastian*, I beg him in my head. *I trust you. Just a bit longer.*

"It won't make any difference, I'm going to die in a minute anyway. Just go to your rooms and let me get on with it," says Gypsy.

"First, you're going to tell us everything," I tell him.

"I'm not going to tell you anything," answers Gypsy.

"Shit!" shouts Iga, grabbing for the blood-soaked towel tied around his leg. She grasps the scissors again.

"What a great friend," says Gypsy.

"Leave it," I say to her. "Take your hand away. Leave it."

"Tell us or I'll kill you; I'll pull the scissors out and dig them into your heart," drawls Iga.

"Leave it," I repeat.

"Iga, the wonderful pal," he continues sarcastically. "The best friend around. Great warrior for the rights of gays, blacks and animals. The revolutionary from the villa in Anin."

"Go on, you bastard, go on." Iga's starting to shake. I go up to her, put my hand on her shoulder; her body's flaring like an old motorbike firing up.

"How many friends have you got left? And how many have you turned your back on?" he asks, and his face turns into that of a crazy puppet. "You remember that demonstration, that trip to Prague, don't you? When was it? Not that long ago. Five years? You remember throwing that Molotov cocktail at the police van? Remember? Then I'll tell you."

"Go on!" screams Iga. I'm holding on to her with all my strength. "Go on!"

"You remember giving everybody's names? Straight away? Because they said they'd let your parents know? Remember?" he asked. "You recognised everyone in the photographs. Everyone."

"Pull those fucking scissors out," says Sebastian, crouching behind Gypsy's head.

"Iga, take your hand away," I plead, but she's gripping the scissors as hard as she can. I grab her wrist. For somebody who's about to die, Gypsy's having a whale of a time.

I went to bed with that man, I think, and just about hold down the contents of my stomach.

"You recognised everybody, including your boyfriend, Gucek." I can see that he's trying as hard as he can to hold his head straight. "He got thrown out of school. Got a sentence. And his parents threw him out. His father was the director of a state treasury partnership. A man of very high principles. Couldn't accept that his son was an idiot who threw bottles of petrol at police cars."

Iga is still clenching the scissors.

"Shut up, Gypsy," I order. "I mean it, shut your face."

"No, let him talk. I'm not scared." Iga shouts again. "Go on!"

"It was fun playing together at fighting for a change, wasn't it?" asks Gypsy. "So Gucek was a bit broken up, lived in a squat and tried some heroin, didn't he? Somebody gave him a smoke and he liked it. And you were probably already screwing his friend, weren't you? The one from Antifa, who did kickboxing?"

I stroke Iga on the head. "I'm with you, whatever he says," I whisper.

"But maybe Gucek forgave you because he somehow understood that the Czech police had threatened to rape you. He forgave you, but he smoked heroin, and you couldn't watch. You started looking at his friend. And the friend liked looking at you. And Gucek watched you looking at each other. And then he got real sad. And jumped out of the window." Gypsy speaks calmly and quietly. "You didn't even go to his funeral, so why are you fucking around telling everybody how awful it was?" Gypsy bares his teeth in a grin. With difficulty but with pleasure, too.

His face is different, I think. *He looks like a caricature of himself.*

Iga yanks the scissors from his leg. Blood splatters everywhere.

I scream, quietly, briefly. Iga, too, backs away. Gypsy doesn't make a sound but presses his hands over the wound and starts to laugh.

From behind our backs comes a brief, rusty squeak. As though somebody was slowly, gently trying to open an old door.

"You hear that?" I ask, but nobody replies.

"You think you're not scared anymore, don't you, Agnieszka?" Gypsy addresses me.

"What?" I ask.

The door to the landing is ajar, I realise. The sound is clearer now, a rattling, scraping. Finally, footsteps.

"You think you're not scared anymore, don't you?" he repeats. "That you've seen everything?"

"Who are you?" Iga is shivering, pressed against Sebastian, not blinking. "Who are you?"

"You'll find out who we are in a few minutes. When they've finished tidying up upstairs." His voice is hoarse, quiet.

Now everybody – Sebastian, Iga, Veronica – turns towards the front door.

Sebastian picks up the bloody scissors. He leads Iga to the toilet door. They stand around the corner. Iga is still shivering. I look at Gypsy. He is dying and laughing.

I'm filled with a premonition that the worst is about to happen. First, it fills my stomach, then the rest of my body. I notice the screwdriver on the floor. Grab hold of it.

The footsteps fall silent.

"Remember the boy your daughter beat up?" Gypsy asks with what strength remains.

Something's hatching. Growing.

"That shitface, Marek?" he asks.

Now I can clearly hear somebody crossing Finkiel's apartment towards the landing.

"He and his friends followed your daughter to the cloakroom after school a few days ago."

"What?" I ask. "What are you saying?"

I lock the front door from the inside, the screwdriver still in my hand.

"They had their smartphones on them." He smiles. "Told her to take off her blouse."

Strong shudders run through me as though I'm being electrocuted. My teeth clatter hard against each other. It takes a great amount of strength not to drop the screwdriver. Somebody walks up to the door of the Institute. Somebody presses the door handle. Sebastian's waiting for a signal.

"There were five of them. They started pulling her hair and spitting on her." Gypsy's talking faster and faster. "And Marek said, 'Really? You say you don't like giving blowjobs, you whore?'"

I swallow. My mouth's as dry as a stone, a nail, a metal slab.

"What's going to become of those shits, eh, Agnieszka?" He shakes his head. Grins again. Looks at the door.

"You're lying," I throw at him. "You're lying."

"I'm not," he says. "The caretaker caught them just in time. Sent them packing. The caretaker at your daughter's school's called Hurrier. But you know that, you laughed at his name. When your daughter said that they shout 'Why the hurry, Hurrier, sir?'"

I grasp my face with my hands; my teeth are just about to snap against each other. He's right. And I thought that I wasn't scared anymore.

The door to Finkiel's apartment opens again, and again somebody crosses the landing. And another person. That makes three. Three people are standing at my door.

"Anything could happen—" He chokes; a little blood dribbles from his mouth. He's losing strength, still pressing his hands against the wound, but he's going to let go soon, he's going to fall asleep soon or else I'll help him.

"Reach into this pocket again, the one the fags were in," he says.

Sebastian holds a knife. Nods at me. Veronica is squatting on the floor with her arms around her as though trying to squeeze herself into a little ball. I reach into his pocket. There's an old phone. One with large buttons for the elderly.

"Call the last number," he says.

Somebody inserts a key in the lock.

"Wait!" Gypsy shouts towards the door. He's trying to shout as loudly as he can. I don't realise I'm grasping the phone, don't realise I'm pressing the green receiver icon twice, putting the phone to my ear. I hear the ringtone, it rings once, twice, three times. The crackle of the call being connected. I hear my own quickened breath, then a voice. All I hear now is the voice.

"Mum." My daughter's sobs echo in the phone. I turn my head towards the door.

"Help me, Mum, please. Mummy, help me." I move the receiver away from my ear. My daughter's voice. I'm beginning to burn from within.

"Mummy, are you there?"

"Yes, I am," I reply, or maybe it's the animal in my stomach speaking, or maybe somebody else. Maybe it doesn't matter anymore. I don't feel much, but I do feel a fire deep within my stomach.

"Mummy, I'm in Cracow, I was coming to see you. I'm sorry, Mummy, I'm sorry. The man in the taxi told me that he was taking me to see you, Mummy. I'm sorry," says my daughter.

"Nice girl. Shame I didn't get to meet her," Gypsy comments.

A metallic rasp, the sound of a broken connection.

"Hello?" I say. No, it's not me, it's somebody else talking – the animal in my stomach.

My hand drops the phone.

Somebody turns the key in the lock. The hand – the one

160

with the screwdriver, the one that is trying to grip it as tightly as it can – takes a swing and drives the screwdriver into Gypsy's throat. I see Gypsy's eyes rolling back in his head, hear a soft crunch, I see my hand pulling the screwdriver out. It doesn't take much strength, didn't take much more strength to dig it into the throat of the man I'd once called Gypsy. I hear a sort of gurgle, air being sucked into the new aperture full of unrestrained fluid. I jump back. My lungs breathe, my mouth is open, my head turns towards Iga, who is staring at me expressionless, not blinking, hunched over like a puppet.

The door to the Institute opens. A woman stands in the doorway, a key to my apartment in her hand.

There's blood all over my face. Gypsy's lying dead on the floor, eyes wide open. There's blood everywhere. Erratic, illegible signs, signatures in blood everywhere. Gypsy is dead but still smiling.

I take a step backwards, then forwards again. I'm shaking. I feel hot.

"Well done," says the woman. "Well done, Agnieszka. But it's the end."

The woman standing in the doorway to the Institute – I recognise her. Suddenly my memory registers where I've seen the symbol of the scout before. The word "jacket" lights up in my memory. There's a badge in the woman's lapel. It's small, but I can see it clearly. Very clearly. Everything else is blurred, shapeless.

My legs take a step forward, then another. I recognise the woman: she introduced herself as Marta in the bar on Bracka Street, when it rained, and she looks exactly like she did then.

"Why didn't you phone?" she asks. "Why did you throw my business card away? Maybe we wouldn't have had to do all this."

The woman pulls a phone out of her pocket. Presses a key.

"Mummy…" A drawn-out voice comes from the phone, the voice of the child I gave birth to and whom I named Ela.

"Mummy, do everything they ask you to, do everything, please. Mummy, help."

"You should never have moved in here," the woman tells me, devoid of all emotion. "You should have been rich and happy."

"Mummy!" somebody calls behind her back.

"I'll kill you, you whore," I shout.

"That wouldn't be wise," assures the woman. Her voice is like a stream of liquid nitrogen: quiet, chilling the walls.

"My daughter," I say, the animal says, every word like barbed wire pulled from the throat.

"Your daughter's here, in this building, and she is going to die if you do something stupid."

My body launches forward. But Sebastian is ahead of me. He reaches the woman in two long leaps as though he'd never sprained his ankle.

He's about a metre away from her. I don't see him fall to the floor. Just hear a sudden, loud blast.

There's a gun in the woman's hand.

"But if you come with me, you'll get your daughter back and I'll let you both go."

She raises the gun again and fires at Veronica. Then Iga.

"Shall we be less formal?" the woman suggests. And then I fall to my knees.

* * *

Ela's father called me at nine in the morning. I'd finished work half an hour earlier and sensed that the holiday was over. This was my fourth nightshift in a row, and when Iga and I got home we felt as if we'd been tied to the rear bumper of a car that was being driven over cobblestones. That night, a famous musician from Cracow had been doing coke on the counter, groping women of all ages, slapping them on the backside and throwing chairs at the wall when we refused to serve him another Jack Daniel's on tab. Papa forbade the security guards from intervening right up to the last round. The musician had once lent him some money and Papa had used it to open the Cat.

At four in the morning, after the musician spat at Iga across the counter and called her an ugly whore, while circling his arms like the blades of a bony windmill, Sebastian approached Papa and asked:

"How much money was it? That he lent you?"

"I can't remember. It was a long time ago and he lent me dollars." Papa shrugged. He looked sad. He was getting worse by the week. Vodka was crushing him into gibbering catatonia. Every evening, when he'd talked to the same people as always about the same things as always, he started to sway to and fro on a bar stool, his eyes closed, extinguishing half-smoked cigarettes in ashtrays shoved under his nose at the last moment.

"And you've paid him back?" questioned Sebastian.

"Two years ago." Papa closed his eyes and knocked back a glass of vodka on ice with a hint of lemon. It trickled down his beard; he couldn't even be bothered to wipe it off.

"So you don't owe him anything," Sebastian concluded.

"Nope." Papa nodded.

Sebastian also nodded, then walked up to the famous musician from Cracow and caught him by the lapels of his hideous, sequin-adorned jacket. The musician tore himself away and threw a punch – a skilled, well-aimed right hook that struck Seba on the brow and made it bleed.

I turned the music off. Silence.

"You ape. What d'you think you're doing, caveman?" the musician asked Seba. Sebastian waited. "So now…" The musician spoke with the typical, exaggerated manner of a drunk ringleader. "Now I'm asking you ladies to kindly pour me a double fucking whiskey on ice, right now. And you, you shithead, bugger off home!" he shouted at a terrified young Brit with a footballer's haircut and a black corduroy jacket, before Sebastian grabbed his long hair and smashed his face against the bar with all his might.

The place fell silent.

Sebastian dragged him towards the door, which I'd opened just in time; otherwise, the rock legend from Cracow would have flown into the cobbled yard in a shower of glass.

This wasn't the end of the entertainment. Half an hour later, one of the barmaids found a fifteen-year-old girl in the toilets downstairs in a state of total collapse. Fortunately, the ambulance arrived quickly and left, sirens wailing. But before we'd found her, somebody had already taken advantage of her. She was lying in a pool of her own vomit, her dress and knickers pulled down.

When I got home, I was pain personified – both of spine and muscles. My tendons were like old, damp pieces of rope. My tongue – from smoke, vodka and coffee – was like the sole of an old shoe. *No game for an old woman*, I thought. *My seventeenth birthday has been and gone.* I drank some water, removed my make-up, brushed my teeth, collapsed onto my bed and closed my eyes.

And that's when Ela's father phoned.

"As you wish," he said, after seconds of silence.

"Wish what?" I didn't understand what he meant.

"Ela's going to visit you for her birthday. For the weekend. I'm bringing her on Friday, picking her up on Sunday. Don't do anything stupid, please."

"Mummy finally let you?" I asked, sitting up, wide awake.

"My mother doesn't know anything about it," he replied after a while. "I told her I'm taking Ela to the mountains."

"Good," I said.

"I'm picking her up on Sunday," he repeated. "Don't do anything stupid. You know I agree with my parents that Ela ought to be here, the way you live is—"

"Shut up!" I ordered.

"We'll be there sometime in the afternoon," he said.

"So long," I replied. I put the phone down, ran down the hall and flew into Iga's room.

"Iga," I whispered in her ear, tugging at her clothes, trying to wake her from her torpor. "My daughter's coming to see us. Here. On Friday. For her birthday."

Iga unstuck one eye – the other was nestling in her pillow – and smiled with difficulty.

"I've got to get some sleep, sis," she moaned. "But that's great, she's going to have a party to remember."

When I ran back out, Gypsy was standing in the hall. He was just getting up for work. Thin, broken and in his boxers, he weighed me up with the look of someone who's just about to do a sixteen-hour shift in a factory while his wife is fatally ill.

"Hi," he said in the same dumb, dull way he'd done every day over the last two weeks.

I suddenly realised that almost a month had gone by since our dismal conversation, and what was he still doing in the Institute? Yet I just said:

"Hi, Gypsy."

He shrugged and went back to his room.

"I hope I get a piece of cake," he called as a goodbye.

Ela was to come on Friday at ten in the morning, and her birthday was on Saturday. On Wednesday, I went to the patisserie and ordered the biggest, trashiest, pinkest cake with ELA YOU'RE THE BEST written on it in icing, pink sugar ponies, pink hearts and a marzipan SpongeBob stuck on top. I spent most of my money on presents: a rucksack, a DVD of the film *Dusk*, a pile of books, a coat and a dress. But I found the best present in a charity shop: a washed-out, greying T-shirt with a poster of *Thelma and Louise* printed on it.

I also wanted to take the Thursday off, but as always when you want to take a day off, the person who was supposed to stand in for me woke up fatally sick. Papa begged me to come in for at least a couple of hours. The couple of hours prolonged itself, relentlessly and without any prospect of ever ending. At two in the morning, I begged Papa to let me go home, but swarms of students were flooding in. There were just the two of us on the bar, me and Papa. People were drawn to the counter like bees to sugar. I felt like a sniper on a besieged tower.

"Do you have children, Papa?" I asked him, shouting over the noise.

"Some, somewhere." He shrugged.

"Do you ever see them?" I slid the ashtray towards him.

"Hey, Hat, what's it to you all of a sudden?" he asked loudly, annoyed.

"I want you to try to understand me!" I shouted, ignoring the outstretched hands in front of me, holding crumpled, wet notes. "My daughter's coming. I've got to look like a normal human being. A healthy human being. I can't look like a slob. Would you go and see your children looking the way you do?"

Papa picked up the phone without a word and called another barman, Goat, telling him he had to be at the Cat immediately otherwise he'd be out of a job, pneumonia or no pneumonia. Fifteen minutes later, Goat appeared in a washed-out tracksuit and with mild catarrh.

I'd started gathering my things when Papa caught me by the arm.

"Hat," he said, "maybe it was easier for me because I was the bad guy."

I shook my head, not understanding.

"I'm the one who fucked things up because, as you can probably guess, I'm the sort of guy who fucks up everything he touches. I haven't seen Iza for about ten years. But I've got what I wanted. It's worse for you. You don't know what the fuck you messed up to end up with all this shit."

I kissed him on his wrinkled cheek, which smelled like a Ukrainian cigarette factory.

"I'd give my mother's heart for a woman like you." He smiled. "And now go home, get some sleep."

As I made for the door, the famous musician from Cracow burst in, digging his way to the bar like a bow saw through human roots. This time he was wearing a white jacket with a black shirt and white tie. Behind him sailed two closely cropped Sebastian clones, though I could see they lacked the warmth that, from time to time, shone through the eyes of my flatmate – when he got a second or third helping of supper, for example, or had smoked two grams of weed.

"Papa!" yelled the musician, parting the people at the bar with his bony hands, then vaulting over the counter. Papa stepped back and held on to a chair. The musician stalked up to the computer and tried to turn off Winamp but decided it would be easier to yank the cable from the back of the computer tower. Everybody turned towards him. "Tell me where that ape is, Papa, you know which one, or you're not going to recognise this brothel," he said, unruffled now, taking Papa's cigarette.

"You shouldn't be here," Goat choked out, and the musician took a swing and punched him in the face.

Sebastian was in the Institute. It was his day off. At that moment, he was probably reading posts on fan forums or *Arnold: The Education of a Bodybuilder*, one of his two favourite books, so he claimed. The other was *The Godfather*.

"Boss," said one of the musician's heavyweights, shoving his way through the frightened and surprised crowd. "I know him from fights. He lives at that slut's."

He pointed at me, and I put my bag down on the floor. Slowly, I walked up to him until we were at arm's length.

"Put that finger away," I said calmly.

"Don't fucking butt in," he retorted in a voice that sounded like a stretched tape.

With all the strength that remained, I kicked him in the crotch with the tip of my shoe. He groaned and curled up like a little boy with appendicitis. Calmly, I walked around the bar and, equally calmly, stood between the rock star from Cracow and Papa.

"You're going to do three things," I said, looking the musician in the eyes as he nonchalantly poured himself a glass of Jack Daniel's from a bottle on the shelf.

He touched my shoulder, leaned over me and announced in a deep voice, reeking of vodka:

"I'm going to do one thing, sunshine. I'm going to be a gentleman and ask you to leave."

"I'm not your sunshine," I said. I removed his hand from my shoulder, took the glass from his hand and put it aside. I pulled out my mobile and entered a number. "And you're no gentleman, but a filthy old prick," I added, putting the phone to my ear.

He burst into laughter and pulled back his hair.

"You're going to do three things," I continued to explain. "Apologise, pay your tab and leave. And you're never coming in here again."

"It's okay, Hat, we'll come to some agreement, don't freak out," Papa pleaded in a rough, tired voice. I didn't even turn towards him.

"Oh, princess, you've got your knickers in a right twist." The musician picked up his glass. "I've been treated like a piece of trash here, and I'm no trash. I'm a serious man, an old-fashioned man. And some things a man just doesn't forgive. And you, you are a tired old-fashioned woman, so go home and tell that darling of yours that he's to come here. Or we'll come for him."

"I'm going," I replied, composed. "As soon as I've called the police."

His expression turned sour. He squinted, eyeing me from head to toe, but he didn't make a move.

"I want to report an assault," I started to say into a silent phone, "in a bar called the Ugly Cat on Sławkowska Street."

The imaginary dispatcher asked for the details and I gave her the name of the musician and the approximate number of witnesses – about two hundred – then hung up, picked up my bag which lay by the bar and turned towards the exit.

"What have you done, Hat?" groaned Papa. "There's going to be bedlam."

The musician still stood motionless.

"Think I'm frightened of the police?" He grinned. "I sat three years in the can during martial law, you stupid cunt."

"If you're not frightened, then wait for them."

I turned towards him. He put his glass down on the bar again. I picked it up and flung the contents into his face, then took another half-drunk beer from the bar and did the same again before he had time to react.

"That's for all the old-fashioned women," I explained.

Everybody accompanied me with their eyes as I left, except for Papa. The next day, Goat phoned and said that they were gone within fifteen minutes, having first paid off everything on the musician's tab. About ten thousand.

When Ela walked into the Institute, she immediately threw herself at me with such force that something cracked in my spine. I hugged her for a good five minutes. We emitted a series of loud, inarticulate sounds, so loud that the remaining residents of the Institute, except Gypsy, came out of their rooms. Ela's father stood in the doorway, silently watching everyone. When he caught Sebastian's eye, he looked away.

There's something weird about two different groups from your life suddenly meeting. It's like on your twentieth birthday when you've invited friends from school and friends from college, or your first dinner with your fiancé and both sets of parents. In situations like that, you usually feel extremely responsible for every misunderstanding or clash between the two groups. But even more than that, you suddenly realise that your life is not actually whole, but rather an incoherent story with serious scripting errors.

Yet, when the past twelve years of my life came together in one place, I felt whole. All I needed was my daughter. Nothing but her needed to exist. When she entered the

Institute and threw herself into my arms, it felt as though my spine, muscles and joints were regenerating cell by cell.

"Hi," Iga said to my daughter, shaking her hand. "I don't think you want to know how much we've heard about you."

"I've heard a lot about you, too," replied my daughter. "It's great, you looking after Mum like that."

"Oh, it's more like her looking after us." Iga stroked her on the head.

Ela's father didn't say a word; he just observed us from the doorway.

"I'll be here on Sunday at five," he said, finally, and closed the door.

I realised I hadn't said a single word to him.

This was possibly the happiest weekend of my life. The sun shone even during the night on Friday; we tried to sleep as little as possible because tomorrow was going to be Saturday and the day after was Sunday, so we tried to grab every single passing second. It was a Sisyphean task because time sped twice, three times, four times as fast. *It ought to be a month, two months, six months*, I thought, when a couple of hours after Ela's arrival, we wandered through the zoo in enormous sunglasses, eating hideously greasy chips, gazing at the sleepy chimpanzees and unwashed tigers. *It ought to be a lifetime*, I thought, as we trotted through the shopping mall, shrieking in the changing rooms, running out of shops selling Chinese trash with dozens of plastic bracelets.

"I've got to tell you something, Mum," Ela announced when we were sitting in the ice cream parlour on Grodzka Street in the evening, staring at the brimming crowd.

"I'm all ears."

"You're extremely frivolous and even a bit crazy," she said quietly, looking around to check whether anyone could hear.

I poked my tongue out and jangled my twelve plastic bracelets. Then I turned to her attentively.

"You really think so?" I asked, seeing her uncertainty. She was evading my eyes, chewing her lips as she always did when she caught herself gearing the conversation in the wrong direction, saying too much, exposing herself.

"No, no…" She tried to smile. "No, you're grown-up, serious, and I love you very much. But you know, six scoops of ice cream…"

"Ice cream with topping," I aimed my spoon at my portion, "is frivolous. I'm too old to eat ice cream. Ice cream is permitted only until you're eighteen. Grown-ups, as I understand, should consume mainly vinegar and salt water."

"Well, no…" she stammered after a while. "It's fattening, you know."

"You're twisting something, my friend." I looked at her carefully, and she turned her eyes towards the window, straining to find something in the crowd to which she could point and exclaim "look at that!" "You really do think I'm frivolous," I pointed my spoon at her. "Because I left you, because I'm here, because I'm living with some odd people who are younger than me and a bit strange."

"No, Mum, no, God forbid. No." My daughter started waving her hands as though what I'd said was smoke from one cigarette too many. "It's not that. You wanted to be happy, and you couldn't be happy with Dad, you never were, I understand."

I looked at her. She smiled again, a little more sincerely, considerably more sadly. I saw in her now something that wasn't visible in the dark hallway of the Institute and through dark glasses in the dazzlingly sunny zoo. My daughter repeated to herself every morning, against her will, "I understand, I understand everything." Again, I had to stop myself wailing and sobbing over the ice cream. What had I done? I ought to abduct her and run away to the far corners of the world with her. Ought to fight for her as hard as I could. I had let myself be bullied and manipulated by people who I didn't respect, who I thought were idiots. I let my daughter be taken away from me and let my life be destroyed.

"Frivolous" and "crazy" was putting it mildly.

"And I know that we're going to be together soon," she said. "And that you're doing everything to make it happen, Mum."

"Yes, we'll be together soon, darling." I stroked her face. "Soon, only—"

"I know," repeated my daughter, but no longer with the same certainty. Her voice was beginning to crumble.

"We ought to go to the cinema now," I decreed, "to see the silliest film going."

So we went to see some American film about people who were in love with each other, during which we, in turn, laughed, cried and invented alternative dialogues so that everyone sitting near us had to move down a few seats, and I wanted, more than anything, the screening to last ten, twenty, thirty hours. Time passed, minutes flew by, and we tried to tear as much as we could from them, as if we wanted to gobble as much of the food that was being catapulted straight into our faces as we could.

The following day was Ela's birthday. We got up early and quickly, although we'd slept perhaps a couple of hours. I didn't even need any coffee; I'd never felt so rested. We went for a walk and when we got back in the afternoon, after a few hours of roaming around Błonie, drinking cola and buying idiotic, useless trinkets, we found Iga had decorated the kitchen with paper garlands, stuck huge cardboard letters spelling ELA on the windows, poured champagne into paper cups and – like it had won first prize in a strange competition – stood my trashy pink cake in the middle of the table. She'd also managed to cook enough chips for an army, fry some soya nuggets, make two sorts of salads and bake some chocolate muffins with hazelnut butter.

"No point in waiting," she said to my daughter. "Let's get this done as quickly as possible and start the party."

"What party?" I asked, watching with horror as my

daughter approached the cake and studied it from every angle as if it was something from another planet.

"The party." Iga waved at the space around us. "I've invited about twenty people. I know, I didn't tell you. Don't get annoyed. The kid's got to have her first proper birthday ball."

"Mum, you're so tacky," said Ela, licking pink icing from her finger. "How could you buy me such a cake?"

"No smoking weed in front of her," I whispered to Iga.

"Mum, Dad's always smoking it in front of me." Ela shrugged, walked up and leant her back against mine. "Give yourself a break."

"Let him smoke to his heart's content," I said and reiterated, "No smoking in front of Ela."

An hour later, the guests arrived: people we knew from the Cat, Iga's friends from her studies, even Yogi, the other guard from the Cat, came with his fiancée and her phosphorescent highlights. Everybody, of course, drank vodka, cheap champagne and beer, and smoked weed, but they were more careful, quieter, swore less. My daughter was over the moon. She talked to practically everyone but most of all to Iga and Yogi's highlightened fiancée, whose sword-length tips made my daughter quake with fear.

When she wanted to try some champagne, I tried to put on the sternest and firmest face I could, even though I'd gone through a whole bottle myself. My daughter stuck her index and middle fingers under her nose, aping Hitler's moustache. I burst out laughing.

After nine o'clock in the evening, we started dancing in my room, moving aside all the furniture, turning Abba, Prince and Michael Jackson up full blast, competing for the silliest moves. At one point, to everyone's horror, Sebastian started spinning my daughter above his head.

A while later, I stopped dancing and just watched. I wanted to stop the moment with my eyes. To give weight to the air, time, surroundings, to make what I saw slow down a hundredfold, so that I could observe my daughter to infinity, catch her smiling, moving and squealing. To make everything unfold at the speed of one frame per hour. I prayed for it. For her to be always happy.

Somebody patted me on the back. I turned and everything grew chaotic, set in fast motion again; the speakers crackled with hits from the eighties, the door rattled with blows from Mrs Finkiel's crutch, and – obeying my orders – everyone ignored her.

"Sorry, do you have a moment?" asked Gypsy.

I turned once more towards Ela, who was now dancing with Iga, executing quadruple pirouettes. I nodded. We went to the kitchen. It was empty.

I sat on a chair; he sat opposite. He was collected, smiling even, probably for the first time since I'd told him to leave, since I'd told him that, even though he did mean a lot to me, the feeling was transitory.

"I understand everything now," he announced, opening a beer.

"So, since you understand, what's there to talk about?" I asked. "I've already said everything. Really."

"Because this 'time being' is still going to last for a while," he added, taking a sip. He stretched his hand towards me but immediately pulled it back. "And it's possible your daughter won't be able to be with you for a long time yet. Possibly for a very long time. Possibly until she can make her own decisions."

"I really don't want to listen to this now." I stood up to return to my room where everybody was dancing and Sebastian, no doubt, had morphed into a DJ, because the apartment was drowning in dance music, the sort you always hear in night taxis.

"But those parents of your husband, you know," he said, looking at me with the same smile, "aren't some sort of omnipotent 'They'. There must be something you can do. They're not omnipotent. I assure you."

"Gypsy, fucking hell!" I shouted. "I don't need your expert opinion. I know who I am, who her grandparents are. I know everything."

"It's just that I can see you're suffering," he replied, unfazed, still not moving.

And suddenly, for a fleeting moment, I thought I saw something slimy, black, terrible in his eyes, but maybe it was simply the weed and champagne in my blood. Anyway, I didn't want to talk to him. I was just about to leave the kitchen but turned towards him once more. He didn't even flinch.

"Let's not talk about my family anymore. Gypsy, it really would be better if you moved out as soon as possible," I said.

The thumping on the door suddenly grew four times as loud, as though an enormous grown man was kicking it at a run, putting his whole strength behind it. I turned and ran into the hallway. Closed the door to my room but didn't tell anyone to turn the music down. *May that old hag finally snuff it*, I thought unkindly.

"Who is it?" I shouted through the door.

"Open up!" croaked Mrs Finkiel. "Open up this minute."

I was furious; I was like a huge cauldron of simmering oil, like an overheated engine about to explode. I opened the door, pushed her two steps away and closed the door behind me. The two of us now stood on the landing.

"Yes?" I shouted, and she aimed her crutch at my solar plexus. I grabbed it. "It's my daughter's birthday. We're having a party and we've got the right. Ear plugs cost five złotys. I can get some from the pharmacy if you can't afford them." I looked her in the face. Mrs Finkiel wasn't outraged like she normally was when I passed her on the stairs. She wasn't as furious as when she'd interfered twenty thousand times before, like when one of us took a bath after eleven at night, for example. Her lips and eyes were clenched; faint, blue but pulsating veins bloomed on her temples. For a moment, I thought the old woman wasn't angry at all. *She's terrified*, I thought. *But maybe it's the weed.*

175

"You've got to get out of here," she crackled, piercing me with crazy eyes, not pausing even to blink. "You've got to get out of here immediately, you idiot."

"Calm down, Mrs Finkiel," I said, "or I'll phone the police."

"You've got to get out of here," she repeated, "otherwise something's going to happen to you. Something bad."

"Are you threatening me?" I burst into laughter. "Go home, Mrs Finkiel. You're mad."

"Listen to me!" she yelled, practically tearing her throat. "Listen to me. You've got to move out of here, you idiot, immediately. You can't even imagine, can't even imagine. It's for your own good. If only you knew! It really is for your own good."

I brought my face up close to hers until it was just centimetres away. As usual, she smelled of mould and resin.

"Please," I said slowly, stressing every syllable. "Please leave me in peace, please go home or I'll tell the police that you're threatening me."

She grew limp, as though someone had tugged a metal string, which had reached to her throat, from out of her backside; she leant on her crutch and lowered her head. She looked at me, but entirely differently, with the hazy and sad eyes of a tired and old woman. Again I saw something, that black something, a strange crack, a break, which had first been in Gypsy's eyes and which I now felt was hanging in the darkness of the stairwell, just behind my neighbour's head.

"As you wish," she said quietly. "Turn the music down a bit."

I went back into the apartment just as my daughter ran out of the room into the hall.

"Mum!" She threw her arms around my neck with the same momentum as when she'd first stepped into the Institute. "I was looking for you, Mum, where were you? I looked all over, but you weren't here. Don't do that again. Don't disappear, and don't leave when I'm not looking."

"I just went outside for a moment. It's okay, darling," I

replied, stroking Ela's head. My hand was shaking. I pulled it away and clenched my fist.

"Dad phoned," said my daughter, and her breath was strangely sweet, like overripe apples, "and wished me happy birthday."

"That's good," I replied, and I walked into the room where the dancing was slowly coming to an end, caught Iga by the hand and whispered in her ear.

"What foul weed is that? I told you."

"What weed?" She looked at me with surprise. "But it's the same as we've been smoking for the past two months. Don't you feel well?"

I shook my head and took a deep breath, switched on "Mamma Mia" by Abba and started dancing with my daughter. When the song ended, I murmured into her ear:

"I've still got another present for you."

I led her to the kitchen and, from the pile of wrapping paper (all the guests had given Ela a present), I pulled out a carrier bag with the washed-out *Thelma and Louise* T-shirt in it. My daughter stretched it out in front of her and was thrilled, although it made her cry a little. Tears were welling up in my eyes, too, so we quietly cried in the kitchen for a while, behind a hastily closed door, just like we had when I was packing to leave for Cracow.

The party ended relatively early, about two, with three of us remaining on the battlefield – me, Iga and Ela, although really it was just me and Iga because Ela had fallen asleep on the table.

"You don't have to give her back to him," said Iga, swaying back and forth on a chair. "They can't do anything to you. It's blackmail; what they've got into your head isn't true."

"If I take her, they'll take her away from me and I'll never see her again," I explained with half-closed eyes, smoking my last slim cigarette. "I told you."

"It's not true."

"I've got to keep my word in all this, Iga. After all, he

did let her visit me here. So I've got to give her back for the time being."

"The time being? Until when?" Iga drummed her fingers on the table. "You don't know that. You've no idea when you'll be able to see her."

"I'm frivolous," I retorted.

"I didn't say that."

"But you think it." I smiled.

"I think you're scared, sis." Iga sighed, stood up and started to carry dirty tumblers, glasses and ashtrays to the sink. "You're too scared. You've allowed yourself to be bullied. I don't know, maybe I'd be scared in your place, too."

"The strategy of small steps," I said, not believing what I was saying myself. "I'll show them that I'm a decent mother. They'll start to trust me and then Ela will be able to come here more and more often and for longer..."

"Fucking hell, who's supposed to prove to who that they're decent?" seethed Iga.

I was too exhausted to answer. Sebastian took Ela in his arms and carried her to my room. She and I fell asleep on my bed. When we got up at about one in the afternoon, it was grey outside, heavy and suicidal. We ate breakfast, picking at scrambled eggs and drinking glass after glass of juice, trying to smile at each other. Ela took a bath, put on some fresh clothes; I threw the rubbish out, washed the floor, washed the dishes, aired the whole place to give the Institute at least the semblance of a respectable apartment.

Ela's father appeared at five on the dot.

He stood in the hallway, stroked his daughter on the head and looked at me with absent, empty eyes. He was unshaven, pale, crumpled. Smelt of alcohol.

"Here are the keys." He handed them to Ela. "Go to the car but under no circumstance look in the boot because there aren't any presents in there for you."

I hugged Ela hard, even harder than when she'd arrived, so

178

hard our bones sounded like a packet of crisps being crushed in a pair of hands.

"Now go." I was trying not to cry again. "Well, go on. I love you very much. We'll see each other soon."

My daughter's wise, too wise, which is probably why she left quickly, taking her rucksack. She didn't want this to hurt more than it had to. She knew there was a right moment when you could still protect yourself from a pain that would later become unbearable.

"Thank you," I said to Ela's father. "Thank you for bringing her."

He didn't answer.

"Thank you," I repeated. "Aren't you going to thank me for keeping my side of the bargain?"

Still he said nothing. He stared at me, or rather through me. He looked like a botched wax figure of himself. I wanted to shake him. Hit him. But I couldn't.

"Since you don't want to say anything," I said, what remained of my composure wearing thin, "just take her and go. Please. Don't draw it out."

"She drank alcohol here yesterday," he finally said with a voice so full of a drunkard's heaviness and cloying hoarseness that it held nothing but faint traces of the voice I remembered. "She was drunk when I called her, Agnieszka."

"I kept an eye on her," I stammered out through a tight throat. "All she drank was a tiny amount of champagne and…"

"She was drunk, you moron," he repeated. "She was drunk and she's twelve. You know what that means."

Now I fell silent.

"You know what that means," he repeated. "That means that you're not going to see her for a very, very long time."

"Casper…" I muttered. "I kept an eye on her. I didn't give her any alcohol. I promise."

"I'll get her to blow into a breathalyser," he said. "I'm going to note down the result and put it in the file marked 'Divorce/Rights of Custody'."

"Casper..." I murmured again.

He turned to walk away, then stopped. Turned his head a fraction in my direction.

"I don't know," he added, not even looking at me. "I haven't the faintest idea how I could have screwed up my life with somebody as stupid, irresponsible and flippant as you. I'd like to wish you all the best. But nothing good's going to happen to you. And it's your own fucking fault."

"Casper..." I said one last time. Almost silently.

He slammed the door. The glass in the front door vibrated. I sat on the floor in the hallway and cried.

* * *

"Agnieszka. His name really was Jacek," says the woman in the jacket. "And my name's Marta. We never use false names." She's staring at me. She still has the same smile on her face. It's permanently stuck there, like a mask – two settings: smile, no smile. "There's no need," she added, standing over Gypsy's body. He's lying in a black puddle, unnaturally twisted as though frozen halfway through an abortive acrobatic act. His blood is too black; it looks like oil. If it was up to me, if I was the make-up artist on the film set, I'd tell them to make it lighter, redder, more human. His face is peaceful, held in a half smile despite the broken nose, despite masses of congealed blood.

This is, after all, a film; it's not really happening.

Sebastian's lying next to him. On his stomach. Also in a pool of blood. The other bodies, the ones behind me, are the same. I can't bring myself to look in that direction for now.

It's a film, it's not really happening.

I can't imagine where I'm going to be when I open my eyes and wake up. But certainly not here. I'm definitely going to be somewhere else.

"Why lie about such an ordinary thing as a name?" Marta shrugs. She's wearing the same jacket with the same badge as she did in the Bracka Street café. The badge with a scout holding a telescope, just like the painting on Mrs Finkiel's wall. Yes, the woman was called Marta. Maybe that really is her name.

"Why should we lie about anything? We can do anything we want. People who can do anything they want don't have to lie. We told you the truth. This apartment is ours."

Her face morph's into something like a child's simple drawing. Lines and dots. Thick and black. *Where's my daughter?* I think. *Iga, I'm so sorry, so sorry, Veronica. Where's my daughter? Ela?? Dear Ela. I'm so very sorry. I'm coming, darling. It's only a film.*

"Where's my daughter?" I ask.

I can still hear a creaking sound, quiet and plaintive, coming from Mrs Finkiel's apartment; it's so silent here that the creaking fills my whole apartment.

"Come, Agnieszka," she says. "Just follow me."

A sound comes from someone's lungs. Someone sighs. Tired. A sigh, from someone old and angry. The sound is far away but also near, at the other end of the building but at the same time right next to my ear. The door to the landing is still open. The darkness on the landing behind Marta makes me imagine that she is one solitary tooth in an enormous black mouth that is about to swallow the entire Institute like a small piece of fruit, like a pip.

"Where's my daughter?" I repeat.

"Follow me and you'll see your daughter, and I'll let you both out. All we want is the apartment."

I nod, walk slowly, but there's something wrong with my balance. It feels like somebody else is moving me, and every move hurts, goes against my muscles. Maybe this is how old people feel. Maybe I've become an old woman. I hold on to the screwdriver.

"You'll see her," she assures me. "You have to know that I always tell the truth. Now you know I always tell the truth."

I'm coming, Ela. Mum's coming. I glance behind me, see

them for a split second: Veronica and Iga. I see their hair, their open mouths, I see masses of blood.

I'm sorry, Veronica. Sorry, Iga. I don't know what to say ever again.

I just want to wake up, I want to wake up anywhere but here.

I'm coming. Mum's coming.

I step onto the landing – cold, reeking, evil. Follow the woman slowly, straight to Mrs Finkiel's open door. It's no longer Mrs Finkiel's apartment. It has stopped being anybody's apartment, anybody's home.

"You've got to understand, Agnieszka," she says, "that all this is for your own good. We're good people. We want to help you, look after you. *Observe and look after*, that's our motto."

"Look after…" I repeat, mechanically.

"Look after you until the right moment comes. That was our instruction," she replies.

Once in Mrs Finkiel's apartment, I follow her into the room with the displaced wall unit and television set, then climb the stairs to the greyish yellow room, where we'd found Anna and Robert's bodies. Marta is wearing high heels and therefore moves slowly, but she still has to keep stopping, waiting for me, turning around to make sure I'm following.

"Come on, Agnieszka," she says. "Come on. Nothing's going to happen to you. Come on."

I nod. Indifferently. I look at my hands; they're covered in blood. From different people, all shades of red.

I see that the chairs are no longer there, and neither are Anna or Robert. Someone else is there. The enormous metal door is slightly ajar. What lies behind is, in turn, black and silvery blue.

In the middle of the room stands a man in a black suit. In front of him is a wheelchair, and in the wheelchair sits a figure who, from a distance, looks like a fatally sick child. The figure is also wearing a black suit, except that it's been tailored for a little boy. I walk towards them, carefully, slowly. Marta gets to them first and stands by their sides. For a moment, her hand rests gently on the shoulder of the man standing. The three of them together look like a hideous parody of a family.

The screwdriver. I'm still holding the screwdriver.

The man standing is my neighbour from downstairs: Doctor Banicki. At least that's how he'd introduced himself when we first met. The figure in the wheelchair is a shrivelled old man, barely alive, who looks like one of those oldest people in the world that they show on TV. On his withered, smooth skull appear wisps of grey hair as though some spiteful person has stuck cotton wool balls on it.

"You look very much like your grandmother," states the man whom I knew as Banicki. "Just as beautiful."

"I'd like to be so beautiful," says Marta, in an entirely different voice. It's as though somebody had ejected a tape from her head and inserted another, with a different person, a different voice – squeaky and stupid, as if belonging to a silly teenager. "We've forgiven her," she adds after a moment.

I squat and start to vomit. I choke; my throat hurts. Chunks of Sebastian's pasta mush. Dirty water, tea. Apart from that, bile.

"My daughter," I try to say between bouts of retching. "My daughter."

"This could all have been different," says the woman.

"But some people don't agree," says the man.

I stand up, wipe my mouth.

The old man in the wheelchair lets out a sigh. When he's finished, the man – formerly Doctor Banicki – pulls a small metal hip-flask out of his pocket and brings it to the old man's lips. The old man tries to swallow, but the contents of the flask trickle down his wrinkled, liver-spotted face. On the finger of one limp hand, which is dangling off the armrest, is a gold ring. I look at the hip-flask and see the same image again – the man on a horse with a telescope. I look at the old man – he, Banicki's hand, the hip-flask, the suits, the ring all seem miles away. I recognise this old man, too. Recognise his hand. It's the same hand that had been dangling off the armrest, attached to a body watching *Clan* on the TV in the depths of Mrs Finkiel's apartment when I'd gone there to ask for the key to the cellar.

"Unfortunately, Mrs Finkiel didn't fulfil her assignment," says Marta.

"I don't understand." Voice, questions, language, all come from me, but distanced, far away, unclear.

"She was supposed to remain silent. But for some reason decided to help you. She'd been so obedient for so many years. Pity." She shakes her head gently.

"Mummy!" The word suddenly bursts from behind the metal door, completely filling my ears. I race towards the door but, at that moment, Marta aims the gun at me again, the same gun she'd used to kill Veronica, Iga and Sebastian. She smacks her lips, shaking her head like a pawnbroker handling a twenty-carat ring.

"Allow me to explain, Agnieszka," says the woman. "It's very simple. We own a great deal. Much more than most people think. And we want to get it back."

"Things are being handed out to plebs. Beautiful houses, beautiful land is being given over to animals who ought to live in sties," states the man whom I met as Banicki.

"My daughter," I say, or somebody beside me says.

"It's unnecessary, terrible. A waste. The place for plebs is the sty. Shelters. Mud huts," adds Marta.

"My daughter," I repeat.

"Decay. Pestilence," comes the voice of the old man in the wheelchair. Hoarse like a worn tape, as if coming from something other than his body. Sick. Angry.

"Besides, they owe us, for so many years of hard work. So many centuries of hard work. Our work in the name of order, something that's never existed here," says Marta.

"Pestilence," repeats the old man, and slowly, with

difficulty, he continues: "There used to be a world, once. Concrete. Timber. Meat. Bones. Now there's only decay. Rubbish."

"Antoni Waraszyl." Marta's voice momentarily changes tone again. Something is breaking it, a trembling, fear. "We owe him everything. It's because of him that we're not animals, that we're human."

I take a step forward, slow and painful.

"Don't move, Agnieszka," says Marta.

"Mum, please, do what these people tell you." My daughter's voice rings out from beyond the metal door.

"Who the fuck are you?" I growl, from fear and fury.

"Your husband's parents," the woman continues, "were probably right to try to get him away from you and save their granddaughter. They probably suspected what was going to happen. Maybe they'd even heard of us. More people had heard of us in the past. We were like a terrifying, terrible fairy tale. But we're not terrible."

"Chaos is terrible. Filth is terrible. Unsuitable marriages are terrible," says Mr Banicki, smacking his lips quietly.

The old man in the wheelchair tries to add something else, but he hasn't got the strength. He just moves his lips like a fish.

"Equality is the most terrible thing of all. The worst," the man standing by the wheelchair continues.

"Who are you?" I strain my eyes as hard as I can to see into the darkness beyond the half-open metal door. But all I can see is a black stretch of darkness. A blue flash every few seconds.

"We're taking back what belongs to us," he explains, "what used to be ours before the war. What was handed out after it. Divided up. Burned. Smeared in shit. What is still being handed out. For a monthly payment they call credit. Handed out to shit-eaters. Slaves. Trash. Handed out to trash like you."

"She's her granddaughter," says the woman.

He shakes his head with repulsion, as though he's sniffed

185

something stale, while the old man wheezes again, traces of dense saliva trickling down his face.

"But what's all this got to do with my grandmother?" I ask quietly. When I touch my face, I notice it's wet.

"Agnieszka." Marta's still pointing the gun in my direction. "If it weren't for your grandmother, you'd be dead by now. It wouldn't have taken nearly as long."

"We'd have bricked up the windows, cut off the power, walled up the doors," says the man. "We'd have done everything straight away. But Mr Waraszyl wanted you to live."

"I don't believe you," my voice tells her.

"Not a trace of you would be left. Nobody would ever have found you."

"Who are you?" I repeat the question.

"We call ourselves the Observers," she explains, pointing to her badge. "There was a time when we used to help kings."

"We see to order. Separating rulers from subjects," adds the man.

"You're talking nonsense," I whisper through a trapped throat.

"We're still hoping that everything is going to be set to rights. That the pigs are going to go back to where they belong. Dogs go back to where they belong," Marta continues.

"And human beings. Human beings go back to their rightful place," adds the man in the suit.

"Equality will come to an end. The time of these monstrosities will come to an end," says Marta.

"Vera?" the old man in the wheelchair breaks in, and briefly there's silence. He'd uttered his previous words quietly, with great difficulty, as though every syllable could cost him his life. But this word, my grandmother's name, is loud and clear.

"Vera," repeats the old man.

"Not long now," Marta, the woman in the jacket, tells him.

"A lot of people mistake us for something else entirely. Jacek, for example, thought that we belonged to the last regime. That we're what one of your presidents liked to call an 'arrangement'. Others call us Judeo-Masons. Others, the conspiracy of Illuminati or the secret service. Some people don't really know what they're talking about, rolling words like 'côterie', 'people you know' around in their mouths like evil spells, like vague signposts to places where they wouldn't really like to go. We never set anyone straight, but, believe me, there are a lot of smokescreens. We're older than all these distasteful and idiotic concepts," explains Marta.

"Than anything," the old man adds.

"Gypsy. Why was Jacek one of you?" I ask.

"He searched for us for a long time. He was one of those harmless clever maniacs who believe that the answer to everything can be found on the internet. He'd read some stupid, old article and then searched for us. He was stubborn. And he found me." After a pause, she adds, "We treated him as a bit of a joke, to be honest."

At the words "a bit of a joke", the old man starts to chuckle; his laugh resembles the squeal of a small animal being strangled.

"He's remembered something." The man in the suit solicitously wipes the dribble off the old man's chin. "He's remembered something. I think I know what." He laughs, too.

"Kiszczak," says Marta, and she gazes at the standing man, for a fraction of a second, with a certain tenderness. "That's it, he's remembered Kiszczak. Go on, tell her, it's a great story."

"Kiszczak, the minister of the interior and prime minister, knew about us. He was very scared of us," explains the man, "but he wasn't stupid. He knew how to evaluate things. Thought that joining forces with us would pay off."

"We had about one and a half thousand properties in Gdańsk, Warsaw, Cracow, and Łódź in 1939," says the woman. "And millions of hectares of land all over the country."

I don't care about anything she's saying. I just want to see my daughter.

"There's history and there's true history," sighs Marta.

"Let's get back to Kiszczak. You're right, it's an amazing story," says the man whom I met as Banicki. "The Counsel and I told him that in order to become an Observer, he'd have to go through an initiation. A ritual to get in. We don't do things like that, there wasn't anything like that, but we agreed to do it as a joke. About two weeks after martial law was declared, Kiszczak came to Cracow at night in a government car, to a villa in Wola Justowska. In civilian clothes. He was guarded by two men from the secret police. He was nervous, kept smoking – Carmen cigarettes. And when he wasn't smoking, he chewed American gum. We don't do things like this as a rule, but on that occasion, we dressed in costumes hired from a theatre. Pretended we were masons. He was terrified."

"It must have been so funny," says Marta, who is still aiming the gun at me.

"So I'm sure Daddy is remembering Kiszczak." The standing man almost chokes with laughter. "Kiszczak in the middle of the drawing room, surrounded by Observers, naked as a newborn baby and fucking his dog."

The old man bursts into fitful laughter. He bounces in his wheelchair as if he's being lifted by a pair of enormous invisible hands.

"We don't like communists. They're vulgar. They belong in the pigsty with the other pigs," adds the younger man.

"A mistake." The old man speaks, inhaling before every word, his half-dead fingers drifting in the air. "My one and only mistake. Vera. Vera…" Saying this, he points at me. "A mistake," he repeats.

"I want to see my daughter," I demand.

"Fine. Let's go." Marta finally lowers the gun and, with a slow movement of her hand, she indicates the darkness beyond the metal door.

"Love is a mistake. Vera," says the old man, quietly again. His chest rises and falls as though there wasn't a body beneath the shirt, only wind.

"Let's go," Marta encourages me. "Let's end all this."

"End what?" I ask.

"Throw that screwdriver away," she orders. She opens the metal door wider. "It'll scare your daughter."

I nod and drop the screwdriver. Hear it hit the floor.

I walk in after her; out of the corner of my eye, I see the younger man follow us, pushing the wheelchair in front of him. The room is quite small. On the opposite wall are several kinescopes built into an enormous wooden cupboard. Something like a console. On the flat wooden surface are red plastic buttons with dirty fingerprints on them. There is masses of dust. I smell a mixture of fungus, dust and mould. There are boxes on the floor, files. And a messy pile of surgical instruments by the wall: nails, pliers, hammers.

The observation room.

Only after taking all this in do I see Ela. She's in the corner, bound to a chair with tape.

"Mummy!" she yells.

She's pale, shivering. She doesn't blink. Beneath her unfastened jacket is her *Thelma and Louise* T-shirt, cut off at the waist with scissors. Between her legs, which are clad in thin pink leggings, is a large wet stain. But even taped to a chair and covered in piss, to me, my daughter is bright, strong, glowing. My daughter becomes a saint from a holy picture, becomes an angel.

"Darling," I say, "darling, it's alright now, it's alright."

She doesn't reply. I tear the tape off her, rip it off with my teeth, throw pieces of it behind me. I press Ela to my breast, crush her into my body and, at that moment, I start to feel like myself again. My body's wet. My breath and pulse are like that of someone who's about to jump from the tenth floor. My heart pounds like a pneumatic hammer. I'm shivering like my daughter. We're shivering together. I move her face away for an instant, stroke her cheeks, her hair. Her lips stop trembling; consciousness is returning to her eyes as she finally finds her way to me.

"Mummy," she says, saliva dribbling from the corner of her mouth.

"Darling, it's alright now, it's alright."

"Dad's dead," she whispers and looks at me. I know her eyes don't recognise me yet, nor do her ears. She knows I'm her mother thanks only to an inner animal instinct.

"What have they done to you? What have they done to you?" I ask, still touching her face, her hair.

"Dad's dead and so are Gran and Grandpa," she says. "I was running for the train. I had to come here, Mum, I had to. I tore myself away from Dad; he was arguing on the platform with Gran and Grandpa. Somebody got on after me, and somebody else followed them. I saw it on the phone. They're dead, Mum. Somebody followed them and killed them."

"We're alive, darling, *we're* alive." I stroke her face; I can't stop, can't stop checking that we really are alive.

"Like Thelma and Louise," she replies, twisting her lips into something like a smile.

"They die," I remind her. "They die."

"No, Mum," she whispers and nestles into me again. "They go to heaven."

I get up and turn away. Only now does it get through to me that there's something happening on the convex screens mounted to the wall. On each screen, there is a different black and white film. Each one is a camera feed. Except for one screen in the bottom right-hand corner, which is switched off. But I'm not interested in the screens. I'm interested in my daughter.

"What have you done to my child, you bastards?" I ask.

"No doubt you want to know why this apartment, why here?" Marta puts the gun away and walks towards me. "Why this tenement? It's ours. It's always been ours."

"What have you done to my child, you bastards?" I repeat, my words like rusty knives.

"Look," says the woman, and she waves her hand at the screens.

People appear on the kinescopes. People in other apartments like mine. Other Institutes.

I press Ela to me, cover her eyes.

"We're getting out now, love," I say.

"That's ours, too. In Lublin." She points to a screen where a young woman is swaying to and fro, cuddling a small child, and a man is smashing a chair against a bricked-up window.

"And this is Zamość." She points to another screen where a large man with a moustache is stabbing an old woman who is hunched over, trying to protect herself with her arms, but in vain. The knife strikes blindly, in her back, face, breasts. A third person, a fat, middle-aged woman, is pressed against the wall, screaming. In the background are piles of shattered plates, pots, cupboards torn from the wall.

On each screen is a different Institute, different people locked in their own apartments, people bricked in with no food, no electricity, people driven to madness, harming themselves and those closest to them, driven to extremes. People being murdered. I see what has been done to us being played out on each screen.

"Why are you filming all this?" I ask.

"Because it's interesting. Didn't you ever enjoy watching ants? Or insects?" asks Marta.

"It's an experiment. Like setting fire to an anthill," says the man I'd known as Mr Banicki, and he adds, "We're experimenting, sort of on the side. We've been doing it for a long time: installing cameras when there's nobody at home, hiding them in airshafts. We observe the occupants for a month, then start liquidating. Carry the bodies out at night. Burn all the furniture. Their relatives quickly learn that there's no point asking questions."

"Everyone knows we've begun and nobody's going to stop us," says Marta. "Nobody. No one in government. Everybody's scared of us. Everyone knows what we're owed."

"This is precisely what the Institute is." The man waves

at the convex screens with clear pride. "The Institute for the Observation of the Lower Classes."

"Let's get out of here, Mummy," says Ela. She presses herself into me so hard that a bone in my leg is about to snap. Let it snap. I love my daughter more than anything in the world. Nothing else matters.

"Don't look, Ela. We're getting out, we're going," I promise.

"Vera," the old man interrupts again.

"Now, now, Dad," replies the younger man.

"This is Warsaw." Marta switches on the screen in the bottom right-hand corner. Despite having no strength left, I scream – on the kinescope I see a man howling silently. He's naked, surrounded by lit candles. Where there used to be eyes and genitals, there is only black emptiness, bloody stains. The man, covered in blood, shuffles slowly like an animal, and only now do I see that somebody's standing behind him with a gun, somebody who, after a long pause, shoots him in the back of the head. The man falls to the floor like a sack of potatoes, and the somebody shoots again at someone cowering in the darkness. I put my hands to my mouth to stop myself vomiting again.

"We did more or less the same to the father of your child. And her grandfather and grandmother," Marta says.

"It's a good way to teach obedience. It always teaches obedience," adds the man. "Cutting off their balls so they can't multiply, the swine. Shit-eaters. An excellent idea. Brilliant." He strokes the old man's head tenderly.

"Vera," repeats the latter.

"Now, now," the younger man soothes.

"But that's only an extra. Only a game. People disappear and there's no way to look for them. Nobody's surprised by bricked-up windows. Nobody's surprised by sealed doors. Nobody's surprised when places change. Everybody gets used to it. Everybody gets used to absence."

"Vera! Vera!" wails the old man, and he points his trembling hand towards me.

As he does, the air in the room congeals.

Marta pulls the gun out of the holster beneath her jacket. Hands it to the younger man.

"Let's get it over with," she says.

The man I knew as Mr Banicki takes the gun from her. Aims it at me.

"I don't understand," I say. Ela is sobbing. I press her to me as hard as I can.

"My father wants vengeance. Revenge for being deceived and rejected. Vengeance is owed to him. According to the old law."

"But it's not me who deceived him, not me who humiliated him," I reply quietly and truthfully.

But nobody here cares about the truth.

"You look very much like your grandmother; you're so beautiful," says Marta, and again she assumes that voice, the squeaky voice of a retarded little girl.

I swallow. Shake my head.

"Wait. Wait. We had a different agreement. We had a different agreement," I repeat. "We were supposed to get out. We were supposed to get out in one piece. Ela and me." I stare at the gun.

"And you really believed me when I said I never lie?" says Marta, in her normal cold voice.

"And if I'd agreed to take the money?" I ask. "The two and a half million?"

"You wouldn't have got any. We'd have killed you anyway. We just wanted to check you out, out of curiosity. We wanted to know whether you're as stubborn and proud as your grandmother was," she answers.

"You're all sick," I murmur.

The old man tries to stand up, tries to touch me with his hand, but falls back into his wheelchair. He is heaving. Froth runs from his mouth. He looks on the verge of death.

"Vera, my love," the old man says to me. "Dearest."

"I'm not Vera. I'm Agnieszka," I say, tasting rust and fear on my tongue, and then the younger man yells:

"Don't argue with Mr Waraszyl, you whore!"

Ela screams. I stroke her head. I'm shaking.

On the screen in the bottom right-hand corner, somebody is squatting next to the man's body and sniffing it. He puts his head to his neck. I can't carry on looking. I focus on the crown of Ela's head, pressed against my hip. She's trembling. I feel tears running from my eyes, an abundant, salty stream. I can taste them in my mouth.

"Agnieszka, the apartment is unique to us, especially to the Great Observer; but above all, it was about you," says Marta.

She stands in front of me. I can smell her. Foul. She smells like vomit, like sugar mixed with shit.

"You're going to die first," says the younger man. He's panting heavily, seems aroused. "It's a mercy granted to you by Mr Waraszyl. You're going to die first so you don't have to watch your daughter die."

"You left me, Vera, my sweet," the old man rasps heavily, and his eyes seem momentarily more open, more present. "And nobody does that to me."

My whole life flashes in front of my eyes, in badly lit, grainy slides. My life is mainly made up of images of my daughter. On the slides in my head, my daughter is growing up, growing up faster and faster, gaining weight, hair, height. She's growing up while standing next to me. I feel her warmth. The gun is at my head. My mouth is full of salty water. I feel faint. Try to breathe. Feel my daughter's warmth. I try to breathe but can only grab shallowly at the air.

I'm scared.

"Ela, my love, calm down. Ela, love," I tell my daughter. I love her more than anything in the world. She *is* my world.

"Dad, look, the time has come. You've waited so long." Mr Waraszyl's son is holding the gun to my head in one hand and still stroking the old man's head with the other.

"Vera, my love, you made an idiot of me. And nobody does that, nobody," groans the old man.

My brain continues to project my life, no longer in frames but in sentences, black words on a white background, clear as lightning flashes. I look at the woman, the old man, the younger man. I'd caused them to be here by making the wrong decision. Because I was scared, because, like most people, I'd spent the whole of my life following instructions. I'd spent my life in fear. I was scared of being disobedient. Scared of taking a step forward. A real step. The words flash before me one after another. We're all here, here in the Institute. All of us. Me. We. You. You, too. We're all treading water. Treading water until we die. I'm going to die in a minute. And then so is my daughter.

"I love you very much, Ela, darling," I say quietly, my head buried in her hair, my voice breaking.

Suddenly I hear a loud, dull thud. Marta screams. Mr Waraszyl Jr's hand droops and the gun falls to the floor.

Marta keeps screaming and I try to understand what's happened.

"Give it to me," says Sebastian, who had unexpectedly sprung up at the door like an enormous white tree. "Give it to me, Hat."

The gun. I pick it up from the floor. It's unnaturally heavy. A gun's weight. That's what comes to mind when you hold one for the first time.

Marta is leaning against the dusty cockpit. She doesn't say a word, just breathes rapidly. Mr Waraszyl Jr is lying on the floor, twitching, his head hammered into his neck.

"Cover your eyes," I tell Ela, but again it's somebody else speaking, somebody concealed in my throat. "Cover your eyes, darling. Don't open them until I tell you."

"Am I to do it, or do you want to do it yourself, Hat?" Sebastian's voice is dull, husky. Half-naked, the lower part of his torso bound with a T-shirt, he clutches his belly; he's pale, trembling.

I look at my daughter covering her eyes. My daughter in her piss-covered leggings. My daughter glowing like an angel.

"Me," I say. "I'll do it myself."

The first time you put your finger on the trigger, you feel resistance, realise that the trigger's like an old, unoiled handle belonging to a door that should never, ever be opened.

Sebastian puts his arm around my daughter and gently leads her out of the room. As they disappear around the corner, I see Sebastian gently, tenderly place his hands over Ela's ears.

I can move my legs and arms. I can move my head.

"Agnieszka, if you do this, something terrible is going to happen," says Marta, glaring at me. "If you do this, your daughter's going to die in front of your eyes. A very slow death. She's going to suffer a great deal, and you won't be able to help her. I promise you. So, think it through. Think it through before you shoot."

The old man in the wheelchair is wheezing, saliva streaming from his lips.

"Vera," he mutters quietly.

"You know that this time I'm telling the truth," warns Marta.

"Shut up, you old whore!" I retort and pull the trigger. Red splatters across the silvery-blue kinescopes. Something pushes me backwards and I rest my hand against the wall to stop myself falling. "Whore," I repeat, but she's no longer there; there's a body lying on the floor. My breathing is even, the gun totally weightless.

Sebastian comes back into the room, holding on to the wall. He stares at the body. Spits on it.

Mr Waraszyl Jr is lying prone on the floor, moaning. He tries to get up, but Sebastian puts his heel on his spine, turning him into a cockroach, an insect, a fraction of a second before it's crushed. It's only now that I see that blood is dripping onto the floor from Sebastian's stomach.

"So, you want to tell me that you can do anything you

want?" I ask Mr Waraszyl Jr, lowering my face towards his. He is moaning but still smiling.

"You don't understand," he whispers with effort. "You don't understand that there are many of us. So many. We don't even know ourselves how many. You're as good as dead."

I can see Ela standing outside. Her eyes are still closed, her hands over her ears. She's still shaking.

"You think you're going to leave now, call the police, file a report, describe everything that's happened." He smiles. "You think the nightmare will be over, you'll get your apartment back, get your life back. But you don't understand how many of us there are. We're everywhere. We're the police who'll come to the scene of the crime. We're the taxi drivers who'll take you to the station, and the conductors who'll check your ticket, the shopkeepers, the owners of your next apartment. You've got to die. All of us know you've got to die."

I bring the gun to his face. He's staring upwards, towards the ceiling, and I realise that he can't see, that his spine is digging into his neck and has deprived him of sight. He continues:

"Besides, they're going to be here in fifteen minutes. Maybe a few of them, maybe more. They'll finish off what we started. They'll kill you and your daughter. Get rid of your bodies. Carry them out during the night. Nobody's going to look for you. The investigation will be closed within a week."

I release the safety catch.

"That's what's probably going to happen if you die," I wave the gun at the old man. "But if he goes?"

"It won't change a thing," he replies. "Absolutely nothing. Having control over their lives is an illusion for most people," he adds after a while. "But it's the privilege of just a few. It's our privilege."

Before I have time to say anything, Sebastian kneels over him and, with one flash of movement, wrings his neck. All I hear is a pop, like somebody pressing a piece of bubble wrap.

The old man starts shaking and silently moving his lips.

"Go," Sebastian says to me. "Run."

I take my daughter by the hand and we go back to the Institute. Sebastian follows, slowly. I let him lean on me.

"I didn't black out or anything when she fired," he explains. "I just couldn't move for a while."

"I didn't hear you coming. Nor did they," I say, guiding the three of us forward. Everything around us fades, grows flat like a photograph.

"I crawled," he replies.

I look down at the pale, bloody marks. I look up at Sebastian again.

"I couldn't let it happen, Hat. Couldn't let those motherfuckers kill you," he mutters.

Something in him goes out. I sense it.

When we reach the Institute, Sebastian slowly drops to the floor. He lets out a deep, loud moan, grimaces and touches the bloody hole in his stomach.

"Ela," I say quietly to my daughter, "close your eyes now, go to my room and don't come out until I tell you to. Don't look." I crouch in front of her, hug her and kiss her hard on the forehead, neck, hands.

Even though she's already closed her eyes, I stand in front of the bodies on the blood-drenched floor – Gypsy's, Iga's and Veronica's – to stop her from seeing them.

"Is everything alright now, Mummy?" she asks.

"Yes, it will be. But stay in my room for a bit with your eyes closed. Don't look until I come in and tell you it's okay," I plead.

Ela goes to my room. I close the door.

"What are you doing, Hat?" asks Sebastian.

"They've got to think I'm dead," I reply. "At least for a while – ten, twenty minutes, half an hour. We need a bit of time, Ela and me. We've got to lead them astray."

"I'll stay here," he says, looking at me, and there's something gentle in his eyes, the eyes of an old animal.

"No fucking deal," I reply.

"I'll stay here, Hat. Look." He shows me the black stain on the T-shirt binding his stomach. "There's nothing doing."

"Wait," I beg him. "We'll go to the hospital." I speak calmly, clearly. "We'll go to the hospital and everything'll be alright."

"Fucking do it, Hat. Get as far away from here as you can," he replies slowly. "I'll stay. I won't make it. If 'They' even try to follow you, I'll throw them down the stairs one by one."

I smile at him.

"Keep an eye on her for a moment." I point to my room.

"Nothing's going to happen to her. I promise." He smiles gently.

That smile changes his face completely, I think.

I go to the kitchen, fetch a bin bag. I go to my room, stuff clothing, make-up silicone, scissors into the bag. My daughter's sitting on the bed. I kiss her on the head again. Then I leave the Institute, run back to Mrs Finkiel's apartment and into the yellow room.

I remove my old clothes, reeking and bloody, and, in my underwear, lean over Marta. She's more or less the same size as me. Her body's not yet stiff or cold. I tear her skirt off, her blouse and, of course, her jacket. *The woman's lost all her features without that jacket*, I think. Then I cram her into my clothes – tracksuit pants and a jacket – manoeuvring her body, lifting limp arms and legs. A dead body is heavy, as if death itself was matter, a weight, black lead. I pack her clothes into the bin bag.

In my previous life, a long, long time ago, I changed people's faces, damaged them almost beyond recognition. I was a make-up artist in films. I know something about faces, how to deform them, how to break them. Make them unrecognisable. I pick up some tools. Spread them out around me, creating a workshop. I take the scissors and swiftly snip the woman's hair, throw the locks into the bin bag.

The old man's still alive, hissing and wheezing, loud, near my ear.

"Pestilence. Vera. Pestilence. Decay," he mutters, spitting phlegm.

I take the woman's tights and shove them down his throat. He starts to suffocate. I ignore him.

Only Ela is left. They'll wonder where Ela is when they arrive. Or maybe they won't. Maybe I'll gain ten, fifteen minutes. Ten minutes is a lot.

I put my hat on Marta's head, wrap my scarf around her neck. I pick the gun up and whack her in the jaw with the butt as hard as I can. Her teeth crack into pieces. I do it again, and again, and again; the gun shatters her face, crumbles it, turns it to mush. I pick up a knife and the make-up silicone and make incisions, puff them up where her characteristic traits used to be, where the small stretches of muscles responsible for her facial expressions used to be – around the nose, under the eyes, around the brows. I improvise. Imagine it's a mannequin.

When I'm finished, the woman could be me. Could be anybody. My hands are covered in blood. I turn around so as not to register what I've just done. I gather all the tools and throw them into the plastic bag.

I turn towards Antoni Waraszyl. I don't know whether he's alive or dead now. He's lying slack in the wheelchair, resembling a bundle of clothes with a wax head and cotton wool hair.

I go back to the Institute, to the kitchen, wash my hands. I try not to look at Veronica and Iga. *I'm sorry, girls, so very sorry.* I go to my room, pick up a bag, throw the gun into it, my passport, bank card.

"Come on," I tell Ela. "Come on."

"Can I look now?" she asks.

"No, not yet. Just a bit longer," I urge. "Come on."

"Sorry," I address Sebastian as Ela and I stand in the hall.

"Sorry for what?" He's trying as hard as he can to express irritation on his face. "Fuck it, Hat. It's not your fault."

"If I'd known—" I try to say, but he raises his hand to stop me talking.

"No time for that now," he replies. "Go, leave."

I pull the mobile phone out of Gypsy's pocket, a new smartphone. I'd never seen him with it before. I put it in my bag.

I scan the hallway. It's as dark and silent as when I'd stepped into it for the first time. The ceiling hasn't entirely lost its cadaverous grey hue, and from beneath all the blood, from beneath the bodies, from beneath the pain, fragments of old, warped parquet are visible.

"See you, Sebastian," I say. He smiles, and I lean over and kiss him on the forehead.

"You're okay, Hat," whispers the huge bald thug who'd saved my life.

"It's you who's okay," I reply and cry as I squeeze his hand.

As I look out to the landing, I notice for the first time that the grating is open. Resting against the wall, it looks just as it had every day that I'd lived here, every day until we'd been locked in.

"We've got to run," I tell Ela. "We've got to run, and fast."

"Can I look now?" asks my daughter, still pressing her hands against her eyes.

"Yes," I reply. "Yes, darling, you even need to."

We leap down the stairs, run through the building, silent and deserted, run past the door to Banicki's apartment and run down to the ground floor, thrust ourselves at the swing door, open it and fall into the street. We continue running. The city is dark, empty and cold. It's night, the middle of the night; there are no cars driving down the street. My daughter is with me, will always be with me, nobody's ever going to try to take her away from me again. She's running along the pavement, one thin, stick-like leg in front of the other, and she's here. She is my life and happiness, she is me.

The city's huge. This city, full of tenement buildings, in the middle of Europe, has never been so enormous. Mighty, with broad streets, with the illuminated edifices of the Academy of Mining and Metallurgy somewhere on the horizon, broad, black, endless. We're running through it, pressing against each other, without looking back; we're running as though it was the first time we'd ever been out, smelled the air. We stretch our arms out, amazed not to be hitting a wall.

"Taxis," says Ela. "Taxis, look!"

I shake my head, but my daughter tugs me towards several cars parked at the taxi rank. Radio Taxi Barbakan. In one of the taxis sits a fat, grey-haired man with a moustache. We're just about to get in, but I pull her away and carry on walking.

Ela points behind us and, further down the empty street, on the pedestrian crossing, I see a few blurred silhouettes, walking briskly in a tight group towards the Institute on Mickiewicz Avenue. I can't make out who they are from here, what they look like. But they're walking briskly.

We go back to the taxi. I open the door. We sit in the back.

"Where to?" asks the driver.

I can't say anything, but my daughter, nestling her face into my belly, says:

"The United States, please. Grand Canyon."

"Please don't take the piss," responds the taxi driver.

"Just drive, please," I say.

The car drives off slowly towards Ruczaj. At the Mickiewicz Avenue and Piłsudski Street crossing, I tell him to turn left. Tell him to go to the train station. I look at the clock on his dashboard: it's three in the morning. I pull the phone out of my bag and call the police. The dispatcher, not imaginary this time, picks up after five rings.

"I'd like to report a crime at 20 Mickiewicz Avenue, apartment 12," I say. "Murder."

"Please give me the details," she replies.

"Please get the police over there as quickly as possible."

"What's your name?" asks the dispatcher.

I grip the phone harder. The driver's going where I told

him to go. I hide my hand in the bag, touching the gun. It's cold and hard but feels like a warm, strong hand.

"What's your name?" she repeats.

"I know you're there," I whisper, gazing at the empty, black city flitting past, "but you're never going to find us."

"What's your name?" repeats the dispatcher, with the persistence of a stuck record.

I hang up, pull the battery and SIM card out and fling them out of the window as the driver accelerates.

I hug my daughter and kiss her hair. It's warm, soft, smells of bed linen. I take her hand, and I'll never let it go.

"I love you, Mum. I love you so much," says my daughter.

My daughter's name is Ela.

My apartment used to be called the Institute. I used to be called Agnieszka. Whoever you are.

THE END

If you enjoyed what you read,
don't keep it a secret.

Review the book online and tell
anyone who will listen.

Thanks for your support
spreading the word about
Legend Press.

Follow us on Twitter
@legend_times_

Follow us on Instagram
@legend_times